BLACK SAILS TO SUNWARD

Sheila Jenné

ALNITAK PRESS

*To Megan
the best plot midwife ever*

Crew of the Mariposa

Officers

George Kim-Johnson, captain
Ivan Brown-Mahoney, first lieutenant
Catherine Vasiliev-Scott, second lieutenant
Alexei (Bing) Abington-Smith, senior midshipman
Lucy Prescott-Chin, midshipman
Margaret (Maggie) Borisov-Harcourt, midshipman

Spacers

Ntumba, surgeon
Maxwell, arms master
Goldstein, EVA master
Hausmann, atmosphere master
Doubek, atmosphere mate
Jenkins, ship's cook
Moira Singh, able spacer
Gomez, able spacer
Nguyen, able spacer
Yao, surgeon's boy
Trask, ship's boy

ONE

It's difficult to get dressed for a business deal when everything hangs on not letting the other person know you're making one.

I had chosen my lilac morning coat, spotless if a little out of fashion, white shirt with a flowing cravat, and buff trousers. It certainly looked like the sort of thing a careless, wealthy gentlewoman might wear to impress a lady. Not the sort of thing the scion of a penniless house might wear to go begging. Though what I was doing was, in a sense, both.

In the sky above, a red streak interrupted the blue: a terraforming capsule burning off. Mars was terraformed generations ago, but keeping our atmosphere was an ongoing fight against the eroding force of the solar wind. An ongoing, expensive fight. The atmospheric gases in the capsule cost a small fortune to purchase from Earth or Venus, and every landowner had to pay our share in taxes. Taxes we could ill afford.

I swung off my horse before Miss Hendershott's front door and carefully dusted off my coat. For a moment I hesitated, my hand just over the wrought-iron knocker. I wished I could have waited longer. I wasn't entirely sure of the lady's feelings. She certainly seemed to like me; the entire summer she had been renting the lake house, she had invited me to every soirée, dinner, and walking excursion that she had put on. And for my part, I had hosted several large (and expensive) events to impress her. The cost had set my teeth on edge, but my mother had reminded me that it was an investment. It would be foolish to lose my chance with her by letting it be rumored we were short of funds.

But there wasn't going to be another chance. Tomorrow Miss Hendershott would give up her lease on the lake house and return to town for the winter season. She didn't know I couldn't afford to follow her there.

I gave the knocker a sharp rap and was admitted. Miss Hendershott's butler dispatched a boy for my horse and ushered me into her morning room. "Captain Black-Medvedev is visiting also," he commented before opening the door.

Unfortunate. I needed to talk to her alone, and besides, Captain Black was a bore. One of the veterans from the last war, promoted beyond his station like so many had been. But Miss Hendershott rose to greet me politely, smoothing her yellow frock.

"Miss Prescott-Chin!" she cried, with obvious pleasure. "I hoped you would come to see me before I left!"

"I promised I would." I lightly touched her fingertips before taking a seat. Dimples flashed in her cheeks.

Captain Black greeted me politely, and I forced a smile at him. Not his fault he was ruining my plans. Unless he, too, had designs on the wealthy heiress. It wouldn't surprise me; she was personable, reasonably attractive in a round-faced, brunette sort of way, and most importantly, absolutely rolling in Martian Imperial pounds sterling. But she would never be interested in him, would she? I hoped not.

Miss Hendershott was talking about her plans for the winter.

Landing City, some distance south of Olympus Mons, was a bustling metropolis at any time of year, but especially in winter, since it was near the equator. Anyone who was anyone had a house there. Even we did—but ours was let. We pretended it was because we didn't enjoy the city.

"I hear the Emprex Themself is having a soirée to celebrate the opening of the new mining station," I said.

"So I hear, though I don't know yet if I'll be invited," she said wistfully. I curled my toes inside my boots, embarrassed to have brought it up. I knew about the soirée because I had received an invitation. My father was the Marquis of Hellas Basin; we couldn't possibly not be invited. But Miss Hendershott's parents had made their money on trade. As far as the Emprex was concerned, she was new money and not someone Their Majesty would know.

"That mining station will change everything," Captain Black declared. "With easier access to the asteroid belt, we won't have to rely so heavily on Earth trade for water. I'd like to see the look on those Earthers' faces when they're forced to admit we're not their lowly colony anymore."

I eyed him up and down. "I'm surprised to hear *you* say that."

"I think every loyal Martian would say that!"

Giving a noncommittal nod, I asked, "Isn't that waistcoat real silk?"

It certainly was; the bamboo imitation never took dye quite well enough to reach that rich berry color. But real silk had to be imported from Earth, since we didn't make it here. And it had been under embargo since we'd won our independence from Earth.

Captain Black's face reddened. In the politest of ways, I'd accused him of disloyalty to Mars by buying smuggled goods, and there wasn't a thing he could say to that. He stiffly rose to his feet. "Somehow the company in your morning room has grown less congenial, Miss Hendershott." With a deep bow to her, and a stiff nod to me, he went out.

She gave me a troubled look. "I'm afraid you've offended him," she said.

I cringed internally. She thought I'd offended him by accident? But it was probably best to let her believe that. She was a kindly soul and wouldn't ever purposefully give offense, even to an obnoxious person like Captain Black.

"I'll have to make it up to him another time," I said. "Today I really came to speak to you alone."

Her fingers twisted in her lap. "Alone?"

"You can't be in any doubt of my regard for you," I said quietly. "I don't think this comes as a surprise."

"No…" she stammered. "At least, I thought—"

"Let me be clear enough to remove all doubt." I cleared my throat. "You have captured my affection with your kindness, your good nature, and your pleasant disposition. Though we have known each other only a short time, I feel confident that we would be an excellent match. Miss Hendershott, will you be my wife?"

A blush spread over her cheeks. "I … Miss Prescott, I am sorry. I don't think I can agree."

I froze. I hadn't prepared for this part. "You don't…but why? I feel we have gotten along very well together over this summer. And you certainly seemed to enjoy my company."

"I do," she rushed to assure me. "Very much. You're a good person, and I confess I did feel some attachment. But I didn't feel it was returned."

"It is," I insisted. "I deeply—like you." Damn it, it would help for all of this if I could be less honest.

Miss Hendershott gave me a pitying look. "I know you do. But I really don't feel…" She trailed off. "I was hoping for a little more than liking. I am too young yet to give up on the idea of a grand passion." She flushed deeply at the words.

A romantic. Conversations we'd had over the summer came to my mind; the stories she enjoyed, the plays she raved about. I should have picked up on that more. I should have brought flowers, maybe proposed by the side of the lake…"Forgive me for being so reserved," I said. "It's never been my way to talk much about my feelings. But I do, I really do very ardently admire you."

She gave a sad smile. "I'm sorry. It's difficult, you see, in my position. I know that it will be hard for me to sort out love from material interest. And maybe you aren't just asking because of my fortune. But I can't be *sure* of that, and if I can't be sure, well—it's really better if I say no."

Now I could feel my own cheeks burning. "It's not as though I have nothing of my own to offer," I argued. "I'm in line for a title; there's the estate to think of. You would gain as much as I would. Not that practicality is the only thing to consider," I added hastily, "but, as far as material things go, we would be a very practical match. I know you would like to rise higher in society than you are. Perhaps to be presented to the Emprex …" I trailed off. Mentioning the invitation I'd received would seem too mercenary to her, I was sure.

"I think you've misunderstood me a great deal," she said, rising to her feet. "I'm not in the *market* for a title. I was hoping for a heart. But I'm beginning to wonder if you have one."

I jumped up. "I do! I swear I do."

"Does it belong to me?" She searched my face, eyes flicking from one of mine to the other. "Does it, Miss Prescott?"

I faltered under her gaze, eventually dropping my eyes to the floor. "It would," I said earnestly, to the rug. "I would be very good to you. You'd never have cause to complain of any lack of attention from me." I raised my eyes hopefully to her face again.

She crushed me with a frown. "I think you've answered my question, Miss Prescott," she said coldly. "Perhaps someday you'll find someone who wants to be a marchioness and have you around all day, *being good* to them." Her voice broke and she fled the room.

I kicked myself the whole ride home. My bay galloped along the bank, just before the ground swooped down to the pebbly shore of the Hellas Sea. In the distance, a jagged red ridge marked the edge of the Hellas Basin. Down here within the caldera was meadowland where wild grasses and clover grew, building the soil in case it should ever be needed for farmland. We should be selling the hay, I thought, and I managed to distract myself with wondering whether the price of the hay would be worth the cost of the labor to harvest it. But perhaps we didn't have enough cash on hand to do even that.

Down the bank, I saw my brother, William, sitting on the gravel beach. Reining in the horse, I left him to crop the wild grasses and picked my way down the bank.

"Good morning, William."

He didn't look up, but he gave a faint gesture with his hand to let me know he had heard me. I crouched down beside him. He had picked out all the largest stones of a particular shade of red and was arranging them in concentric circles. Smaller rocks of a browner color formed rays radiating out from the center.

"I like it." He didn't answer—he does not speak. He has what we on Mars call the noble condition; although he is older than I am, I have understood since I was small that his abilities and habits would always be different from mine. But our family speaks to him regardless. He understands, at least when he cares to listen.

I often tell him the things that are on my mind—when I had to sit the exams at New Oxford, when I had quarrelled with my mother over a party she was throwing that I didn't want to attend. It was nice to talk to someone, and I didn't mind that he didn't offer advice. So I had come over with the thought of unburdening myself over my financial worries. My fear that, with my hopes for a good marriage dashed, our family could lose everything.

But as I examined his circles, I realized I couldn't possibly tell him any of this. If he did understand it, it would terrify him. My exams had no real importance for him, but this? It could change the entire course of our lives, if I couldn't find some other solution, and any words that might introduce that worry into his mind died on my lips.

So I sat with him, for the better part of an hour, and found him rocks. The regolith was sharp enough to cut your hands; the sea hadn't been lapping at that shore long enough to round them much. William wanted the roundest ones from right at the water's edge, that were softened on the corners like sea glass.

A crisp breeze came off the sea, a first hint of the long, cold winter ahead. All the neighbors would soon head to Landing, where the dry season would be setting in. We'd be left here in the cold and the scanty snow.

"I had no luck with Miss Hendershott," I said at last, as I deposited a small harvest of stones at William's feet. "She wanted someone more romantic."

He carefully began a new circle a handspan out from the previous one. "I feel maybe Miss Hendershott was right," I said. "She asked if I had a heart at all. I know I did have one. But now? I feel nothing. Nothing for her, nothing for anyone."

I held out a good stone on my upturned palm, and he took it, brown eyes passing over my face to focus on the rock. "Well, I feel something for *you*," I said. "And Papa and Mama. But not for Miss Hendershott or anybody else. I don't feel the kind of passion women expect from me. Maybe they think I'm some kind of machine, wound up with a key to parrot words at them, without any soul behind them. But it's just that I don't have room in me for anyone else."

He paused for a moment, his hands in his lap. The wind

ruffled his light brown hair. He was out here in only his shirt-sleeves. Quite improper, but he hated coats. In the winter, he would grudgingly accept one, because it meant he could still come here. He would skip stones across the ice or sweep the light snow into patterns. This was the place where he could be happy—and alone, though I could see his companion swinging his legs against the bank a stone's throw away. We could never be entirely sure William wouldn't get lost, too interested in his art or exploring to notice how far he'd gone.

I held out a stone before realizing he hadn't been reaching for one. He was waiting, because he thought there was something else I should be saying. Which there was; I'd been trying to avoid it. "So you *are* listening. Don't believe me?"

He gave a small gesture with his hand and took the rock.

"It's true," I said softly. "I used to be different, at least."

Once, you'd have never seen me anywhere alone. There were always two of us: one plump tow-headed girl and one lanky dark girl, running through the wild grasses. My hair had darkened to old flax and the plumpness had settled around my bosom, but she had changed more than I had. She had disappeared altogether. Left me. Gone.

I could have languished, torn my heart to pieces with missing her. But she hadn't been worth it, not after the things she'd said and done. Instead I had shut my heart down, silenced it with a pillow over its face. Maybe it was dead. Who could say.

All I knew was that I had tried to court any number of beautiful women and felt nothing. They were too accomplished, too finely spoken, too well dressed. I wanted someone honest and blunt. I wanted someone who would lean in close, in the middle of one of these fussy parties, and whisper something obscene.

But not Moira. I didn't want *her* back again. Not ever.

When I arrived home, my mother was pacing the floor. One look at my face answered her unspoken question, but she still clutched my arm. "Tell me everything!"

I told her, in as much detail as I could recall, what had been said. She frowned and shook her head. "Why, *why* couldn't you put a little more passion into your proposal? You *know* she's a romantic!"

"It wouldn't be right," I said. "I couldn't start this on false pretenses."

"None of us knows everything about the other person when we get married."

I sat down heavily on the sofa. "Anyway, I couldn't have pulled it off. I'm not that sort of person."

"You *are* a terrible actress," she admitted. "So what is next?"

Yanking off my white gloves, I balled them together and threw them onto the coffee table. "Next? There is no next. That was my last idea!"

"Surely there is somewhere on Mars another wealthy gentlewoman who might be interested."

"I don't think so." In my room, I had a list of every single lesbian with any fortune to speak of in *Who's Who*. I hadn't tried with all of them, but I nearly had. "What else is there? Another season in town to try to meet someone? The town house is let."

"Perhaps if we borrow—"

"No. No borrowing. That's what got you into this mess."

"Not only," she said mournfully. "This place was deep in debt when Papa and I inherited it."

"From generations of Prescotts and Chins borrowing."

"And the land is poor. If only our Founder ancestors had gotten a mineral assay before claiming this land…"

"There could have been a perfectly good living in it if they'd focused on farming, especially once the terraforming was done.

But no, they wanted to live like dukes and spend all year in Landing."

"Well, it's too late now." She sighed. "I'm sorry to have nothing but this mess to hand down to you. I'm afraid we won't be able to stall the creditors much longer. Just this morning, Mr. Lopez was by to see Papa again. Nasty money-grubbing little *krepostnoy*."

"Mother!" I cried, aghast. That was *not* a nice word for a colonist—someone whose ancestors had come to Mars after the first settlement.

"I'm not sorry," she said. "How can these people come after us like this? Why can't they give us more time?"

Privately, I felt it was unfair to blame Mr. Lopez, the colonist collections man, over the gentlemen who actually owned the bank. It was always easier for her to be angry at a commoner than someone of our own class. But I couldn't get into that with my mother, or I'd start talking about whose fault this actually was, and get more angry at her than I wanted to be.

"I will simply have to find some kind of job," I said. "Perhaps a governess … some kind of companion …"

"That won't pay the mortgage."

"It'll give me a place to live, when …" I trailed off, looking around the elegant sitting room, with the French doors that overlooked the sea. I couldn't bear to say, "when we lose the house." Generations of my family had built everything I saw, from the first underground bunkers, to this house, and even to the sea glimmering outside. They had come to Mars when Hellas Basin had been nothing but an empty crater of red rock, and now there was blue water slowly lapping at the red gravel shore and a green lawn running down as far as the bank.

"And what about your father and me?" my mother asked tightly. "To be put out of our home … I worry what that will do to your father." Her eyes went to the dueling pistols in their rack over the fireplace.

"You will simply have to lean on one another," I said shortly. I hoped my father was better than to take such a coward's way out. Better men than him had been poor before. "William, I will keep with me. He'll be my responsibility soon in any event."

"He can't live in some garret with you, with nobody watching him!" she cried.

I got to my feet. She was right, but I didn't know what else to do. There was simply nothing else to be done. Either I would find some situation where I could live with my brother, or … There was no *or*. I would. Somehow.

The door swung open and my father strode in. "Agatha, you wouldn't believe what I just heard from Singh."

My mother scowled at him. "This is hardly the moment, Henry. Our daughter's just had her heart broken, again."

I prickled. Heart broken? I was understood to have none. "I'd like to hear the news."

"War," he said, eyes wide. "Earth has declared war on Mars. Didn't I always say they'd take that mining station as a provocation?"

"That'll mean more taxes, for certain," said my mother.

A slow smile spread across my face. It was the best news I could have possibly heard.

"What *are* you smiling about?" my mother demanded. "With all this money trouble, and now a war …"

"Don't you see?" I said, scooping up my gloves from the table. "The one solves the other. In wartime they'll be desperate for officers. And war means prize money. Quick promotion." If a man like Captain Black could rise to the top, surely I could.

"What are you saying?" asked my father. "You don't mean *you*—"

"I do." I said. "I'm joining the Imperial Navy. I'm going to space."

Two

Of course there was much to do before I could ship out. Letters flew back and forth between my father and various friends, seeking a recommendation for me as a midshipman. I dug my grandmother's chest out of the attic to take what I could from her old Navy kit: stopwatch, spyglass, a little round mirror for light signals.

Most importantly, I needed money. A commoner could go to space just by enlisting, but as a gentlewoman, I needed to pay a number of fees and outfit myself appropriately. Thank the ancestors we had the horses to sell.

I broke the news to the stablemaster myself. He had worked for my family since he was a boy and was one of my father's closest confidants. Nothing was as important to my father as those horses, and he reposed absolute trust in the man who kept them.

Shafts of light fell through the dusty air and onto the straw-strewn floor. The smell of horses filled my nose and for a second I had to stand still, chest aching, hands in fists. I hadn't been here since…well, in years. When I needed to ride, I had someone else prepare the horse and bring him to me. It hurt too much to be here.

But there was Ramesh, examining the hooves on my father's big bay. My father had hoped to make money racing him, but he hadn't been lucky enough to cover the cost of his keep, and now he was too old to race. Ramesh loved him, and so did my father. This wasn't going to be pleasant.

"Ah, Miss Lucy," he said, straightening up. "I don't see much of you these days."

"But I see nothing has changed here." I leaned against the stall door. "Did my father tell you I'm going to space?"

"He did, and I wish you luck. My daughter's a spacer now, you know. Though with the war starting, I'm glad it's a merchant ship and not the Navy."

I stammered vaguely. Of course he would bring her up. I shouldn't have thought I could come in here and talk to her father and not have him talk about her.

"But then maybe you've had a letter from Moira since I have. Weren't you two thick as thieves, back in the day?"

I swallowed hard and regained command of myself. "When we were little, I suppose," I said casually. "I haven't heard from her since she left here." On my eighteenth birthday. Five years, eight months, and twelve days ago. The morning after my coming-out ball.

"Well, she likes it," he said. "Though I miss her so much. She doesn't come down long enough to take the train out here. My husband and I go to the city and visit her when she does come down."

I had a strong feeling the amount of leave she had wasn't the real reason she wasn't coming to Hellas. I wouldn't have wanted to come within a thousand miles of her either. "Does my father talk to you about his debts?"

He bent over and went back to inspecting the bay's hooves. "Yeah, I know about all that. Is it time, then? Are they repossessing the place?"

"Not—not quite yet." I hesitated. This was so hard. "I am hoping to save some of it with this Navy idea, but . . . well, the horses are the only thing we have left to sell that isn't mortgaged. And I need money for my commission."

Ramesh kept his head down. His hair was white all over now and I felt a crushing sadness for him. "I understand." His voice quavered.

"Is it—is it better if you do the selling yourself? You could find someone you would trust with them."

"I s'pose."

If Moira and I had still been friends, I might have opened the stall door and gone in there with him and squeezed his shoulder. A friend's father is almost like a relative. But instead I was only his employer.

"You always have a home here," I said. "Even without the horses. As long as we still own the estate."

"That won't be much longer." He straightened up, wiping his face with the back of his hand. It only smeared his tears into mud. "I'll move on if I can. See if I can stay with the horses."

"Of course," I said. "My father will want to talk to you more about it. I only wanted to tell you myself, because it's for me they're being sold. So that I can join the Navy and see what I can save. Maybe enough for William and me to live on."

At that he forced a smile. "It's all right, Miss Lucy. Really. You do what you have to."

I folded my lips together and looked down. He was much, much too kind. My family had used him up and wasted the patrimony that supported him and dozens of others. I thought of having this conversation over and over, with the housekeeper and the driver and the farmhands and everyone, when the house was repossessed. No wonder my mother worried about my father losing the courage to see it through. I made a mental note to sell those dueling pistols too.

Once the money was raised and my recommendation accepted, I said goodbye to my parents and bought a train ticket to Landing. A friend in town put me up for a few days; at least I did not have to stay in some cheap boarding house. I needed the time to buy the essentials in the handbook my father's friend had sent.

That part I enjoyed thoroughly. I hadn't been to town in a Martian year, and I hadn't been shopping in longer. I had stretched out my wardrobe by carefully scrubbing out stains and making over old frocks. My friends had simply thrown away their out-of-fashion clothes, clothes I would have been grateful to have, but asking for them would have revealed our poverty.

The boots I needed for zero gravity were soft leather, with the upper thicker than the sole, since I would have to hook my feet under loops to keep myself in place. The spacers went barefoot, but officers must be dignified. I was measured for a pair before heading to my favorite part of the city, the clothiers' district.

Several happy hours later, I took possession of the last parcel and returned to the main street. Two pairs of buff knee-breeches! Two waistcoats, one buff and one blue! One long navy jacket, with gold buttons! Three white linen shirts!

I was skeptical about that last one. I couldn't imagine the ship would be turning over laundry often enough for me to have clean shirts every three days. Probably—I shuddered—I would be expected to make those three shirts last a week. But I couldn't afford to go beyond the list. I would have exactly what the other midshipmen had. If I smelled bad, at least we'd all smell the same.

Wrinkling my nose, I darted into a shop for one last, guilty purchase: a very small vial of bergamot cologne.

The shoes were ready in a few days, and I packed them into my bag with everything else. Shirts, stockings, a notebook, pencils. It wasn't much; the bag itself was made of thin canvas so that the whole thing massed under five kilos. Five kilos to last me a year or more till I might return. I couldn't even predict what I might be homesick for, but there was no weight allowance left for sentiment in any case.

I wished vainly for a friend to see me off at the elevator, but I was close enough to no one else. I had plenty of friends here in the city, but no one I wanted near me at a time I might be tempted to cry. So I said goodbye to my hostess at her house and walked.

The district around the space elevator bustled with activity. A few weeks since war had been declared and everything had changed. Whole new warehouses had sprung up. Trucks full of sheet metal and cables and hydrogen tanks and unlabeled crates waited to get close to the elevator, and shouting longshoremen passed boxes from hand to hand to get them onto the pier.

The pier was simply a broad, concrete platform where cargo rested until more expert stevedores could pack it into an elevator car. One car, unfastened from the cables, was being loaded, while a steam-driven crane carefully maneuvered a full one into place.

I couldn't see where passengers could wait, and yet I'd been assured this was the place to report. I stood around awkwardly in my uniform, hoping someone would notice me and tell me where I was supposed to go.

"Lookit that toff!" cried a male voice, and I spun around. A number of navvies were looking at me, faces scowling, but I couldn't tell which had spoken. They looked away again and a voice muttered, "Fucking useless prats."

I stood stricken, staring after the men. What could possibly have gotten into them? I wasn't accustomed to being addressed like that by commoners. Or anyone, for that matter.

"Do forgive them," said an urbane voice beside me, and I turned to see a naval officer. He wore a dark blue coat, but no epaulets: a lieutenant. "There's been some unpleasantness lately over the war. It isn't personal."

"Thank you, sir," I said. "Is this where I should wait for the elevator?"

"It's where I'm waiting," he said. "No point in getting closer till they finish hitching up the car. Once they've done that, we'll get in that lower hatch." He gestured.

"This is my first time, sir," I admitted.

He raised a thin black eyebrow. "That much was obvious by your lack of a salute."

I felt my cheeks redden as I switched my bag to my other arm to make an awkward attempt at one. "Sorry, sir."

"You'll have time to study the regs on the way up," he said with an easy wave of his hand. "I'm Lieutenant Brown-Mahoney."

"Prescott-Chin, sir."

That earned me an evaluating stare. Had he heard of me? My family? But instead he simply said, "You want a piece of advice, Mister Prescott?"

"Of course, sir."

"Always respect the chain of command. You're from a good family, right? Pretty rare that someone tells you what to do. On the ship you'll have to learn to obey promptly. You're old for a midshipman."

"I know that, sir, but—"

"I was speaking. You're old for a midshipman, and that means it'll be harder to pick up the right habits. Some things have got to become instinct for you, and that means they've got to crowd out whatever instincts have gotten you through so far. Right now, your reflex when someone criticizes you is to interrupt. You need to have the reflex to sit tight, take your medicine, and then say yes, sir."

I paused, to be sure he was finished. "Yes, sir."

"That goes the other way, too. You're being trained for command and that means you can't take any guff from the men. But I'm less worried about that. You're a gentlewoman. You know how to manage your servants. It's the same thing, though in the Navy there's less leeway for insubordination. You'll soon see why. Spacers are a rough lot and space is a dangerous place. A bleeding heart risks everyone's skin. If something happens, we all die horribly in the vacuum." He gave a friendly smile. "But I'm not worried about that. You'll learn fast."

I licked my lips with a dry tongue. "Thank you, sir."

Just then there must have been a signal, for he strode forward. A small crowd began to gather near the hatch he had indicated, and I hurried to join it.

The trip up took most of a day. I didn't see more of Brown; my ticket entitled me to a little private compartment that must have been in a different section than his. But I followed his advice and studied the regs. There were two hundred pages of them, many of which I couldn't understand. No sexual activity along the chain of command, that was clear enough. Just as on the ground it was strongly discouraged to have a relationship with an employee or, for that matter, anyone but a social equal. But no drunkenness? How could one even get drunk when reg. 4.15.871 set the alcohol ration at four ounces of strong liquor per day? If one stole the alcohol to get drunk on, that was a whole separate offense, 6.34.267, theft from stores.

Well, I was sure it would all become clear in the proper context.

THREE

Phobos Station, at the top of the elevator, was a bewildering hub of cargo and people. There was just enough gravity to make things drift slowly downwards, but not enough to actually walk. Some people pushed off walls and floated out of the car, but I crept tentatively along the handholds. It would show me up as a landsman, but a mishap would be even more embarrassing.

Phobos was all pre-Singularity construction, meaning stone and dark metal, with hollows on the ceiling where the electric lights had been. The tunnels had been carved perfectly smooth and round by robots, but the new fiber-optic lights left them dim and half-shadowed. Modern construction would have left more windows.

Teams awkwardly dragged nets full of canisters and crates down the concourse—still the easiest way to get things around on Phobos. It wasn't like you could conveniently bring a horse up here, and the anti-electricity laws made no exception for space, not when there was any option to get the same work done without power.

My ship, the *IMS Mariposa*, was too large to dock at the station directly. I would have to take a small launch. I should try to find one directly, but I found myself strangely uneasy. For all the lightness of my body, there was a cold weight in my stomach. Was I ready? Shouldn't I get my space legs first? Or do they call it space legs at all, when in space nobody uses their legs for much? Was I going to humiliate myself in front of my new crew, the crew I'd have to be with for the next year?

I crept along with the crowd that flowed around the station. This area seemed to be mainly for passengers. I spotted small, spartan restaurants and a busy area labeled CORRESPONDENCE. It turned out to be a place for writing letters and having them posted down to the surface; you could also rent a mailbox or purchase a money order. I sent a postcard so my parents would know I'd made it this far. It would be months before they had any other word from me.

At last I saw the information desk, at a crossroads where several concourses came together. Behind the desk, a black board with magnetic letter tiles spelled out departing ships and airlock numbers.

I pushed off from the wall to see more closely. The *Mariposa* was listed at P-6, and P concourse branched off to my right. That should be easy enough. I tried to turn around and return to the wall, only to twist awkwardly in the air. I had pushed off too far from the wall, and now nothing was in reach.

My cheeks heated. It was the most basic landsman's mistake. You were supposed to keep within reach of a wall, and if you needed to cross an empty space, you made sure you had enough momentum to make it all the way across. Otherwise you got trapped in the middle of a room, as I just had.

At least I did know enough not to try swimming motions;

that wouldn't work in a thin medium like air. And I was pretty sure blowing wasn't going to do it. The obvious solution was to ask the man behind the desk, but I couldn't possibly embarrass myself like that. No, I was lucky to have done this here, instead of aboard ship. Phobos's low gravity would drift me back to the ground eventually. All I had to do was act natural.

I read the departures board a second time, and a third. My foot was less than an arm's length from the floor now. I was starting in on a fourth read when I heard a commotion and half turned to look.

A man in plain clothes hung in the air a little way off, one hand grasping a ceiling strap to keep himself in place. Below, a small crowd was gathering to listen. The man shouted, "Let them try waging a war without our labor! Let them try forcing our labor without our consent!"

"Nobody bothers asking for it," a heckler shouted back. "Were you born yesterday?"

The man kept shouting. "Not our war! Not our empire! God fuck the—"

He was interrupted by a woman in uniform, who had come up behind him and grasped him by the arm. "That's *quite* enough of that," she said. "I've got you on disturbing the peace already. If you finish that sentence, I'll have you under the Sedition Act."

The man didn't finish whatever he had been going to say. He turned to follow the constable, but turned over his shoulder to shout, "No war for the Emprex! Mars is the planet and people!"

The crowd began to disperse. I felt my foot brush the floor and pushed off toward the wall. The scene I had just observed troubled me. It was like the men who had heckled me at the elevator. Something was definitely stirring and I wasn't sure what. Everything had been calm the last time I'd been to the city. But now we were on a war footing, and instead of throwing their efforts toward victory, some were spreading discontent. Why?

The last line, at least, I remembered. It was a slogan of a social reformer a few years back, who had campaigned for class equality. Not a revolutionary like this fellow—he never spoke against the Empire. Even I had thought he made sense, when Moira had lent me his pamphlets.

The memory of her made my stomach turn sour. The social reform movement had petered out years ago, when the man at its head had died. But I had stopped keeping up on it by that point anyway, since Moira was gone. It was always something we had done together. Without her, it felt hollow.

The launch was beginning to load when I reached the correct airlock. It was the shape of a tin can, big enough for twenty or so, with bubble windows at either end. There weren't any seats, just a number of handholds spaced regularly around the cylinder. I selected one on the floor so that Phobos's weak gravity would keep me near it until we left.

Two spacers came in, maneuvering a massive netted bundle of packages which they stowed near the rear. "Give me that duffle, sir, and I'll stow it for you," said one of them, and I glanced around for a man they might be speaking to. Then I remembered that in the Navy, male honorifics were used for everyone. Gender, like clean laundry, was a luxury the Navy expected you to do without. I carefully lobbed my bag across the launch.

A number of drunk spacers came next, guiding the slack body of an unconscious companion. They reeked of cheap alcohol and ribbed each other loudly about how much they had drunk and how they had behaved at the station bars.

A commotion at the hatch preceded the next party: three miserable-looking people in civilian clothing, followed by a spacer and a lieutenant, both carrying swords. "Please," begged one of the civilians. "I've been in space for a *year* and I need to go *home*. My little girl—"

"Shut your moanin'," said the spacer with them.

More diplomatically, the lieutenant added, "The law gives us the right to impress you in wartime. Anyone who makes their living in space is liable, as you should be aware." She gave a tight smile. "Just hope for a quick end to the war, and then we can all put our feet back on the ground."

Once the impressed spacers had found places within the launch, the lieutenant looked at me. "You're our new midshipman?"

"Yes, sir."

"Catherine Vasiliev-Scott," she said, extending her hand.

"Lucy Prescott-Chin." She clasped my hand briefly, careful not to pull either of us off our feet.

"Don't mind these complainers," she said, gesturing to the three she had brought in. "They'll be paid better here than on the merchant ships, and when the war is over they'll go home with prize money, most likely." She moved to the transparent bubble at the front. "It's your first time, right? Come up here."

I joined her in the bubble and gasped. Much of the view to the right was blocked by the station, but beyond that I could see Mars spread out below, a green and red jewel. The blue scar of the Valles Marineris dominated the view: once a massive canyon, now a narrow inland sea.

The airlock was closed and Lieutenant Vasiliev began to give commands. Spacers at the sides and rear of the launch pulled levers to fire each thruster at her mark. Slowly we drew away from the station, and the faint gravity of Phobos faded. As the launch pivoted away from Mars, I saw the ship.

"That's her," said Vasiliev fondly. "The *IMS Mariposa*. Ninety-six feet stem to stern, forty-two in the beam. Of course she's more beautiful under sail, but we'll be on board before that happens."

To my landsman's eye, she wasn't beautiful at all. The ship looked like a stubby cigar, slightly fatter at the back, all dark metal except for clear bubbles at either end and a shiny translucent panel along one side. As we drew closer, I could see the complex framing of the sails, folded flat against her sides. That was her main method of travel, with propulsion fuel carried only for emergencies. If all went well, we wouldn't spend a drop—or so my reading had told me. Now that it was wartime, it would be surprising if things went that smoothly.

Behind me, the drunk spacers were singing, "Fare thee well, my own true love," in raucous voices. The impressed spacer who had begged to get back to her little girl was crying quietly, tiny diamond drops scattering away from her as she wiped her eyes.

This was it, I thought. I was going to space. Goodbye to the city, to the old estate, to the sea. To parties where I had socialized like it was my job. Goodbye to Miss Hendershott, and may she find someone who loves her the way she wants. Goodbye to my family, and may they keep the creditors from the door long enough for me to get paid.

We docked at an airlock on the main level, just in front of the rear bubble. I followed Vasiliev out of the launch and stopped dead in the air, gawking.

The main deck, where the sails were controlled, was a single broad room, running the entire length of the ship. It would have been very spacious, except most of the space was taken up with massive wooden beams, fifteen feet long and four inches thick, tilted upward from the bottom edges of the room—the levers for raising the sails. Between these were cranks, pumps, and smaller levers, for other adjustments. Only a narrow column in the middle was clear, where spacers were easily launching themselves back and forth, as comfortable without gravity as fish in water.

To our left was a raised deck with a railing, where blue-coated officers stood with their boots hooked into mesh loops on the floor. "Permission to come aboard, sir!" cried Vasiliev, saluting, and the center officer looked up. His epaulets showed me that he was the captain, as did his bearing. He was middle-aged, my father's generation, and the braid floating behind him was white. Prominent cheekbones gave his face an elegant look. His name had been in the letter I had received: George Kim-Johnson, captain. Scion of the Xanthe Kim-Johnsons. Decorated several times after encounters with pirates. I had landed quite a favorable first post.

"Granted, Mr. Vasiliev," said the captain. "Is that the new middie? Bring them up here."

The lieutenant made it up in a single leap; I followed less gracefully. I saluted the captain carefully, so as not to launch myself into the air. He nodded and ignored me at first, asking Vasiliev, "Did you find enough new men?"

"Yes, sir. Though not all of them are happy about it."

"They don't have to be happy. They have only to serve the Empire," he said shortly. "As I have no doubt they will do, once they accept their duty. You, midshipman. Prescott-Chin, yes?"

"Yes, sir."

"You're old for a midshipman."

I had learned my lesson from the officer at the elevator dock. "Yes, sir."

"Well, in war we take all kinds. Just remember: everyone on this quarterdeck outranks you. Abington-Smith here is senior midshipman."

I followed his gesture. Abington-Smith was a lanky young man, with carrot-red hair and an unfortunate complexion. He must have been about seventeen. I gave him a tiny smile. Of course people younger than me would outrank me—I had no experience. I only hoped he was more competent than his age would suggest.

"Show her your berth, Mister Abington," said the captain. "And then be back here in twenty. We'll assemble the hands before we start to make sail."

I took my bag from the spacer who had claimed it earlier and followed the young midshipman off the quarterdeck, down the empty center of the room. As soon as we were out of hearing of the captain, Abington began to chatter. "You'll like it here, Prescott. *Mariposa*'s a good sound ship and the captain's aces. Mind your head. Here, don't swing yourself on that, you'll pull a sail out. Grab this. My first name's Andrei, but they call me Bing mostly."

"Lucy Prescott-Chin," I said. "Who calls you Bing, the officers or the men?"

"The other middies, and the men if I'm not commanding them at the moment. It's funny for us. We technically outrank them but they also know a lot more than us, so it's good to hang around and be friendly. Not *too* friendly, that's fraternizing. But you know, listening to what they say so we can learn. We're not scary to them like the real officers." He jerked a thumb behind us, at the quarterdeck. "This we're on now is the sail deck. Our berth is on the gun deck, up forward where the bow chasers are. That way's the forecastle, the clear bubble at the bows where we can see where we're going. There's always somebody there and on the quarterdeck."

"Is the gun deck up or down from here? Or do we even have up or down?" I stared down at my feet. My brain told me that was down, but I had turned somewhat in my efforts to follow Bing, and I could see the quarterdeck below me. Or behind me. I felt suddenly giddy.

Bing looked back at me and circled back to hover in front of me. "You're not going to toss your lunch, are you? First thing you should learn is maybe where the sacks are, because that'll be a mess otherwise."

I shook my head. "No, I just got turned around. How do you manage without up and down?"

"Oh, there's up and down all right. In space there's no direction to speak of, but we invent directions to make sense of it, 'cause otherwise we'd be lost as a pigeon on Mars. See, look. Where my feet are pointing is ship's down, right? That's why I point my feet that way when I could be pointing them anywhere. And that way, toward the sun, is ship's up."

I oriented my body perpendicular to the decks above and below, to match his. He was right; it did help. "How do you know which way the sun is?"

"Because we always point ship's up at the sun, unless we're in a battle or something and we can't. See, at the very top is the water store, which helps block some of the radiation. And under that are the algae tanks, which need the sunlight that filters through the water. Then water filtration, laundry, air quality, that kind of housekeeping thing. After that is this deck. Sails are right in the middle, coming out from sides of the sail deck here. Like a butterfly, right?"

We reached a small opening in the wooden deck and he dived down toward it, pulling himself through with his arms. "And this is the gun deck. The men berth all along here." I looked, but only saw a low-ceilinged room full of torpedo tubes. There was barely room to stand upright, if one wanted to attempt it, and the tubes were less than two feet apart.

"They berth where?"

"Between the guns," he said, as if it were obvious. "Or above or below them. Wherever. Remember we can use any surface. Anything's a ceiling, anything's a floor, whatever you need it to be. Look, here's the forward gunroom."

A small sliding hatch, about two feet around, was the door to our berth. Midshipmen couldn't be broad-shouldered, I supposed.

Inside was a torpedo tube with a tiny porthole beside it, and not much room for anything else. The walls were knobbled with clips and handholds, and a few boxes and sacks were strapped on. But I didn't stop to look at those, since there was somebody already in the room. She was dressed like Bing and me, in dark blue tailcoat, knee-breeches, stockings, and soft leather boots. Her three-cornered hat floated beside her, and her dark braid was mussed from pulling off the clips that were supposed to keep the hat on. She was curled up into a ball, making quiet whimpering sounds.

As we entered, she raised her face from her knees and regarded us. She was maybe twelve years old, freckly, her eyes wet and puffy from crying. "Buck up, Maggie!" said Bing, in what I supposed was meant to be a bracing tone. "Look, you aren't the only landsman in the berth. Here's Lucy Prescott-Chin! She may be grown but she's never been to space before, any more than you have."

The girl dragged her sleeve across her face, leaving a shiny trail on the dark wool. Depending on laundry, that mark might be there a long time. "Margaret Borisov-Harcourt," she said shakily, trying admirably to regain her poise. "Pleased to make your acquaintance."

"The pleasure is mine," I said, sketching a bow. Her presence instantly made me feel ten times better. I wasn't the rawest recruit around; here was someone even less at ease than I was. And that meant I had a use beyond simply trailing after Bing, trying to learn things. I could support this child and perhaps make her transition to shipboard life easier. First step was to pretend I hadn't noticed her tears, to avoid embarrassing her. "The Argyre Borisov-Harcourts?"

"The Lowell ones," she said, with a loud sniff.

Bing finished strapping my case to the wall. "There we are, shipshape and ready to get under way."

"Where will we sleep?" I asked, eyeing the six walls of the room.

"Take your pick," he said. "This wall's mine, the hammocks are in there. When it's your watch below, you clip up yours wherever suits your fancy."

The three of us went back out. "Nothing to see below this level, only stores," said Bing. "Food stores, fuel stores, ammunition, cargo. When you're on watch, you'll sometimes be posted to watch the stores. The men need to get down there sometimes to get something, but you have to keep an eye on them or they'll take things."

By the time we regained the quarterdeck, a loud whistle was sounding a series of notes, and spacers were appearing from hatches everywhere to gather in the center of the sail deck. On the quarterdeck, another officer had joined the captain, one with a black braid and thin black brows. He spotted me. "Ah, the elderly midshipman!"

"Lieutenant Brown," I replied, saluting. I should have realized anyone coming up the elevator at the same time as me might have the same goal. I wondered if having him on board was better or worse than any random officer it might have been. Or were they all like that?

The captain began to address the crew about the ship, the officers, the voyage. Lieutenant Brown, it seemed, was new to the *Mariposa*, as were many of the forty spacers on board. The mission was to take a cargo of minerals to Venus in exchange for the light, strong carbon fiber they produced there. It was used in cables, grapples, sails, even the space elevator itself. At the best of times, the voyage was months long and plagued by pirates; this time, crossing Earth orbit would be a dangerous business. Earth itself was on the far side of the sun now, or would be by the time we crossed its orbit, but Earth ships trawled the area in an attempt to blockade us from Venus, an ostensibly neutral planet.

As he spoke, my gaze roved over the spacers, all turned out in their smart linen uniforms: loose white trousers, white shirts buttoned down the front, and blue kerchiefs. Their feet were bare. They were a rather frightening lot, all things considered: tattoos on every exposed piece of skin, rings in their ears, stubble on all the male faces. Given that some of them didn't want to be there in the first place, I wondered how three officers and three midshipmen would keep order among so many. Perhaps that was what Brown had meant about strict discipline.

One face in particular caught my eye. It reminded me of—but no, so many faces reminded me of hers. I kept seeing her everywhere. But as I inspected the thin brown face, the wide mouth, the high cheekbones, and the wispy dark hair—cropped short and floating around her head, not long and brushing her cheeks on either side like I remembered—she looked back at me.

My heart pounded. No. It couldn't be. Not here, not when I'd just left all the worries of the past behind me. But she smiled slightly, a dimple appearing in her left cheek, and I knew. It was her. It was Moira.

The blood rushed to my face. Smiling? How dare she? After five years with no word, no letter. After the things she had said that night. After what *I* had said. Had she forgotten all that? I certainly hadn't.

I forced my eyes away from her. Could I convince her I hadn't seen her at all? That I didn't recognize her, didn't care? Composure ought to be simple—nobles all learned it in boarding school and I was stoic even for a gentlewoman. But I didn't usually have so many warring feelings going on at the same time. I wanted to look at her more, see how five years had treated her. I wanted to hurt her any way I could. I wanted to ask her, what in the ancestors' name happened? Why didn't you come to me the next morning and talk it over? *Why are you smiling?*

The crew began the naval hymn, and I carefully unclipped my hat to hold it over my heart. With my other hand, I dug my nails into my palm. I had to be cool and blank. I was her ranking officer, technically. I was going to have to order her around as if I didn't even know her, for a year or more, and I had to begin as I meant to go on.

"Martians never will be slaves!" the crew bellowed, and I sang along voicelessly, shutting my eyes as if in piety.

A moment later came my rescue. Lieutenant Vasiliev brought Maggie and me to the long, curved aft window as the spacers began to disperse to their stations. "Since it's your first time, you have to get a look at it," she said.

The view from here was stunning, better than in the launch. I could see Phobos Station—half lump of rock, half metal structure—and below it, the delicate, shimmering ribbon of the elevator. Beyond was the planet, still in exactly the same view. Since Phobos had been moved to geostationary orbit, it always stayed over Landing. But the dayline had crept across more of the planet's face as the station swung into sunlight. We would have to leave orbit at the right moment in order to use as much as possible of our orbital energy to push us sunward.

Lieutenant Vasiliev floated near the outer edge of the bubble and pointed back toward the side of the ship. "Look, there go the sails!"

Gazing up the length of the ship, I could see the spacers, all along the sail deck, hook their feet to the floor and haul the levers downward. If I understood my reading, the levers would push hydraulic fluid through tubes that pierced the skin of the ship and out to the sail arms.

I moved nearer Vasiliev to look outside. Slowly the masts unfolded like a pocketknife, the port mainmast near us, at the stern of the ship, and the port foremast farther away. Then, as the bosun shouted and the men moved to other levers, each mast unfolded like a fan into several splaying ribs, unfurling between them the shining fabric. It glinted here and there where it caught the sunlight, though as the masts stretched it out it grew dark, pointed as it was away from the sun. The sails were massive—miles wide, so that if the ship were shaped like a butterfly, it was a comically tiny one in proportion to its wings. The way they stretched on and on till they cut off the stars reminded me of the night sky over the

Hellas Sea. They arced over the window on either side, almost but not quite meeting in the middle.

The lieutenant pulled Maggie and me sunward, until we were looking at the black backside of the sails. "You can't look at the lightward side when the laser's going," she explained. "Hold up one hand to block Phobos; the light is much brighter than the sun."

I did as she said. A moment later, my hand was turned almost translucent by the light spilling through it. I could see the capillaries at the edges of my fingers. Turning to look at the sails, I could only see faint glimmers at the edges.

Maggie's mouth wavered, tears pooling in her eyes again. "Don't cry," I said quietly, perhaps to myself as much as her. A lump had tightened in my chest and I wasn't sure if it was made of tears or rage. "Look at the sails; they're beautiful. You don't want to miss this." I squeezed her hand and she squeezed back gratefully, gulping back her tears.

It was good advice: focusing on where I could find joy might help me keep my composure and do my job. And the sight was stunning. But it was hard, trying to fix my gaze on the horizon of sail when all I could see behind my eyes was Moira's face. Smiling. What business had she to be smiling?

One thing was certain: thrown together by fate or not, we were still as we had been. Nothing had changed. She had betrayed me in a way I had thought she never could. And for that, I could never, ever forgive her.

Four

I awoke my first morning aboard ship with a pounding headache. Bing was shaking me awake. "You forgot to crank up your fan," he said.

"My fan?" I mumbled, fighting my way out of my hammock. My hair had worked loose from its braid and drifted around in all directions. What a way to wake up. At least I didn't have to heave myself out of bed.

"Oh. Um. I guess I'm the one that forgot to tell you." He showed me the small oscillating fan in the corner of the berth. "Here in space, air doesn't move around much on its own. You have to run a fan so you don't get a headache from rebreathing your own air."

"Thanks," I said, rubbing my temples. "Am I late for watch?"

"No, it's seven bells of the forenoon watch. You have half an hour. I just popped in to wake you."

We were running three eight-hour watches, which I understood was luxurious to the men. Sometimes they had only two groups of men serving four watches, which meant no one ever got to sleep a whole eight hours at a time. As second midshipman in seniority, I was assigned the first mate's watch—Vasiliev's.

I reported to the quarterdeck before eight bells. Vasiliev greeted me with a sharp nod. "Good to see you're punctual, Mr. Prescott."

She brought me to the upper deck with a small party of spacers. "Every day, we have to service the bilgewater plant. The men know what to do. You only need to supervise, but you should take the opportunity to learn the procedures. By the time we reach Venus, you should know intimately every process on this ship."

She turned to go. "Sir!" I protested.

Turning, she looked me over. "Are you going to tell me you don't know what to do?"

I gave a tiny nod.

"It's not the Navy way to let you dip your toes in while we hold your hand," she said, without rancor. "Our way is to drop you in the deep end. You'll swim, believe me."

Then she was gone, and it was only me and half a dozen men. I took a deep breath. "What do you do first?"

The bilgewater plant was a complex series of tanks and pipes, all filled with wastewater of various degrees of murk. It all appeared to be airtight, but somehow the smell of the contents pervaded the entire room. My eyes watered with it. I swallowed hard to avoid humiliating myself by gagging or covering my nose. If the men could handle it, I should be able to do the same.

The men cast glances at each other, till finally one spoke up. "Sir, we pump the contents of the fermentation tank into the centrifuge, and the contents of the holding tank into the fermentation tank."

That seemed simple enough. "Carry on, then."

He touched his forelock. "Aye aye, sir."

As I watched them, I began to see how the process worked.

All the pumping and cranking was a substitute for gravity. On Mars, you could just have the sewage flowing from one pool to the next, and a settling tank would do instead of a centrifuge. Here, everything had to be complicated and use manpower.

They finished the pumping and looked at me. I chose one of them at random, a wiry young man with a scrubby beard and gold rings in both ears. "What's your name?"

"Nguyen, sir."

"What do you do next?"

"Crank the centrifuge, sir."

"Carry on." I relaxed, hanging in the air and watching them work. I could do this. They knew what to do and they automatically treated me with respect. No different, really, from managing my own servants or my father's tenants. They knew how to do their work, and they wanted to please.

The centrifuge ground to a stop.

"Is something wrong, Mr. Nguyen?"

"Shit's gumming it up, sir." At first, I thought he was only using colorful language. But no, that was exactly what it was.

I peered through the glass side of the barrel. "Can you fix it?"

"I don't know, sir," he said, eyes wide and innocent. "This doesn't usually happen. What should we do?"

I bit my lip. I could get Lieutenant Vasiliev in here and ask her. But I had a feeling I was being tested, and if I took that approach, I'd fail. I pushed closer to the centrifuge and examined it. All along the sides of the glass cylinder were dark solids, while the middle was mostly clear. If there was a blockage, I couldn't see where.

There was, at least, an opening on the side, covered by a screw cap. Was that to reach in and clean it out? I glanced around wildly. In a slot on the wall, there was a thin rod about three feet long. Yes, exactly, that would be for probing for blockages. I gestured to the cap, carefully not touching it. "Can we open this up, Mr. Nguyen? I think we could use that rod there to move things around."

He looked around vaguely. "What rod, sir?"

My lips pressed together. He had to be playing stupid. He must have noticed my reluctance to touch anything and was going to make things difficult. Well. I wasn't going to be an infant about a little mess. I took out the rod and handed it to him.

Nguyen slowly turned the cap. The smell immediately got a lot stronger, the sour ammonia smell overpowered by an earthier one. Inside, there was only the flat brown surface of the liquid, kept inside by surface tension.

Nguyen moved aside. "Could you do it, sir? I can't understand what you're asking."

I scanned the other men. They looked back innocently. "Really, sir, this never happens," said one.

They were watching me to see if I was a coward. Trying to see if I was afraid to do what they knew how to do. I knew it was a test; the question was whether I could do it.

I had a horror of dirt and grime. I certainly was never raised to deal with plumbing. But this was the price I was paying so that my family could be kept at the level they were used to. This surely wasn't the last duty I'd have in the Navy that I didn't want to do.

"All right," I said. "Watch closely; next time you'll be the one to do it." I held my breath and tried to imagine I was…stirring up the mud at the bottom of a pond, maybe. I slid the probe into the liquid.

For a moment I was too absorbed in pretending I was somewhere else to pay much attention to what I was doing. And then I was moving the probe around, trying to find anything like a blockage. So the first I knew of my mistake was a cold, damp touch on my hand.

I had disturbed the surface tension of the liquid inside by putting in the probe, and the liquid had done what liquids do in space: it crawled. Up the probe and up my hand. I glanced down and saw the brown goo flow over my hand and onto my shirt cuff.

Letting go of the probe, I screamed. It was on my *hand*. I needed to run to the sink to wash it, but there were no sinks. It would spoil my handkerchief.

I stared at my hand, gagging and crying, aware the whole time how ridiculous, how childish I looked. Why couldn't it have been a terrible physical injury instead? At that moment, I felt I would have preferred to lose the hand altogether.

I took a shaky breath and looked around for some kind of a towel. Nguyen handed one to me with a smile. I froze, in the act of cleaning my hand. He wasn't just smiling. He was laughing, a silent, repressed chuckle. Tears twinkled in his eyelashes.

The others burst out laughing too. Loud guffaws at my expense. An angry glare from me only set them off more. I looked back at my hand, scrubbing it as best I could. It would take a wet towel, soap, and several washings to really get it right. And the shirt needed a change. At least it hadn't gotten my uniform coat. My cheeks burned with humiliation and rage.

Lieutenant Vasiliev re-entered the room, and the laughter cut off instantly. "I heard a shout; is everything all right, Mr. Prescott?"

I looked at the probe, still slimed with sewage and buried in the access port. "We had a blockage, and I was trying to fix it," I said carefully. I wanted to tell Vasiliev the trick they'd pulled, but I felt that that probably wasn't the Navy way. The deep end, she'd said. Was this sort of thing standard? The test was how I coped with it. Perhaps I'd already failed by being taken in by it. "I see now this probably wasn't the right way."

Did I detect a twinkle in her eye? "Oh, that port is for evacuating the solids into a container, to be moved to the biochar vat," she said. "This valve here has a rubber seal, so you can insert things while keeping the contents inside. You should have asked Nguyen. He's had to service this thing any number of times."

I shot Nguyen a dark glance. His face was again polite and innocent. I looked back at Lieutenant Vasiliev. "I'll remember that next time, sir."

It took the rest of the watch to get the sewage handled—properly this time. I didn't touch anything anymore. The men knew I wasn't afraid to do it, and they also knew I absolutely could not handle doing it. For better or worse, I had nothing I could prove to them at this point.

I got off duty and immediately took off my shirt to begin a thorough scrubbing of my hands and, while I was at it, the rest of me. I wanted a shower more than I had ever wanted one in my life. All I had was a wet towel and some thin, slimy soap.

Bing entered while I was still scrubbing. "Be careful with your water ration," he said. "It's mostly for drinking."

I hurried a clean shirt on. "I got very dirty today."

"The men haze you?"

"How'd you know?"

"They always do it. They want to see what you're made of, when you first come on board."

"I think it's horrible," I said hotly. "I have never been treated that way by a commoner, never!"

"The Navy isn't like anywhere else," said Bing, shrugging. "It's always a bit of a power struggle between them and us. Them seeing what they can get away with, us showing them it isn't much. You have to always show them you're not afraid of them."

"I'm not afraid," I said. "I'm furious."

"Well, let that go, too. Old grudges are no good. Let's mess belowdecks tonight. We're allowed. The food is better in the officer's mess, but the conversation leaves something to be desired. You'll see. The men will have no hard feelings by now, and you shouldn't either."

Reluctantly I followed him onto the gun deck, where already the cook, Jenkins, was scooping something out of a vat and handing it out. Breakfast in the officers' mess had been rehydrated eggs and a foil pouch of something that was allegedly sausage. If what the men ate was worse than that, I wasn't sure I could stomach it.

It turned out to be beans, rice, a black glob of yeast paste, and a green glob of algae. I mixed it around inside the bowl. Unlike the sewage I'd dealt with today, it was sticky enough to stay put. But I wished I hadn't thought of that comparison.

A squeeze bottle sailed through the air toward me and I caught it. Looking up, I saw Nguyen had thrown it. "You need that," he said. "Otherwise it tastes like shit. And you know all about *that*." He grinned.

All the men crowding the gun deck wanted the story. They packed into the spaces between the guns, perching on the ceiling, the floor, the wall, and on the guns themselves. So Nguyen told them all, complete with imitations of my disgusted horror.

I could feel my breath speeding up, my fingers tightening on the sauce bottle. Bing nudged his shoulder against mine. "You have to show you can laugh at yourself," he said, low. "If you get mad now, they'll hate you."

I unclenched my fingers and tried squirting the sauce onto my food. It was red and smelled villainously spicy, but I gave my bowl several squirts anyway. Better to taste that than to actually taste the food.

A big, dark-skinned man with tattoos all over his face was laughing the loudest of all, wiping his eyes. "Well, you know Founders!" he said cheerfully. "All a bunch of super geniuses."

I gritted my teeth and smiled.

The man added, half under his breath, "Except the ones that are morons."

Rage poured hot through my body. Morons. That's what they called people like my brother. I'd heard the jokes. Too many smart genes makes you stupid, that's what they said.

I shot off the gun I was perched on without thinking. The air rang with a crack and my right palm stung. I had slapped the big man across the face.

The laughter died like a snuffed candle. The man only stared, raising his hand to his cheek. I hung in the air, fuming. He was bigger and stronger than me, but I was dying to fight him. I didn't care if I lost. It was just something I had to do.

Bing grabbed my arm and hauled me bodily out of the cluster of people. Once out of earshot, he hissed at me, "You never do that, Prescott! Do you understand me? Never!"

"No dueling in the service. I remember," I said dully. The adrenaline seeped out of my muscles, leaving me feeling shaky and let down.

"It's more than that." He led me through the hatch up onto the sail deck. "He's not your equal. He couldn't have fought you back. What's the penalty for a spacer striking an officer, did you read that bit?"

Understanding dawned. "Flogging," I said. "And dismissal from the service, if it's to the point of injury."

"You see," he said. "It's not like dueling back home. It's like beating a dog. It'll let you, but you shouldn't."

"Are you going to tell the captain?"

"Somebody's going to even if I don't. Probably best if it's you."

I found the captain in the officer's mess, finishing after-dinner drinks with Vasiliev, and I poured out the whole story.

"I wouldn't have done it if I'd known, sir," I finished, "and I can assure you, it won't happen again."

He nodded solemnly. "You understand, I'm sure, that being a Founder is a sacred trust. Our ancestors left Mars in our care because they needed someone who would be utterly dedicated to the terraforming project and the good of the Martian people. We're not a bunch of careless elites, even though some people seem to take that attitude. We are in this position out of responsibility, not out of selfishness."

Of course I understood that. I had learned it at my mother's knee. Everyone did. Some people didn't take it to heart, but I always had. "Yes, sir."

"In the Navy, it's the same, only more so. A ship would never survive if it was a number of disparate individuals, each doing what they felt like in every moment. They need to be organized, led, disciplined. They don't exist for us. We exist for them. They rely on our leadership just as we rely on their labor. I want you to think of that trust the way you think of your duty to Mars. This ship is a project, like Mars is, that will only function with us keeping it fixed on its goal. And to do that, you must never, ever make a personal quarrel with the men. If you ever discipline them, it must be without anger, without malice, and without any personal motive. Do you understand?"

I felt my cheeks burn with shame. I shouldn't have needed this lecture. I should have understood it from the beginning. It was only what we all knew, in a different context. I never would have struck a servant either. "Yes, sir," I managed.

As a punishment, my alcohol ration was stopped for a week. I didn't mind; it only felt fair. And in any event, it didn't matter, because the following evening, a pouch of rum was floating outside my berth when I came out.

"Whose is this?" I asked a ship's boy nearby.

"Yours," he said. "From Maxwell. He wanted to say, no hard feelings about yesterday, and he won't say things like that no more."

Five

After that, I had no further trouble from the men. If they'd been testing what I was made of, the results hadn't been flattering, but they seemed satisfied. Perhaps they had only wanted to put me in my place. I might be an officer, but I was completely green and ignorant, and I was well aware of that now.

When commanding the men, I had the right to order discipline—the bosun's mate, Schmidt, would "start" any man I asked, with a rope's end across his back. But I never did that. After the lecture I'd had from the captain, it didn't seem right. I simply found out the proper procedure—from someone *other* than Nguyen—and gave the orders, and the men carried them out without complaint.

The launching laser from Phobos shut off after the first few days, and the sails had to be heaved about into a new orientation: the dark side to lee and the reflective side toward the sun. But always at an angle, which Bing explained helped brake the ship against its orbit, letting gravity pull us slightly sunward as we barreled downstream.

Our first Sunday of the voyage, we had services. The men turned out in fresh uniforms, or as fresh as they could manage. The captain, intimidating as ever in his gold epaulets and cocked hat, read the Mars Colony Charter and led the crew in the recitation of the names of the Ancestors.

At the end was an odd ritual I didn't understand. Lieutenant Brown cranked up the radio till the light came on, and the captain read into the radio a series of ship names. "To *Dauntless*, *Excellence*, and *Harrison*; to *Judgment*, *Liberation*, and *Lexington*; to *Marineris*, *Mindful*, and *Newton* ... to absent comrades, still on patrol: steady sails, and a clear orbit."

Everyone hung in silence until the little red light on the radio went out. Then the bosun's whistle shrilled to dismiss the crew, and the men scattered, back to their work or below.

It was still my watch for a few hours yet, so I couldn't find Bing yet to ask him about it. Instead I circulated around the ship, supervising the men hard at work. Perhaps in the forecastle I could look for neighboring ships we might be calling to.

But Maxwell was on watch there, scanning the stars through the glass. My cheeks burned and I turned to leave. He might have had no hard feelings over my striking him, but that didn't mean I was over the shame of it.

But he had already seen me. "You didn't know about the memorial, eh?"

I braked myself against the wall and reluctantly turned around. "With the ship names?"

"Mm." He put the glass back to his eye. "Some ships never come back, you know. No prisoners returned from the Earthers, no distress call anyone hears. Maybe the masts all got broke. Maybe they ran out of air."

"So we were calling the lost ships?"

"Still on patrol," he corrected, putting the glass to his eye. "See, nobody knows how long a crew might survive on one of those. Space is too big to have much chance of finding them all. Till they're found, you don't know they're dead. And even after they're dead, the ship goes on. Round and round their orbit. Maybe out past the belt. Still patrolling."

A chill ran up my back. "Full of dead bodies?"

He dropped the glass to waist level, casting me a sidelong glance with his sharp dark eyes. "I saw one once."

More hazing. Well, this kind I could take. I've never been frightened by a little ghost story. I crossed my arms. "What was it like?"

"You can tell 'em 'cause the sails are full of holes," he said. "Without anybody inside steering, they plow through every fucking comet tail in the ecliptic. This one's port masts were both broke and the starboard sails were in tatters. It was going near the same speed as us, so we took the time to go over to it. See if the log book was still there, if we could figure what ship it was."

He put the glass back to his eye and surveyed the darkness, faintly alleviated by the solar glow—dust in the light of the sun.

"And?" I demanded.

"I wasn't on that EVA," he said. "But they told me it was a fucking nightmare. The men were all still there. You know, bodies don't break down in space. The air slowly leaks out, if nobody's putting more in, and the algae dies. But the people are all still there. Floating like they don't know what hit them. Clinging to the walls 'cause that's the last place they fetched up."

I swallowed, rubbing my arms to smooth down the goosebumps. "And was the book still there? Did they find out what it was?"

"The *Aldrin*," he said. "Lost in the last war. Some of those bastards' kids had grown up and joined the service, in the time that ship had been missing."

"That's terrible," I breathed.

"Oh, I don't think so." He pursed his lips. "I like the idea of still going on, after. Just round and round the sun. And every bunch of years, somebody calls out on the radio, wishes us a clear orbit. Feels like my ghost might like the hello."

He finished his scan of the stars and deftly scrunched the spyglass back up. "None of them in sight today, anyhow. Nor the enemy, more's the pity."

I nodded. It seemed he really had put our whole quarrel behind him. "Sorry," I said. "About striking you."

He shrugged and strapped the glass back against the wall. "It wasn't much of a punch. You'd better not try that shit on the enemy."

I smiled in spite of myself. "I can handle a sword, at least."

"A cutlass? In no gravity?" I shook my head. He grinned. "I'll be starting my class soon. See you're in it, if you feel like surviving your first boarding party."

Right, he was the arms master. Responsible for caring for the cutlasses and training the crew in combat. No question, I could use the help.

I left the forecastle to continue my watch. Sundays, it seemed, a minimum of work was done, but even that amounted to quite a bit. The bilge pumps had to be run and the results centrifuged. The atmosphere master had to test and correct the oxygen levels. Someone had to aerate the algae.

At last my watch ended and I went below. Bing was there already, getting undressed to sleep. "No clean shirts, still," he complained, rifling in his duffel. "I'm the last thing from picky, but four days is too much for anyone to tolerate."

I felt a cold prickle at the back of my neck. "I get a new one every day," I said. "I've never had to rewear a dirty one. I thought they were very efficient."

"The laundry crew must like you," he said. "It's my watch that handles it, mostly. The spacer that runs it now is new—she was just impressed. Name of Singh."

Of course it was. Of course. "Well, that explains it," I said, undoing the gold buttons on my waistcoat. "She used to work for me."

Used to work for, what an understatement. Used to be everything for, would be closer to the truth. My only friend. But also, the person who had parted with a torrent of angry words and left the whole planet to get away from me. I couldn't see how that squared with doing my laundry.

"It's my fault if I don't have a clean shirt," Bing was saying. "I should get on their backs more."

"Probably," I said absently, taking off my waistcoat and carefully folding it. May as well sleep when Bing did, during the middle watch when the ship was quietest.

Had she intended me to notice and find out it was her? That was the real question. If so, the whole thing was a signal, an opening gambit, and she would eventually try to talk to me. Which seemed odd considering she had had my address these five years. But in any case, I would have to be on the lookout to shut down any such conversation. I didn't want it. I had nothing to say.

But if she didn't mean for me to notice, if she only wanted me to be comfortable . . . what did *that* mean? We had parted in anger, both of us. What would have had to change for her to feel any different now?

Bing cranked up the fan, which started buzzing softly as it pushed the air around, and crawled into his hammock. "Night, Prescott. Put out the light when you're done with it."

I took off breeches and shirt, stowed them, and slid the little cover over the fiber-optic light. Not that there was any chance of me sleeping now. No, I was going to hang in the dark, missing the pressure of a bed, any bed, and think about Moira. Think about the last time we'd spoken. The fight that had ended it all.

It had been the night of my coming-out ball. The time when

a young person enters society, declares their romantic inclination, and is courted for the first time by potential suitors.

I had already been made aware of my family's straitened circumstances, and the whole thing felt like a farce. Why must we organize our affairs by elaborate costumes, subtle flirting, and intricate dances? Couldn't we just put on a marriage market like a stock exchange? Five hundred pounds sterling for my daughter! A title for my son! Sold!

Instead I had been decked out within inches of my life, as traditional. A rose-colored frock to set off my paleness; my ashy blond hair done up in a painful coif. And I had endured hours upon hours of dances; women who all looked the same, thought the same, talked the same. It might as well have all been the same woman, for all I cared.

Jaded and exhausted, I had slipped out through the french doors that led off the ballroom, where light spilled out onto a little paved garden. Little benches sat under grapevines, where in the daytime my mother liked to host small parties. Now the vines cast dark shadows in the light from the windows. Inside, a few dancers still whirled about the floor. The rest clustered to the edges of the room, drooping with weariness. They would be calling for their carriages soon.

"How's your party?"

I spun around. For a second I saw only darkness, and then my eyes adjusted and I saw Moira, legs drawn up on one of the benches. With a rush of relief, I came over and sat down. After all the elegant strangers, here was my best friend. Here I could relax. "You can see how it's going from here, can't you?"

Moira shrugged. "Well, it sure *looks* fun."

"It's going well," I answered vaguely. I didn't want to confide my thoughts, not right now. Not to Moira, who wouldn't relate at all. It would only sound like ingratitude for my privileges.

Wouldn't Moira love to be dolled up like this, have every eye on her like I'd had tonight?

"I haven't decided yet whether to be mad at you," said Moira, her voice light. "You never told me."

"Told you what?"

"How you were coming out. All these years I just assumed you must be into men."

"Oh." I picked a grape, tasted it. Too sour. "No, I'm not."

Moira looked down, shrouding her face in darkness. "All those years. I kept going on and on about girls I thought were pretty and you never said one word. Not one word!"

I shrugged. "What would be the point? I try not to look at people like that. I don't have the privilege—" I stopped myself. Poor choice of words. "It's just not going to be important to my life, who's beautiful and who isn't."

She was quiet a minute. "You know who's beautiful?"

I looked in the window, watched the dancers. "Who?"

"You are." She tucked a loose curl back into my ridiculous updo. "You were the prettiest girl in the room."

I smiled despite myself. "Well, of course *you* think so."

"I do," she said, dropping her voice and leaning a little closer. "I always have." She closed the rest of the distance and touched her lips to mine.

I froze. For a moment I couldn't move at all. She had kissed me. Moira. My best friend. Had kissed me.

Then I recovered my senses and pulled sharply away. "What are you *thinking*?" I hissed.

"I was thinking," she faltered, "that after all this time, having feelings for you, that I was going to let you know."

"And what," I demanded, "did you think I was going to do with that?"

"I was sort of hoping you'd say you felt the same."

I shook my head, rising to my feet. "How could I? If you were someone I could ever—ever be with, you'd be in there." I flung my arm toward the window, where couples still glided across the floor.

"I see how it is," she said angrily, standing up. "I'm not good enough for you."

"No!" I cried. "Have I ever treated you like you weren't good enough?"

"Never till tonight." The light glowed golden on one side of her face, leaving the other side in shadow. "But it's not like I'm going to forget it in a hurry."

I pressed my lips together. "Fine. Decide on your own what I meant."

She started to turn away. I exhaled. I knew her well enough to know that if she stormed off now, she'd be back in the morning, full of apologies and ready to listen. But I also knew that if she stayed now, angry as she was, we'd have a real fight.

But then she turned back. "No. I'm not going to slink away after that. I'm tired of being told I'm not good enough to be friends with you. That I'm not worthy to be at your parties or talk to your friends. Why did I bother wasting my time on a hopped-up princess who thinks she's better than me because of how she was born?"

I gasped as if she'd struck me, too angry to speak. At last I managed, "You have to apologize for that."

"Oh, I'm sorry," she fired back, her voice dripping with sarcasm. "I'm sorry for the *idiocy* of being in love with *you*!"

Then she did storm off. I stared after her in shock, wondering what I could have said or done. Was her reaction predestined the moment I had told her no? Accept her love or admit I thought I was above it?

But that wasn't the part that hurt the most. We had fought before; I knew we could talk it over in the morning. Somehow, some way it would be all right. If we could find some way to put the cat back in the bag. She could tell me she had been confused, that she didn't mean it, that we could somehow still be friends. But I lay awake all night, doubting it. She had broken something important between us, and I didn't know how to mend the wall of glass I had so carefully protected. Something that said friends, not lovers. Never lovers. Only friends.

In the morning, she didn't come. Or in the afternoon. I waited for days, casually letting myself be seen in places where she'd find me. At last Ramesh, watching me saunter through the stables for the tenth time, told me she was gone. Off to space. Yes, a sudden decision, but why not? She's old enough to seek her fortune. I'm sure she'll write.

I went outside, collapsed in a patch of overgrown grass, and cried. It was over. The only real friendship I had ever had.

SIX

Bit by bit, I learned the ropes, from the words fore and aft, port and starboard, to how to hand myself along the sail deck without stranding myself far from a handhold. It was a relief when finally, a week out, Lieutenant Vasiliev summoned the midshipmen to the quarterdeck for navigation classes. At last I would be taught something useful. I was tired of being the least knowledgeable person on the ship.

Vasiliev was a striking woman: tall, pale face, dark hair and eyebrows. In one hand she had a slate; the chalk floated near the other. "In the future," she said, "we will be meeting here every day, on my watch. You will bring your estimate of the ship's position, which you will have to work out on your own time. I don't expect that of you landsmen yet, but I'm ready for yours, Mr. Abington."

Bing rifled madly through his notebook, sweat visible on his forehead. "I think … it's … um. Two hundred twelve by seventy four sixteen by sixty nine, sir?"

"Units, Mr. Abington."

"Two hundred twelve *leagues* by seventy-four *degrees* sixteen minutes, by sixty-nine kilometers north."

She frowned "I'm afraid that's incorrect. Not just incorrect, but so far off I haven't the faintest idea how you arrived at it."

He made a clumsy gesture to show her his notebook. She refused it. "Just tell me what you got your sightings off."

"Jupiter, Earth, and the sun, sir."

"Let me guess. You always use those three because they're the only ones you can consistently identify."

He gave a nervous nod.

"Earth is on the far side of the sun right now. It's almost impossible to see. You probably took a bearing off Venus instead."

Bing turned beet red. "I ... I see how I may have done that, sir."

"Learn another object to sight off of. Venus will work well. Or Saturn. You can tell it by the ears." She touched one of hers, with a twinkle in her eye.

I relaxed. If she hadn't shamed Bing for a mistake that bad, hopefully she wouldn't be too terrible to learn from.

"Question, sir?" asked Maggie. "Why is the middle one measured just in degrees? If there's a north and south in space, why not an east and west too?"

"Here's a question for you, Mr. Borisov. When we lay at anchor off Phobos, were we moving?"

"No, sir."

Vasiliev sighed. "Mr. Prescott, do you agree?"

I stiffened slightly to attention. This had to be a trick. After a second, I saw it. "No, sir. We were moving because Phobos is moving. And because Phobos is orbiting Mars, which is moving. We were only standing still in reference to Phobos."

Vasiliev nodded. "You see, Mr. Borisov, space isn't like a flat map. Space is like a river. Everything is moving in relation to everything else. The solar system can be thought of as a river flowing around the sun. The planets are all hurtling downstream, each at its own pace. Mars is traveling at twenty-four knots, so we were traveling at twenty-four knots.

"The upshot of it is, we measure our position in leagues from the sun, in kilometers north or south of Mars' equator, and in degrees of a circle. The center of that circle is the sun. Zero degrees is in the direction of Regulus. We're nineteen degrees around that circle from Regulus, so that's the middle number."

She explained, on her slate, the math required to take a bearing. We followed along in our notebooks. Once we had it written down, she said, "That should be all you need to take a bearing," and left for a turn around the ship, to check on all the crews.

Bing went first, carefully measuring the position of each of the celestial bodies he'd chosen through the stern window with a sextant. "I hate navigation," he said, as he turned to the chart book to check each planet's position. "Math isn't my wheelhouse."

Maggie was even more confused. "I never got this far in school," she wailed. "We only barely studied trigonometry!"

"Did you do the lighthouse problem?" I asked. "It's just like taking a bearing off two lighthouses, only the lighthouses are planets."

"No," she said sulkily. "I only just learned sin, cos, and tan."

It was a relief to me not to have much trouble, once Bing showed me how to use the sextant. The math was laborious, but I had studied math at New Oxford. That and political science, which turned out to be no use at all. At the time, I had had hopes of running for Parliament. But you needed money for that, a lot more than I was likely to ever have.

Vasiliev's watch ended, and Bing and I went back to our berth, leaving Maggie to go on duty with Brown. "I don't know if I should sleep or study," said Bing. "I bollixed the calculations today like I always do. I'll never make lieutenant if I don't get it right."

"You're only seventeen," I said. "I'm sure no one expects it."

"They do, though." He gave me a piteous look. "Once you've been in the service five years, people start to wonder about you, no matter how old you are. Whether you've got the stuff."

That did sound dire. "Give me your notebook," I said. "Let's see if we've got the same numbers."

We didn't, and I was pretty sure mine were right. We were deep into rehashing the whole calculation when Maggie tumbled into the room. "Isn't it your watch?" asked Bing, rubbing his eyes.

"I just asked the captain if I could switch with one of you," she said all in a rush, large eyes blinking nervously. "He said yes, if one of you would agree to it."

"I will," I said, quickly stowing my notebook and pencil.

She hesitated. "I was thinking maybe Bing—"

"It's fine. I don't mind Brown." By now Brown's reputation as a disciplinarian was well-known. If one was going to get into trouble, best to be caught by Vasiliev if you could manage it. If not, the captain. Brown least of all.

But I felt I could handle him. What was he going to do if I disappointed him, put me in irons? I knew the regs; I wasn't going to give him anything to punish me for.

Given how abruptly Maggie had gotten her post changed, mid-watch, I half expected to find Brown berating some poor spacer or having the bosun's mate lay his rope into everyone. But things were calm. I found him in the forecastle, peering through a glass at the stars ahead. "I've taken Borisov's watch, sir."

He turned and raised an eyebrow at me. "Did the captain give permission for that?"

"Yes, sir."

Heaving a small sigh, he returned his glass to his eye. "Go make a round of the ship, then."

Moira was on Bing's watch, not this one, or I'd never had agreed to the switch. I had no interest in commanding her. Of course I knew where she must be, just as she had known how badly

I would want a clean shirt. If she wasn't sleeping, she'd gravitate toward any window she could find. She hated the indoors; it made her claustrophobic. Just as I hated to be untidy, which she had quietly remedied without a word.

I patrolled the top deck, where spacers aerated the algae tank and fed the yeast. The room was bathed in white, indirect light, like a cloudy day, from the sunlight passing through the thick layer of transparent aluminum and then the water tank below. It smelled like a brewery in the middle of a swamp.

I passed through the second deck where water, oxygen, sewage, and laundry were all processed. I watched a crew under the direction of the gunner service the torpedo tubes. I spoke to the man looking out at the forecastle. Moira was nowhere to be seen; she must have been below.

Lieutenant Brown joined me while I was watching a crew polish the levers on the sail deck. When he appeared, everyone increased their pace, though I hadn't noticed them lagging before. He stood for a while watching them, feet hooked into the loops on the floor and hands clasped behind his back. Then abruptly he barked out, "Schmidt! Start that man!"

The bosun's mate obediently braced himself and lashed out with his rope. I flinched as it connected, though the victim, a scrawny man with wiry black hair, didn't cry out. Brown spun to face me. "You have a problem?"

So he'd been watching me, to see how I'd react. "No, sir."

"I expected this of you," he said. "Borisov never tried to judge the way we do things here. But I can see that you do. You're used to your cozy life on the ground and you're old enough to think you know everything. You think you have nothing to learn from your betters."

My eyes widened slightly. How could he make such wild assumptions on such trifling evidence? Of course I didn't like seeing the man punished, mostly because he hadn't even been slow. He had only been the slowest of the group, and someone had to be the slowest.

"You need to keep better discipline than this," he went on. "The second I came out of the forecastle, they all worked faster. Why? Because they fear me, and they don't fear you. That has to change."

My lower lip trembled and I stiffened it resolutely. I wasn't going to give him the satisfaction of upsetting me. "Aye aye, sir," I said crisply.

I worked out my frustration the next day at sparring practice. Bing and I were there most days, along with most of the off-duty spacers. Zero-g sparring was unlike planetside fencing or any other sport I'd practiced, but it would be necessary if we were ever boarded.

"Fighting in space is like fucking in space," Maxwell pronounced, in his rounded city accent. "You gotta hold on tight or nothing's going to happen."

A laugh ran through the group. Bing's ears turned bright red. "Why'd he have to say it like that?"

I pushed over to him, short wooden cutlass in one hand, and grabbed his arm with the other. "To distract you so I could get the jump on you," I teased.

He quickly parried with his sword, trying to push me off of him. But I made a second jab and got a touch in that time. We parted, panting.

"How was Brown today? Do you know why Maggie wanted to switch?"

"I don't know. Sounded like he wanted her to stay." I curled my feet up against the wall, ready to fire myself back toward him.

"He doesn't like me. He says I'm too old to understand Navy culture."

We collided again in midair, this time winding up in a spin that made me too dizzy to stand a chance. After scoring his point, he pulled me back upright and gave me a moment to get my bearings. "Navy culture—what does he even mean by that?"

"Beatings, I guess." I rubbed my ears, as if that would somehow make the fluid inside stop whirling around. "He thinks we'll have a mutiny if we don't keep the upper hand."

Bing shrugged. "I mean, you do need discipline, for sure. Like if people are actually causing trouble."

"But they *aren't*. Not since that first time hazing me. I was friendly with the men of my old watch. If I'm always having the spacers beaten, they'll hate me."

"You can't want to be liked too much. I mean, better for them to hate you then not to listen."

"Brown says he wants the men to be afraid of me. I just … I don't know if I can be that intimidating."

Bing grinned. "You're intimidating all right. *I'm* scared of you. Ready to go again?"

A week later, I felt certain Brown was right after all. I could never adapt to Navy culture. Not if Navy culture was what he said, and it seemed it was.

It had started with Gomez, the spacer who had cried on the launch. Her daughter, it turned out, had recently been diagnosed with cancer. She had been hurrying home when she was impressed. Many of the crew felt sorry for her plight, and she had become very popular.

Unfortunately, the way they expressed their admiration was by giving her some of their alcohol ration. Probably they felt a good, stiff drink before bed would help her get to sleep instead of lying awake homesick. But since she stayed awake drinking, she was far from sobered up when she reported for duty at her next watch. Brown had reported her for drunkenness and she sat in irons until the next morning when the bosun's whistle shrilled to call all hands to observe punishment.

Funny they needed all hands to watch, I reflected as the bosun's mate brought Gomez to a grating that ran down the front of the quarterdeck. In boarding school we were often paddled, but at least it was in private. Having the punishment where everyone could watch would add humiliation to the pain.

He stripped off her shirt and tied her by the wrists facing the grating. Then he stood by, waiting for the captain to read off her offense and sentence. I stared at the woman's bare back, wishing myself anywhere else.

" ...Do your duty and spare not your shipmate, or by God you'll take her place." Bing's elbow caught me in my ribs, and I saw everyone else had taken off their hats. I rushed to unclip mine.

The formalities duly observed, the bosun's mate hooked his bare feet to the ground and began the blows. The first swing of the cat left red marks, and the bosun called, "One." By the second the blood beaded up. Red drops scattered off the cat and were carefully swiped out of the air with a cloth by the surgeon's boy, a dark-eyed girl as small as Maggie. I tried to look away, but saw Brown's eyes on me. Breathing slowly in through my nose, I forced my chin up and watched. *I'm not scared or weak*, I thought. *But this is barbaric.*

When they cut her down, she had to be pulled off the grating, too weak to move. Her messmates took charge of her from there, faces white and hard. Did they blame themselves, or Brown?

Afterward I wanted to talk it over with Bing alone, but instead it was time for breakfast in the captain's mess. Brown's eyes pinned me over the foil packets of ham and potatoes, and I kept my eyes on the table as much as I could.

"I'm really very pleased we'd gotten as far into the voyage as we did without any serious infractions," said the captain cheerfully. "It's a good crew we have."

"Or else we've been slack when it comes to catching infractions," said Brown.

"Why do they assemble everybody to do it?" asked Maggie.

Vasiliev frowned. "Midshipmen are not to speak at table unless spoken to. You know that, Mr. Borisov."

"It's a fair question, though," said the captain. "The answer is that it's instructional for the crew. It helps them keep in their minds what will happen to them. I'll wager we don't see anyone else drunk on watch for a long time."

SEVEN

We entered Earth space soon after, and the ship hummed with tension. Earth itself was on the far side of the sun from us at the moment, but Earth ships were known to patrol its entire orbit, to say nothing of pirates trawling for cargo ships. Both were supplied out of Halfpoint Station, directly opposite Earth. We'd be passing within a league of it.

The captain had us exercising the guns many times a day. The torpedoes were self-propelled, to avoid throwing the ship into a spin with their thrust as they left. The spacers hauled them across the deck and into the tubes, attached a timed fuse, and shut the inner door before venting the outer hatch to space. Once outside, a rocket started accelerating them toward their target.

Or would in a real fight, anyway. During the drills, the crew mimed the priming and firing, taking the same torpedoes in and out of the tubes. We couldn't afford to waste firepower we might need in a battle.

The crew of my watch, perhaps motivated by the flogging,

worked with a will and no slacking. Which meant Brown gave me no further trouble, even though I had not had to become any stricter.

One day he summoned me to the quarterdeck. I climbed over the rail nervously, finding the captain already there with him. Was I in trouble? But the captain saw me and smiled. "Ah, Mr. Prescott! I was hoping you'd get to see this." He handed me his spyglass. "Have a look, just upstream and two points north, in Taurus."

I put the glass to my eye and surveyed the darkness outside. Where he had indicated, I saw a tiny gap in the stars. "That's a ship? That little shadow?" I had stood watches here before, looking for ships, but I could never have spotted this one at such a distance without him pointing it out. I blinked and refocused. No glitter of sails, or their characteristic circle or diamond shape. Just an elongated dot, which meant a blunt cylinder, seen almost exactly end-on.

"Time to see how much you've learned so far. You worked out our position, bearing, and speed already today?" I nodded. "Work out theirs. And if you can, when they'll catch up to us."

It was a difficult problem to solve even with a pen and paper, which I didn't have. There were, at least, a slide rule, clock, astronavigator, and chart. My lips moved as I did the calculations. If I could pull this off, even Brown would have to be impressed. But if I dropped a digit, trying to carry them all in my head, he'd have something else to crow over me for.

It took several rechecks through the spyglass, at timed intervals, but I finally had something. "If the ship is about the size of ours, it's about five hundred kilometers away, bearing almost straight downstream, gaining at a rate of point two knots. So it will be close enough to fire on us in forty minutes, sir."

The captain raised his eyebrows, impressed. "And is it friend or foe?"

Confused, I looked back at the other ship. Friend or foe? From here, it was a dark shadow against the stars. With the sails furled, there weren't any differences between our ships and Earth's that could be recognized at this distance. And pirates might well occupy a Mars-built ship; they weren't particular.

Then it dawned on me. The captain knew I couldn't read the name off a ship's side at this distance. He would expect me to use information I did know. All I knew was its position, bearing, and speed, relative to ours. Would a friend be plowing straight down Earth's orbit like that?

"Foe, sir," I said at last. "It's patrolling Earth's orbit, sails furled, not going anywhere. If it were a friend, it would be bearing either sunward or leeward, getting past Earth as fast as it could."

He nodded. "Go tell Mr. Maxwell to beat to quarters."

The crew responded to the summons with enthusiasm. I had worried they'd be afraid, but almost everyone wore a smile as they rocketed through the sail deck to their battle stations. "Finally a chance to kick some Earth ass," I heard somebody say. And—I reminded myself, to soothe my own nervousness—a chance for some prize money also.

I took up my station over the port hatch to the gun deck below, to relay orders. Maggie manned the starboard hatch. Brown went below to the weapons locker with Maxwell and came up with cutlasses to distribute. The men heaved on the levers to take in the sails, to save them from damage when the enemy came into range.

The other ship proved its hostility by burning emergency fuel, slowly decelerating so it would be near our speed when it reached us. Thus it was more than forty minutes before it arrived; minutes we spent in anxious anticipation. At last Bing, stationed in the quarterdeck, cried, "They've fired their bow chasers!"

"Brace for impact!" shouted the captain.

Across the sail deck, Maggie hesitated, though we'd drilled this a thousand times. After a second, she pulled herself together and shoved her arms and legs through the straps on the grating behind her. I managed to do the same before the impact hit.

The torpedoes used in ship-to-ship combat weren't meant to damage the ship itself. The radiation shielding was far too strong, and besides, each side wanted to take a prize, not only destroy an enemy. Instead they were concussive charges designed to shake everyone inside to death with the acceleration.

The impacts struck, four quick slams that thundered on the hull and wrenched my arms painfully. But I heard no screams or crashes; everyone was properly secured. "Quick, fire the sternchasers while they're reloading," ordered the captain, and I repeated the order down the hatch. The gun crew went through their smooth ballet of steps and a faint whoosh signaled the torpedoes venting.

The other ship slowly pulled along our port side, moving past us at a walking pace now. Their first broadside caught one of the gun crew unsecured, and he flew into the ceiling of the gun deck. The surgeon passed me at the hatch and a moment later reemerged with the man trailing limply. Dead or only unconscious? The surgeon seemed to think he stood a chance, because she belted him tightly to the wall of the cockpit, just below the quarterdeck.

As soon as we'd fired our own broadside, the captain shouted for Vasiliev to take the starboard gun crew and head to the launch to board the enemy. As she passed me, she grabbed my arm. "You're with me. Borisov, man the port hatch."

Maggie watched me go forlornly. Twelve years old, and bloodthirsty enough to want to be on a boarding party. Or perhaps just hating to be left out.

Vasiliev piloted the launch expertly out of the path of the weapons fire and around to the other side of the enemy ship. We clamped to the airlock gently as a kiss, though they'd surely seen us coming anyway.

I clutched my sword in sweating hands. On Mars we would have used guns, but guns were more of a danger to yourself than your enemy in space. The recoil would fling you backward, and the bullet would ricochet around the metal ship till it killed someone, maybe your enemy but just as likely you.

But a sword made the whole thing that much more intimate. Soon I'd be grabbing for a handhold on an Earther, hoping to slit his gut before he slit mine. Not something for which my upbringing had prepared me at all. Maybe Brown was right and I was too old to learn new tricks.

The men at the airlock braced their feet, set their crowbars, and levered the inner door open. We exploded inward, trying to push as far as possible before the enemy could stop us. Gaining the area around the airlock would be the hardest part of the fight. We'd had mock boarding melees a dozen times, and that had always determined everything. If you could get your entire party in before they pushed you back into the launch, you stood a chance at winning. Otherwise not.

But we had rehearsed this well, and our momentum carried us several yards in before the Earthers managed to force us to engage. Vasiliev put her back against mine and we shoved off in opposite directions. I aimed straight at a short, stocky man with a beard. Well, that described all of them. Their triple gravity made Earthers grow muscular and broad in the shoulders.

Unfortunately it also made them stronger than us. The man threw me off easily before pushing off to slam back into me. The air huffed out of my lungs, but I grabbed his arm with my left hand, remembering Maxwell's instruction, and slashed with the other.

Bloody drops filled the air and I blinked, bewildered. I had been riding on adrenaline and muscle memory—I hadn't quite remembered my sword was real and sharp. The man thrashed in the air, hurt but not dead, and my second slash stilled him.

Around me, other battles were playing out the same way. I looked for another opponent, but no one seemed to be attacking me. After a second to size up the layout, I launched myself forward. That was where Earth captains were stationed, rather than an aft quarterdeck.

Vasiliev was right behind me, handing herself along the sail levers. "These Earthers are cowards," she said, curling her lip. "They thought they were attacking a soft cargo ship, and now that we're on their deck, they run and hide."

The Earther captain was a plump woman with short blond hair, shouting into a speaking tube, "We have unfriendlies heading toward the bridge, I repeat, we have—"

I slammed into the spacer nearest her, while Vasiliev engaged the captain herself. The man braced his feet and threw me off him, but I hit the ceiling feet-first and came back at him, sword held in front of me like a lance. He was too slow parrying. One good hit to the neck was all I needed.

By the time I had regained my breath and turned to look at Vasiliev, the Earth captain was handing over her sword.

We were the heroes of the hour when we returned to the ship, splattered in blood. Three of the boarding party had died, plus the man from the gun deck, who had never regained consciousness. But the Earthers had lost three times that many, and now we had their ship, the *Andromeda*, as a prize.

Extra rum was broken out. The port gun crew, who had done most of the work, and the boarding party were allowed to celebrate first. Obviously it would be disastrous if another ship came upon us with the entire crew drunk at once.

Bing and I took our drinks—really only grain liquor, called rum for tradition's sake—off to an upper corner of the sail deck to drink alone. The heavy sail levers fenced us off from the rest of the deck.

"You look a little peaky, Prescott," said Bing, after knocking back a swallow.

I tried it myself. It was harsh enough to scour the sail levers with; it couldn't be doing any good to my insides. In the captain's mess, we drank wine. "I don't feel anything," I said. Which was true; I felt blank. Nothing, where my emotions were supposed to be. But I couldn't say that. "I mean, unwell, I don't feel unwell."

"Get drunk before it hits you, then."

I cocked my head. "What?"

"Whatever it is that hits you after a fight. You've never been in one before, so you don't know how you handle it yet. So get drunk. It's what everyone does."

I managed another burning swallow. "I thought it was to celebrate."

He shrugged. "That too."

"How do you handle battles?" I asked.

"The first time I was in a boarding party, I hid on the sun deck and cried after," he said. "Which was stupid, because I'd been longing to go since I first shipped aboard. I was fifteen and finally big enough not to get killed offhand. But I was scareder ... more scareder ... more frightened than I thought I would be."

I had another drink and turned myself upside-down. Now it looked like the quarterdeck was pinned to the ceiling. I used to get vertigo when I failed to orient myself around ship's up, but I had my bearings now. "Why'd you go to space, Bing?"

"Second child. You know the drill. You too?"

"Yes," I said, because I was the second child, and then, "No," because I was still due to inherit. But then I remembered that I didn't want to tell him the real reason, and said, "Yes," again. This whiskey was stronger than I was used to.

He laughed loudly. "Your father's the Marquis of Hellas, right? With all the horses?"

My heart pounded. "You know him?"

"Not to talk to. Didn't know he had kids. But I remember he had that bay, Orbital Resonance, that won the Ascraeus Stakes that year. He was fifteen to one, and I wanted to bet on him, but Father said I was too young to know good horses and would only waste my money."

I smiled and slowly rotated myself back right side up. Moira had had a hand in the training of that horse. She was light as a feather on his back; he didn't seem to feel her. I remembered the rush of my heart as he had gone thundering by, and pretending to myself as hard as I could that it was because I was so interested in horses.

"My father shouldn't get all the credit for that," I said. "Our stablemaster is amazing. Ramesh Si—"

Then I suddenly remembered where I was, and who else was here.

"Silva," I finished. "You wouldn't have heard of him." I suddenly felt very sober and very cold.

Vasiliev came over, smiling. "I have the command of the *Andromeda*, to take her back to Phobos," she told Bing. "You're to come with me."

He managed a passable salute. "Right…now, sir?"

"Finish your drink, then go get your things and sober up. Say an hour."

"I'm not going to be sober in an hour," said Bing, when she had moved away. "That stuff is strong. They should serve it in thimbles."

"I'll be sorry to have you go," I said. I meant it; Bing had made everything on board make sense. He didn't mind explaining everything, and he was too young and cheerful to make anything sound as serious as it was.

"Me too," he said sadly. "Not likely to be much action between here and Mars, and then I'll need a whole new posting. Doubt it will be as good as this one."

On the other side of the row of sail levers, Vasiliev was telling Maggie the news. She burst into tears and threw her arms around the lieutenant.

"Come now," said Vasiliev, "our ancestors have given us a noble heritage. Don't shame them with childish tears." But she squeezed Maggie tightly.

The celebration continued as the prize crew sobered up and gathered at the airlock. The spacers sang and skylarked around the sail deck. But Brown came to the captain, as the men were cheering him, and murmured into his ear.

The captain's expression clouded, and he called Bing and me into his cabin for a private word. "Brown has reported to me that not all the cutlasses have been returned to the weapons locker. Did you return yours already, Mr. Prescott?"

"Yes, sir. I gave it to Mr. Maxwell. So did everyone that I saw."

"Ten are missing. Too many to be an oversight."

"Should we ask the men?" asked Brown.

The captain shook his head. "I'd rather as few people as possible even realized it could be done. No, search the ship quietly. Five pounds of my own share of the prize money to the man that finds them."

The watches were reduced to two, six hours on and six off for everyone. There was some grumbling from the crew, now that no one got eight hours of sleep in a row. And I didn't get to see much of Maggie anymore, since anytime I was off watch, she was on.

The next day I spent my free watch in the laundry room,

trying to clean the bloodstains out of my clothes. They came out of the coat reasonably well, and the dark color hid the rest, but the shirt seemed hopeless. After several cold rinses, it was still blotched and splattered with light brown.

I blinked hard as I scrubbed at the stains with a brush. I hadn't cried over the battle, or the dead spacers, or Bing leaving. And this was only a *shirt*. But I only had three; I couldn't afford another. The shirt I had such a short time ago been so proud to buy…

Something nudged against my arm and I lifted my head, clearing my throat and sniffing. It was a bulb of peroxide. I spun around, catching myself before I could twist out of control.

It was Moira, floating in the doorway. "That'll do the trick," she said. "Though I would have done it for you if you'd just left it."

My tongue felt like a dry rag inside my mouth. How to make it form the necessary questions, like *why* and *why did you leave* and *what are you trying to do?* She looked the same as ever, wispy dark hair standing a handspan out from her face, dark eyes sparkling. What, did I expect her to be haggard, pale with grief, like I had felt for days, months…well. Like I still felt?

All at once I felt cold fury. How dare she come here and help me with my shirt and make me feel taken care of when I was lonely? What could that be but preying on my weakness? I didn't even want her to *know* I was weak. Still worse that she let me know she knew.

I turned from her coldly. "Thank you, Mr. Singh," I said, because it was the cruelest thing I could think of to say. Let her wonder if I even remembered her.

She came closer—I could feel her, a warmth all down my left side. In a low voice she said, "If anything happens, lie low. Stay in your berth if you hear a commotion."

It was so unexpected I looked back up at her, even though I had just been resolving that nothing she could possibly say could make me do that. "Anything?" I repeated. "What's going on? If something is going on, I need to tell the captain!"

"I have nothing to tell the captain," she said in the same quiet voice. "Just you. Lie low if you can at all. If you stay out of the way, nothing's gonna happen to you."

I opened my mouth, trying to think of what to do. Threaten to tell the captain anyway? Damn her, she knew I wouldn't betray her. She knew I couldn't even if I wanted to, because it's not my way. Nothing at all to do with her, or how I felt about her.

"You still smell the same," she said in an ordinary voice, pushing off and away. "Best smelling thing on this whole reeking ship."

She passed through the open hatch and was gone, and I was left with my pounding heart and conflicted feelings.

EIGHT

I searched the ship whenever no one was paying attention to me. I crawled into lockers and slid my hands underneath torpedo tubes, without luck. I had to be the first to find the missing cutlasses. I wanted the captain's five pounds, of course, but I also wanted to be the one to find them in case Moira had had something to do with it. I could retrieve them without getting her in any trouble.

That was definitely the right thing to do: stop any possible mutiny, but quietly. I could see why some on the ship might be dissatisfied, what with Brown's harshness and the flogging of Gomez. Moira herself had been impressed recently, so Bing had told me. Perhaps she would be tempted to cause trouble. I could forgive that. I could even save her from making such a stupid decision that would get her airlocked.

But most likely it wasn't her at all. I eyed the spacers with a more suspicious eye than before; any one of them could be plotting our deaths at any moment. Sometimes I floated into a room and heard suspicious snatches: "could never succeed against" "have to sleep sometime" "never return to Mars again." When I drew close they would fall silent. Maybe those clauses could fit innocently into a normal conversation. Maybe not.

The officers stopped eating together; we made sure half of us were always on watch, cutlasses at our sides. The friendly camaraderie that had sprung up briefly after the battle had vanished. Maggie was nervous and withdrawn, and I spent as much of my off-duty time as I could keeping an eye on her as she stood watch. She was so little, even without a weapon any of the big men could easily overpower her.

The only bright side to all of this was that Brown stopped harassing me about being harder on the men. He remained as strict as ever, if not more so, but he was far too busy watching the men to watch me.

Not that the four officers were entirely alone. The warrant officers—Cheong the bosun, Maxwell the arms master, Ntumba the surgeon, and Goldstein the EVA master—were veterans of many years' service. Presumably they would be on our side, at least, if it came down to it. But the captain wasn't quite confident enough in them to share what we knew. They might be elevated above the rest of the crew, but they were still commoners, not officers proper.

After two days of searching, the captain assigned me to a spacewalk with Goldstein. "Officially, of course, you're going out to check for damage to the hull, and so that Goldstein can train you in proper procedures. But I want you to check if there's anything hidden out there."

"Do you really think someone could have hidden them out there, sir?"

He rubbed his face, looking worn. "I don't know. I wouldn't think so, but I feel like we've ruled out every other place. We've searched everyone's effects, every storage locker, every part of stores that isn't locked. It's not impossible that someone could have somehow slipped them out through a torpedo tube, kept them on a cable or something to reel back in. Just—have a look. If they're not there, I have no idea where to check next."

Goldstein was a quiet man; I hadn't dealt with him much before. He helped me through the tedious process of donning the space suit. A heavy battery went on the back. By law, almost everything on the ship was run by manpower or crank, but electricity was necessary in the suits to run the scrubber. It's not as though a single battery would be any danger. But I still felt leery as it went on. I'd been raised on terrifying tales of robots and artificial intelligence wreaking havoc. Anything that could power a computer unnerved me just a bit.

At last the whole suit was on, and the master's mate helped him don his own a great deal quicker. "Can you hear me?" he asked through the radio.

"Loud and clear."

The airlock thumped and wheezed as the mate pumped the air out. While we waited, Goldstein quizzed me on procedure. Where would I attach my tether? Was it safe to slide my hands along the railings? What should I do if I found myself untethered?

I answered promptly. I had studied the manuals, but book knowledge was nothing compared to experience, and I wanted to see the outside for myself.

When he levered the door open at last, I hovered in the hatchway, awed. The view was little different from what I could see from the forecastle, but somehow, seeing it through only my thin faceplate, it felt more real. We were on the port side of the ship, which pointed south, so I could see most of the stars I had grown up with on Mars' southern hemisphere: Canopus, Alpha Centauri, the Jewel Box cluster, the Magellanic Clouds. The long, black arc of the port foresail cut through the southern starfield and shaded us from the sun.

Fastening my tether, I joined Goldstein at the handrail that ran the length of the ship. "Watch those," he said, gesturing with his suit's big mitt at the long, thin sail masts. "They're not hand-rails. They won't hold you and you'll damage them. Stick with these."

"Understood," I said. It was one of those moments when, despite my higher rank on the ship and in society, I had to defer to him. He had the knowledge that would keep us both alive.

An hour later, I was merely bored. The concussive shells the Andromeda had fired at us had left only blackened dents, no real damage. The sails, of course, had been folded and protected by a metal cover during the battle. And there was no sign of the missing cutlasses anywhere. One by one, we checked the hatches of the torpedo tubes. Nothing unusual. They all opened and shut exactly as they should.

"Can I ask you a question?" I finally ventured, after the eighth torpedo tube.

"You can ask."

"Is everyone in the crew . . . doing all right? I've felt some uneasiness."

He gave a short sniff, not quite a laugh. "Oh, it's uneasy all right."

"Is it because Gomez got flogged?"

This time his snort was more pronounced. "Gomez? No. She took her licks like a man and nobody thought the less of her for it. We've all had a checked shirt some time or other. If we weren't in suits right now I could show you the scars of 'em. It's just the way things are in the Navy. You get used to it."

I turned my body toward him in surprise, since I couldn't turn my head. "Then what's the matter? I know Lieutenant Brown is a little strict . . ."

"Strict, my ass," said Goldstein, slamming down the hatch on a torpedo tube and moving to the next. "He raped Yao."

"He *what?*" I jerked so violently my tether snapped taut.

Good thing I kept it fastened at all times, or I'd be spinning off into the black. "The surgeon's boy? How old is she even?"

"Fourteen," he said. "Fourteen and the bastard couldn't keep his hands off."

"You should tell the captain!" I protested.

"Oh, he knows. Lieutenant Brown was docked a week's pay for it."

"A week's pay ..." I trailed off. I was thinking of Gomez's "checked shirt," of the little drops of blood flying off the ends of the cat, and Yao there patiently whisking them out of the air with her towel. That brutality for drinking too much. A week's pay for assaulting a young girl.

"The rules are different for you lot," he said.

"Not that different," I said. "That's a court martial offense in the regs."

"The captain didn't see it that way."

"I'll talk to him," I said. "There's got to be something else that can be done."

He gave a gusty sigh, which made the radio go to static. "You think that because you're new here. Give it a year, two years in the Navy and this kind of thing won't surprise you anymore. That's what I tell the men when they talk about it. But ..." He sighed again. "Well, they're still bothered by it and that's why you might sense some frustration. It won't come to anything. They'll learn eventually. Just like you will."

I didn't ask any more personal questions during the rest of the walk.

I confronted the captain about it as soon as I was back in my uniform. "Sir," I said, approaching him in the sterncastle where he was taking bearings, "I heard a rumor about Brown and Yao."

"It's probably true," he said. "She reported it, at least, and I don't think she seems the sort to make things up. I gave Brown quite a lecture over it and stopped his pay."

"With all due respect, sir . . ." I hesitated. So far I had never questioned an order or decision of the captain's, and I wasn't sure how he'd react if I did. But somebody had to say something. "Article 5, section 6, paragraph 789 of the naval code—"

"Sets the penalty for this at court martial and dismissal from the service, yes. I am aware. But look at our situation. We started out with six officers and forty crew, and now we're down to four officers. I can't afford to put my only lieutenant in irons till we're back to Mars."

"I suppose not, sir."

"And even if I did. I could take him back and we'd do the court martial, and the Admiralty would expect witnesses. The girl doesn't have any. At that point the Admiralty would be very eager to return an innocent verdict, because they're in the same boat I am in, at a bigger scale. We're at war. There aren't enough officers, especially not enough *trained* officers. I'm allowed to impress the merchant spacers, but I can't walk into New Oxford and impress a whole graduating class of mathematicians, more's the pity. Perhaps the Admiralty will eventually see its way through to elevating officers from the ranks, though I'm not sanguine anyone who isn't Founder stock is even capable of the math required to navigate a ship."

I nodded. Mars was founded by some of the greatest scientific minds Earth had been able to send. Naturally those of us descended from those first colonists had superior aptitude. But it was just as natural that most of us would prefer to stay home, on the estates our ancestors had claimed, rather than brave the cold vacuum. Even though they wouldn't have those estates at all if Earth had their way. I could feel pride in myself for being out here, protecting my home. Maybe my reasons hadn't been patriotic at the outset, but something had changed. I was proud to be an officer of the Martian Empire, to be here while others had stayed home.

The captain picked up his sextant again, idly sliding the index arm back and forth. "So I chose to make sure Lieutenant Brown got at least some penalty. I marked the offense down as harassment, which I'm allowed to punish myself, and stopped his pay. It's not perfect, but it's what I can do."

I bowed my head. "I understand, sir. Thank you for taking the time to explain."

I slept uneasily that night. Too many thoughts whirled around my head. Fairness. Punishment. Mutiny. Maggie shyly asking me to switch watches—had Brown done something to her? His taste seemed to run that way. It made me sick just thinking about it. All those comments about me being too old.

But my mind, being less than completely selfless, kept returning to the present danger to myself. Ten cutlasses; not enough to give every man one, but more than enough to overpower the four of us. Three of us, if they made a move while I was asleep. I couldn't ever sleep. Not when it meant leaving the captain and Maggie alone to face whatever they might face alone.

Could Maxwell be trusted to defend them? He had taught me to fight; I knew the strength in his corded muscles. If he were on our side, I could sleep easy, but could he dismiss what had happened to Yao as easily as Goldstein had? I remembered his comment about Founders being morons, and the bowl of food spinning out of my hand as I lunged through the air to slap him.

I woke up with a start. While I'd been thinking, I'd been half dozing, but my mind had finally reached some kind of revelation and jerked me awake.

I knew where the missing cutlasses were. Where they had to be. Where no one had thought to check.

I dressed and made my way up to the sun deck, where the algae and yeast tanks were. The deck was warm with diffuse sunlight and the huge glass tank glowed green with algae. Along the edges of the room were the round openings, about the size of a shilling, of the mirrored fiber-optic cables that brought light down belowdecks. No one was there at the moment, which was exactly what I wanted.

I passed the algae tank. It was clear enough that I could see almost completely through it, which meant nothing could be hiding in there. What I wanted was the yeast tank, a large metal rectangle topped with a round lid.

Dealing with liquids in space is a messy business at the best of times. And the hatches were designed for emptying in sacks of barley meal or removing the yeast to add to the pot at mealtimes, not for rooting around. I took off my jacket and white shirt and carefully tucked them into a strap on the wall. If my stays got dirty, I could live with that.

Without gravity to draw any foreign objects to the bottom, the cutlasses could be anywhere. I unscrewed the lid, releasing a smell like a bakery, and carefully set it to float against the wall.

So far, the black treacly mix inside didn't seem inclined to float away. Part of the point of the yeast was that it was sticky enough to keep the beans and rice from floating out of the crew's bowls. That and the vitamins.

Taking a deep breath, I carefully reached inside. The goo clung to my arm, but didn't creep like water. I felt nothing but warm viscosity as I slowly felt around inside. Only when I was almost up to my shoulder did I finally brush something.

Triumphantly I pulled it out. The cutlass shone black with the tarry yeast, but it was there. Exactly where no one but a spacer would ever look. They didn't expect officers up here.

Of course that didn't narrow down the suspect much. The cook would have to be in on it, wouldn't he? His galley was here, at the aft end of the deck. Then again, what were the odds he would be reaching around that deep when all he needed per day was a few quarts of the stuff? And if I spread the net to include anyone who worked here, I might as well also consider everyone else who had access to this room when no one else was in it. Which, considering I'd just wandered in and found the place empty, was everyone.

But I was getting ahead of myself. I had found the cutlasses. I would bring this one to the captain, claim my five pounds, and come back here with help to dig out the rest of the swords. There was nothing to implicate Moira, so no reason to handle anything myself.

I found a rag in a locker and was starting to clean myself up when I heard movement over by the hatchway where I'd come in, on the other side of the tanks. Whoever it was couldn't see me yet. If it was a conspirator, it was best if they never did. Let them learn I'd found their weapons stash when it was too late to move it.

But that was easier said than done. My shirt and jacket hung on the wall, high enough up that the intruder might spot them. I had to get them down and get moving to the aft hatch before they caught me.

I stared at my hands, dismayed. Both were completely smeared with yeast. The thought of touching my nice clean shirt with those hands horrified me, but I supposed in the interest of not tipping off the mutineers it would have to be done.

Or . . . I nudged myself into a slow spin with one foot, till my head faced down and my feet kicked toward the glowing glass roof. It didn't feel like being upside-down; it felt like I hung over a shining pool, a roof of metal over my head. With my feet, I carefully extracted my clothes from the loop where they hung.

"Hey!" cried a male voice. The cook, Jenkins. Of course; it

was almost seven bells of the morning watch, time to make break-fast. "Who's skylarking up here?"

His voice was close. If I came out from behind the yeast tank, he'd be on top of me before I could get past him to the hatch. Reluctantly I turned myself back over, so I could see over the tank. "It's only me, Midshipman Prescott," I said. "On business for the captain."

I smiled, hoping for a friendly word that would tell me he didn't know anything. Instead the stout, bearded man kicked the wall behind him, shooting toward me.

I shook the shirt and jacket off my feet, leaving them to float, and grabbed a loop to push off aft. But he was too fast for me and snatched me by the ankle.

For several seconds, I only stared in shock. He had assaulted a superior officer. That would get him airlocked for sure, if it was in an attempt to mutiny. He had crossed the rubicon with that action. It was too late to talk him down, and surely his plan now was either to begin the mutiny right now, or to kill me to hide the evidence a little longer.

Coming to my senses, I struck down with the cutlass in my hands. It dug deeply into his arm, and he hissed with pain as the blood seeped over his skin. No shout. So he meant to kill me secretly. If he had hidden the cutlasses in the yeast tank, he could hide a body there just as well. The thought flashed through my mind with a cold clarity, even as I raised the cutlass again.

This time it rang against another blade, metal on metal. Not a cutlass; he had pulled his kitchen knife. Now my ankle was free and I made a grab for the wall. My fingers fell short by half a yard. The horror of every landlubber, getting stranded out of reach of handholds and having to be helped down. Only this time there was no one to help me, only a murderous cook.

He darted in with his knife and I parried. I might not be able to reach him, but my blade was longer than his. I could keep him at arm's length at least.

"You don't want to do this," I said. "If you mutiny, you'll never go home again. No way back to the ground but the elevator, and no way to pass through Phobos Station without them catching you."

"I don't care," he said, with another lunge. "I'm a dead man anyway."

"I can give my word." I shoved his knife away. Had I edged myself close enough to the wall? Not quite. "I won't say you attacked me. I'll give the cutlasses to the captain and no one will know you were involved."

He spat, a messy blob hovering in the air. "Is that how you toffs run things? Hide and sneak and lie? Like Brown?"

I parried again. "I'm nothing like him. I hate him. But that's beyond my power to fix. I just know turning on the Empire isn't the answer."

"Fuck the Empire," he said, punctuating his words with jabs of his knife. "God fuck our gracious Emprex. None of this is for us. It's all for you. Your empire. Not mine."

I wished I could have heard more of what he had to say. I wanted to understand what he meant. Why my Empire and not his? We were both Martians!

But his blows against my sword had driven me closer to the wall, and I turned my body to bring my legs in reach. With one kick against the wall, I closed the distance between the cook and me. My sword went in between the third and fourth ribs. The final look on his face was surprise.

I made my report to the captain as I was, half dressed and covered in yeast and blood. Jenkins wouldn't have acted alone, and

I couldn't risk anyone else coming on the scene before the captain was informed.

He looked grave. "Well done, Mister Prescott," he said heavily. "You did the right thing. Go clean yourself up."

When I returned to the quarterdeck, the ten missing cutlasses were assembled in a row, hanging in the air. Nine black and tarry, one bloody. That made three men now I had killed. I had the idle thought of mentioning that kind of thing back home, at one of my mother's garden parties. The ladies and gentlemen would edge away from me. I had changed so much in a few short months. The old me would have been no less horrified than them. Now I felt—what? I probed my feelings, but could find none. Something about the Navy made it hard to have feelings, to even consider my actions my own. Orders came and I carried them out, that was all.

The bosun's whistle was shrilling to muster the ship's company, and they came hurrying through the hatches to assemble on the sail deck. Every face was carefully blank as they regarded the ten swords. Not one looked shocked or asked a question. They knew. They all knew.

At first, I felt my breath knocked out of my body. Every sailor was in the mutiny? Every one? But then I breathed again. No. They all knew, not all had agreed. That was the meaning of those whispered arguments. Some schooled their faces to blankness to hide disappointment, others relief. And I would never know how many had been ready to kill me.

The captain stood at the railing looking out over the men. "It seems one of your number has plotted a mutiny. We have already dealt with Jenkins, the cook, who concealed these weapons. But I don't believe he worked alone. I am ready to hear any information about his co-conspirators."

There was a long, painful silence. Every man in the crew was careful not to so much as twitch, for fear of being seen to volunteer. They gazed ahead, afraid to either meet the captain's eye or appear to avoid it.

Moira was in front, ramrod straight, wispy hair circling her head like a starburst. My heart contracted. She knew, and she knew I knew. Would she think I had told the captain about her warning? Would she come forward now, for fear of being caught out later? But no, she had to trust me more than that. She wouldn't have warned me if she hadn't. Would she?

If she trusted me that much, she knew more about me than I did. Because I would have put myself down as a person who would tell everything she knew. I would have sworn to it. And here I was, silent.

"May I remind you of article 19 of the Articles of War," the captain continued at last. "'If any person in the fleet shall conceal any traitorous or mutinous practice or design, or if any person shall conceal any traitorous or mutinous words spoken by any, to the prejudice of Their Imperial Majesty or government, or being present at any mutiny or sedition, shall not use his utmost endeavors to suppress the same, he shall suffer death.'"

Someone stifled a cough. I saw Moira's shoulder press against that of her neighbor, a ship's boy by the name of Trask. Comfort? A warning? But again no one spoke.

Suddenly the captain's voice was raised to a shout. "You are all guilty! Every one of you! You all knew about this, I would swear to it! Every one of you should die!"

The crew flinched at his volume, but there was still no answer. Beside me, Brown glanced at the captain. The captain only stared back, as if unsure of what Brown was asking.

Vaulting over the railing, Brown came face to face with the front row of men. One by one he looked into each one's eyes. They stared back blankly. I could scarcely breathe, wondering which of them would crack. He stopped a long time by Moira, looking her up and down.

I bit the inside of my cheek till the blood came. If she spoke, if she moved, if she batted an eyelid, he'd be on her like a bulldog and I didn't think the captain would stop him. My muscles ached with the effort of being still, all to will her into the same stillness.

Brown's hand snaked out and made a grab. There was a muffled squeak, but not Moira's voice. Brown had the boy, Trask, by the arm. Hooking his feet on the floor loops, he dragged Trask to the airlock and shoved him inside. As the door shut, Trask threw himself against it, pounding on the glass window. "Please, sir, I had nothing to do with it."

"Mr. Goldstein," Brown said crisply. "Man the pump."

Goldstein stared at him, stricken, and sought the captain's face for confirmation. But Captain Kim was staring straight ahead, as if pretending he knew nothing of what was going on.

"Promptly, Mr. Goldstein. You may join him within if you prefer."

The EVA master's voice was barely audible. "Aye aye, sir." Bracing his feet, he hauled the long handle of the pump down, and back up again. Down. Up. The air hissed out of the lock.

"Please, sir," begged the boy.

"Give me a name," said Brown. "Give me the name of the man who took the cutlasses."

Trask was silent. The pump developed a soft squeak on the downstroke. The crew barely breathed. I tried to force my lungs to go in and out, but I felt like I was suffocating too. What name was it Trask wouldn't say? Was it Moira's?

At last the boy pounded with an open palm on the window. "Maxwell," he gasped out. "Maxwell took them."

Brown waved for Goldstein to stop pumping and open the lock. With the hiss of the seals I found I could breathe again. But among the crew, there was a flurry of movement as the arms master shot up from the floor, handing himself along the sail levers forward to get away.

"Detain that man, Mr. Prescott," the captain murmured, and for a second I froze. I had been so absorbed with watching, I had forgotten I might have a part to play. I braced and pushed off, calling the names of a few of the men to help me.

This was the moment of decision. Either the men would help me and we would apprehend Maxwell, or they would make up their minds to stand their ground and refuse. Or worse, resist. I had only a cutlass, not enough to go against almost thirty men.

That worry was loud enough to drown out the sick feeling in my gut that told me this was all wrong, that I didn't want to be a part of this at all. That part didn't matter. I had an order, the choice wasn't mine, any more than Goldstein had had a choice to man the pump.

The men whose names I called rose into the air, moving to cut off Maxwell from any of the hatches. We caught up with him on the gun deck. He fought like a wildcat, completely ignoring the blade of my sword. And why shouldn't he? Surrendering wouldn't save his life. At last, the men had him restrained, whipping a piece of cable around his wrists and hauling him down through the hatch, back onto the sail deck.

Maxwell did not bother to defend himself. Not that it seemed likely anyone would listen if he had. Brown wanted someone air-locked for the treason of stealing the cutlasses and he wouldn't stop until he had his culprit. The captain read the section of the regulations on treason and mutiny, pronounced a guilty verdict, and gave the order. Brown pulled the emergency lever to open the outer hatch. For an execution, the Navy allowed the small mercy of a quick evacuation instead of the slow pumping it would take to recover the air.

Back at the captain's side, I struggled to believe what I had seen. Maxwell? A veteran of twenty years' service? He had seemed the perfect example of what a sailor ought to be. He had forgiven me for striking him, my first full day on the ship. He had fought by my side in the boarding party just days ago. How could he turn his back on his duty like that?

The captain dismissed the company and I numbly groped my way to my berth. Maggie trailed beside me, openly sobbing. I couldn't manage to chide her, given my own cheeks were wet. All I could do was squeeze her hand. There was nothing to be said. This was the way things had to be in the Navy, and nothing could make that easy.

Nine

A few weeks later we left Earth space, having met no more hostile ships. The mood on the ship was quiet, sullen. I guarded my words when I spoke to the men, and they chose theirs just as carefully. I didn't know which of them had been ready to mutiny, but I knew full well it hadn't just been Maxwell. The captain had chosen to endorse the delusion that Maxwell had acted alone only because he had no way of finding the others.

I longed for someone to talk to. We resumed our formal dinners in the officer's mess, but I could hardly bear to sit quietly and watch the captain and Lieutenant Brown make small talk. I sometimes talked to Maggie, but I could tell she was valiantly trying to forget everything that had happened. I couldn't bring it up. I wasn't even sure I wanted to. I just didn't want to have to carefully avoid it. I wanted to have a relaxed, easy conversation, like Bing and I had used to have. How would he have handled it? Had he seen anything like it before? Maybe this was just the way it was, and by the time one had been in the Navy as long as Bing had, you felt nothing about it.

I threw myself into my studies, memorizing long tables of planetary positions just to have something else to think about. I took a stopwatch with me when I went to take bearings, trying to beat my previous speed records. If the captain called on me again, I wanted to answer promptly and with confidence.

One day, Maggie cried out that she'd spotted a sail. I was off duty, but rushed to the forecastle to see. She handed me the glass. "I'm almost sure," she said, hesitating a little.

When I squinted through the glass, I understood her confusion. Instead of the bright shine of a reflecting sail, or the solid black diamond of the leeward side, there was a confusion of broken glints.

The captain, arriving a moment after me, took the glass and had a look. "Ah," he said. "The sails are slack. Broken mast, I'd expect." He glanced at his watch and then back at the glass, taking its bearing.

"Is it a ghost ship, sir?" blurted Maggie.

"Still on patrol, Mr. Borisov," the captain corrected. He glanced at his watch again. "Its bearing is near enough to ours. Mr. Prescott, you will command the boarding party."

"Sir? What are we to do there?"

"Find out what happened to the ship. See if it's worth anything, not that we have the manpower to take it if it does. And, if there are any remains there…I would like to bring our men home if we can."

I saluted and went to suit up. My hands felt cold and I could feel my cheeks paling. A boarding party to fetch corpses, ancestors knew how old. I didn't feel competent to command the mission, but I supposed the captain hadn't wanted to send his only lieutenant.

Goldstein joined me after a few moments. "Cap'n assigned me to your party, sir."

I breathed a discreet sigh of relief. "Good. I'll need your knowledge. Have you done one of these before?"

"Twice, sir."

Nguyen was our third, serious for once. I hoped we'd see no pranks out of him today. Lastly came Trask, half drifting through the air. "I'm to join you, sir."

Goldstein and Nguyen both turned their backs to him. The crew had shunned the boy after his half-airlocking, calling him a Jonah. His messmates had thrown him out, and he ate alone now.

I could hardly blame them. With a completely united front of silence, they could have shielded Maxwell indefinitely. The captain couldn't have killed them all. Everyone had loved Maxwell. Even I had.

Not that it was the boy's fault he'd broken. For all I knew, Brown would really have killed him if he hadn't given up the name. But Trask was a shell of his former self. He drifted from station to station like a man asleep.

Goldstein and Nguyen helped each other get into their suits. I helped Trask, since it was obvious no one else would. "Are you all right?" I murmured before putting his helmet on.

"Don't be kind to me, sir," he muttered back. "It only makes it worse."

Valiant, read the name on the side. The ghost ship's sails hung in tatters, holed all over from asteroids. They'd do the ship no good even if someone had been inside to steer. I wondered if the *Mariposa* had enough sail cloth to make the repair. If that was the only thing wrong with the ship, she might be salvaged.

The main airlock was open when we arrived. No question of

testing the air, then. Inside, the sail deck was a mass of shadow. With no one to keep the top deck oriented toward the sun, the fiber-optic lights weren't working.

Goldstein led the way out of the launch, panning a battery-operated light. The sail levers were a hopeless tangle. "No bodies here," he said.

"I assume they were dragged out when the airlock blew," I said. "There might be some on the other decks."

"Ain't that a cheery thought, sir," said Nguyen.

"Mr. Goldstein, Mr. Trask, check the gun deck," I ordered. "Nguyen, this deck. I'll go aloft."

"Isn't it dangerous to split up, sir?" Nguyen asked in a small voice.

"We have the radio," said Goldstein. "You frightened?"

Nguyen turned his helmet to glare.

"I'd just as soon be finished and out of here as fast as we can," I said, by way of explanation. "We'll only be in easy range of the *Mariposa* for an hour."

It wasn't as if I'd even given Nguyen a challenging task. I'd chosen the sun deck for myself, where spacers' bodies might be trapped. I didn't crave the opportunity, but I could see Nguyen was on edge. I didn't want to put him in a position to humiliate himself.

The hatch stuck a little as I slid it open. Here, some dust still lingered, winking in the light of my hand-lamp. The water tank overhead was dark, turned away from the sun as it was, but my light cast a greenish ray. Still full.

The algae had died in the tank, leaving it full of gray water. The yeast tank was dry. I moved forward through the deck, feeling strange. It was enough like the *Mariposa*'s sun deck to be surreal as I handed myself along the wall in my thick spacesuit gloves.

The *Valiant*'s galley was on the bow end. I passed the partition and let out a yelp.

"You all right, sir?" came Goldstein's voice, dry as ever.

I took a deep breath to steady my pounding heart. "Yes, Mr. Goldstein. I've just found the first of the…remains."

There were five of them, clinging to the walls where their drifting had left them. Their white uniforms still looked fresh, a few grubby marks showing their daily wear. Their faces…less so. The vacuum had slowly desiccated each, drying the skin to leather and pulling the lips back to show horrible grimaces.

I could tell the cook by the black yeast smears on his uniform. His hair had been long, tied back in a messy pigtail. By his side, against the wall, was an oxygen tank, gauge reading red. The mask dangled in his hand.

When the locks blew, the air wouldn't have rushed out, like on the sail deck. It would have slowly seeped around the hatches and through the vents, thinning while the men clustered together around the emergency oxygen. They'd taken it in turns, five men to one mask. Hard to hold your breath long enough to make that work. They'd have known the whole time there was no remedy. No suits up on the sun deck, no way to creep below and fix the airlock.

The oxygen had run out before the pressure got too low for them to breathe it. I wasn't sure if that was better or worse.

"I've found a few down here also, sir," said Goldstein after a while.

"There should be suits down there. Any sign that they tried to come up and fix the airlock?"

There was a brief silence. "No, sir," he said at last.

Strange. It's what I would have done. Perhaps they had panicked. "Mr. Nguyen, your report?"

"I've found the log book, sir," he said. "The captain will want it."

I glanced around at the grisly company. "I'll come down and take a look."

Nguyen was carefully flipping pages when I entered the captain's cabin. The paper was brittle from exposure to the vacuum, but it didn't crumble. "The captain was a Boris Xiao-Hamilton, sir," said Nguyen. "But on this page, it says Captain Xiao was killed in an engagement, and a Lieutenant Henry Vasiliev-Scott took command."

I joined him beside the captain's desk. "Relation of our Lieutenant Vasiliev?"

"I think so, sir. She's said her father was lost at space when she was a child. Dates would be about right."

I scanned the log. Bearings, supply levels, punishments. Vasiliev, senior, had been competent enough, it seemed.

Then things started to go wrong.

Aquariad 15. The last engagement exhausted our emergency fuel. Repairing the harm to the sails has taken our whole fabric supply. I pray they take no further damage before we reach Venus.

February 21. I believe we are in the vicinity of the Leonids. I can't be sure, & there's no one I can ask. I don't fully trust my navigation. I was never supposed to take command this soon. I will steer 10 kilometers north & pray that will be sufficient.

February 24. It was not. Port foremast struck by meteor. The whole sail is torn. We haven't moved sunward enough; we'll miss Venus. I have set a man on the radio around the clock, calling for help. Right in the middle of the shipping lane as we are, I have to believe someone will hear.

Piscead 16. We've drifted out of the shipping lane. No one would be this far leeward of Venus at this degree of orbit. And that's if I calculated our course correctly in the first place. I've sketched out the entire thing. By my calculations, we should cross the lane to Venus again in nine months.

We do not have enough food, oxygen, &c for nine months. I have ordered rations to be shortened.

Piscead 17. There is grumbling over the short rations. Clearly everyone knows why. I do not speak of it. I pretend I have a plan. The men do not believe me.

Piscead 28. I have abandoned military discipline. Since we shall never see Mars again, I care nothing anymore for my own dishonor. I am glad at least that my wife & daughter shall have my survivor's benefit. The men seem to appreciate my honesty.

March 6. I have asked the crew their wishes. They wish to continue calling for help until the food is gone, but they were adamant they would not die as the Navy commands, gasping on stale air until the last. When we are near the end, they would like to make it a quick one. I promised them I would do so. If rescue does come, I will destroy this page of the log.

Ariad 9. We scraped out the last of the yeast tank, since we have nothing left to feed it. We took most of the algae out. I broached the last keg of rum & shared around the officers' rations. We sang till our voices were rough. It was a beautiful time. You would have liked it, Eunice (see, I pretend you will read this. Grim realism is no longer any help).

A few of the crew are panicking & have locked themselves in the sun deck. They say there are still some specks of algae left, that it isn't time to give up hope. The rest of the crew has voted to overrule them. I don't know what to do about it.

Ariad 10. It is time. Those men who most ardently wanted a quick death, I passed the word to gather on the sail deck. The rest may stay below, for a slower death but a better chance the Navy finds their bones.

I love you, Eunice. I love you, little Catherine. I go to do for my men what I think my captain would have done for me, had he been fool enough to bring us into this nightmare. I commend you to the ancestors.

The log ended there. I looked over at Nguyen. Large globes

of tears clung to his eyes, and he jerked his head back and forth to dislodge them. I swallowed the lump in my throat and switched off my radio.

Touching my helmet to his, I asked, "Does the Navy expect us to report this?"

He sniffed loudly to clear the last of his tears. "They'll want the log, sir."

"And if a page is removed?"

He pulled back to search my face. At last he moved back to touch helmets and said, "They might prefer it, sir." He opened his cloth specimen bag toward me.

I carefully tore out the last brittle page and placed it in the bag. "It could be mailed to Lieutenant Vasiliev," I suggested.

"You can leave it to me, sir."

Our little plot settled, I switched my radio back on. Goldstein was saying, "Sir? Midshipman Prescott?"

"Go ahead."

"Trask and I split up for a while, and when I came back—well. Can you come?"

When Nguyen and I reached the gun deck, I could see the problem. Trask hung in the air just outside the forward gun room. His helmet was in his hands; his face a purple bruise. His wispy brown hair, chin-length in gravity, scattered around his head like a halo.

I couldn't process it. We had come for corpses, but not this one. Not like this. "Why—"

"He was just a boy," said Goldstein, his voice choked. "We were too hard on him."

Nguyen's voice was hard. "*We* weren't the ones who started it."

Goldstein clasped my arm. "Be careful how you report this, sir," he said, low and urgent. "Don't speculate. Say a suit breach.

Let the captain draw his own conclusions. It's the best way to preserve something for his family."

It took me a moment to piece together what he was saying. At last I understood. Trask had taken his opportunity to end his life while he could. Goldstein hoped it would be ruled an accident, so Trask's family could receive his survivor's benefit.

Something burned in my chest, something I couldn't put a name to. Or didn't want to. Brown had broken the boy, taken him away from his mates, who could have given him courage. It hadn't been fair of them to blame him for it.

But had Brown even had a choice, with the men arrayed before him like that? We had our duty, and our own lives to protect.

"Of course," I said to Goldstein at last, moving to put the dead boy's helmet back on. The Navy could at least do that much for him.

Ten

Venus grew from a dazzling star to a bright disk, and at last to a colossal gold sphere. The thick clouds, boiling with acid, scattered the light till I could barely look at them.

At last we reached orbit and the captain mustered the crew. "We will lie at orbit for a week, as I arrange the purchase of the carbon fiber and cables we need," he explained. "There will be shore leave for those who have merited the privilege. I must warn you, the Venusians are not like us. Stay in the area of the Martian embassy and do *not* go wandering. Watch out for Earthers. This is neutral territory and the Venusians have no tolerance for fighting and stirring up trouble.

"If anyone is thinking of desertion, put that thought from your mind. The Venusians do not want you. They don't want any of us. They will deport you back to Mars, and the penalty for desertion is death."

After the captain dismissed us, Maggie asked me, "So are we going down to the surface?"

I shook my head. "Nobody can go down to the surface. It's hot enough to melt lead and crush a ship."

"Yes, but the floating cities!"

"Only the Venusians get to go there. They don't like outsiders. We'll be going to Aphrodite Station."

Her face fell. "I just *really* wanted to go somewhere with gravity again."

"It has gravity. Or, well, it's supposed to feel like gravity. It spins."

When the launch docked, we felt the false gravity immediately. I had been floating, holding loosely to the handrails, and now I was pulled backward, hanging by my arms. I had to climb down to the new "floor" to get to the hatch.

The station was a vast wheel. From the concourse where I stood, I could see ahead and behind me to where the ground curved upward and cut off my view. Everywhere around were flashing signs—advertising restaurants, bars, brothels. "So much electric stuff," breathed Maggie. "Isn't that dangerous?"

"Not really," I said. "Electricity isn't dangerous without computers running off of it. But it's better not to get too used to it. If the Venusians get too comfortable with it, they'll forget. They'll start wanting to do more and more with it. That's what our ancestors did, and the AIs killed billions of them before they learned. I think our way is better, never to use it when we don't have to. That way we will always remember."

I shepherded Maggie beside me, scanning the flashing neon signs for what I wanted. It seemed the Venusians had a very low opinion of what comforts visiting sailors might be looking for.

"What's exotic dancing?" asked Maggie. "I love dancing but I only know the quadrille."

"It's nothing for you," I said, pulling her along by the elbow. Good lord, how did I end up the nanny for a twelve-year-old in what appeared to be the biggest den of vice in the solar system? Bing would have been a better guide. "Ah, there's what we want."

The glowing blue sign read "BATH HOUSE." An animated neon display showed water pouring out of a shower and into a tub, proving it was a literal bath house and not—well, the other kind.

Maggie took my guidance in good humor and we each spent five shillings for a private bathroom of our own. "Don't wander off," I said firmly. "The captain made me responsible for you and if you get into trouble, it'll be my back that gets it."

The bath was heavenly. I started with a hot shower and moved on to a long soak in a tub big enough to lie down in. It had been months since I'd felt clean at all. I scrubbed my scalp with the plain shampoo they provided, pumiced my heels, everything. When I finally forced myself to get out and dry off, I felt like a new person. Or rather like my old self, who was clean and smelled like bergamot and had never killed a single person. A person who was fit for the drawing rooms of Mars, where I hoped one day to return. I had to remember that person, lest I return and no longer belong there.

I emerged from the bathroom with an apologetic smile, looking around the waiting area for Maggie. But there was no sign of her. I checked the room where she'd been, but the door swung open freely. No one there.

"Excuse me," I asked the attendant. She was wearing a silver garment tight enough to be a second skin and had blue hair. "Do you remember the girl I came in with? About this high, dressed like me?"

The woman's eyes flicked up and down, sizing me up. "Preteen? Brown hair? Yeah, she went off like twenty minutes ago."

"Any idea where she went?"

"Out. She didn't tell me."

I sighed and rubbed my forehead. Either she was extremely absent-minded, to forget to leave me any message, or she had deliberately shaken me off, in search of some kind of vice or other. I suspected the latter.

Four bars, two opium dens, and a casino later, I finally found her in the exotic dancing club. She was sitting at a small table with a drink in front of her, eyes like saucers. And no wonder. There were two women dancing and one man, none of them wearing more than you could cover with a postcard, if you didn't count the numerous piercings and tattoos. One of the women had her entire skin dyed green. Her hair was a shimmering silver, which matched the studs in her navel and nipples.

For a second I too just stood there and stared. I had heard Venus described as a planet of vice, but I had assumed they meant all the electricity. Not…this.

Tearing my eyes away from the green woman, I pulled up a chair. "This really isn't appropriate at your age. I'm shocked they let you in."

She turned her large brown eyes on me. "I saw a man killed in front of me. If I'm old enough for that…"

I grimaced. "I don't make the rules," I said at last. "If I did, you'd still be in school."

"Well, I'm not." She turned back to the dancers. "I just thought, look, if my head is going to be full of those memories, I need to make some better ones. Something to fill up the space and maybe drive that stuff out." She sipped her drink and made a face. "I thought this would, too, but it's horrible."

I took the glass from her and knocked it back. It was pretty vile. "Fine," I said. "We'll stay a little. But you stay with me, all right? This is no place to be alone."

I ordered her something different to drink, a fizzy thing with just a little alcohol, and watched the dancers. She was right—it was better to watch this than think about Maxwell. Or Trask. Or Jenkins. Though now that I was thinking of them, the warm feeling from the girls and the drink vanished. I could see now why

sailors needed such a large alcohol ration every day. It took more than a little to be numb enough not to think.

We stayed on Aphrodite Station a week. Maggie and I rented a cheap hotel room, and I occupied her time on educational pursuits—museums, concerts, videos about Venus's terraforming project. It was a massive undertaking, carried out from huge floating cities.

The minerals we had brought were a contribution to that: calcium and magnesium would pull carbon dioxide out of the air, binding with the carbon and freeing up the oxygen. That was one way to get rid of it; another way was manufacturing carbon fiber and cable to sell to us.

It was the opposite of Mars's terraforming project, trying to subtract ninety percent of the atmosphere instead of trying to thicken it. And it would take thousands of years longer. But the Venusians were fiercely dedicated to it. I supposed you had to be, to choose to live in a place so wildly inhospitable.

"It's not that bad," said the guide who was leading us through a display explaining the process. "I mean, we're in space right now. If you punch a hole in the side, the air is sucked out and we all die in minutes. Whereas on Venus, at floating altitude, the pressure is almost equal so it's more of a slow leak. You have plenty of time to patch it before the sulfuric acid starts to bother you."

Maggie's eyes bugged out. "Is that a thing that happens?"

He waved a hand dismissively. "Oh, hardly ever. But of course we drill for it all the time."

I gazed at a diorama of a floating habitat, like a city packed into a giant zeppelin. "For me, this is like stepping back in history. I mean, it's all very different. But my ancestors were the ones building a livable world for us. You're doing that for your descendants."

"And we have nothing but admiration for you," he said. "You could say Mars is like our big sister. What we are, you were, and what you are, we're gonna be. It'll happen. Rivers, oceans, grass growing. Just like Mars."

I had a sudden pang of homesickness. Galloping through the wild grasses, under a clear blue sky, the wind in my hair…"Funny, I'd always heard Venusians didn't like Martians. Or any outsiders, really. You don't allow immigration."

"Well, I mean, think of it," he said with a little laugh. "You've got millions of people who would rather be here. We'd be swamped with people."

"Really? Millions of people who'd rather float surrounded by toxic gas than stay where they are?"

"You wouldn't *believe* the number of requests we get. Every time a ship comes in, half the crew tries to request asylum. Imagine if we said yes to all of that. We wouldn't be able to build the habitats fast enough."

We left the museum in a thoughtful silence. I wondered if any of our crew really would ask to remain here. Not that it mattered, if the Venusians wouldn't accept them. But after the voyage we'd just finished, it wouldn't surprise me.

The day we were to leave, about ten bedraggled sailors made it to the dock. This seemed to be usual; Brown and I were sent out with a few sailors apiece to find the rest of the crew. My team trawled one side of the street while he took the other.

We found several drinking heavily in a bar, singing bawdy songs. That was an easy one. The ones we found in brothels were harder to extract. But as I approached the end of the port district, I began to worry. I hadn't yet found Moira.

Brown met me in the middle of the concourse. "Time to return to the ship," he said. "The crew were told not to go past here."

I blinked at him. "But … sir. We don't yet have everyone."

He gave me a withering look. "Whoever we don't have, has deserted. We will simply write up their names as deserters and move on. If they were interested in leaving with us, they knew the time and place."

"Yes, sir." I fell in beside him. Between the death sentence from Mars and Venus's refusal to accept immigrants, I had assumed no one would be foolish enough to try desertion. Least of all Moira. What could she possibly be thinking? Or had something happened to her?

I dropped back to speak to the men. "Do any of you know where any more of the crew might be? This is your shipmates' last chance to return without punishment. If we can find them before the *Mariposa* sails, they won't be in any trouble."

The ones sober enough to listen looked around at each other. "All of my messmates are here," said one.

"What about Singh and Nguyen and that lot?" asked another. "I haven't seen any of them."

"Nguyen got in a fight with an Earther," said the man next to him. "The Venusians took him off."

I rejoined Brown. "Sir, is there a prison here? Or where would someone be taken if they got in trouble with the law?"

He sighed. "You won't let this rest, will you? Fine. We'll check out the security office."

Sure enough, several of the missing men were there. Not Moira. The Venusian police were extremely polite. "We do not allow fighting on Aphrodite Station," the chief said earnestly. She was a short dark woman with vivid pink hair and silver tracery going around and through her earlobes. "And these men started the quarrel."

Brown stared down the four men sitting, abashed, on a narrow metal bench. "Is this true?"

"It's true that we threw the first punch, sir," said Nguyen.

His hunched shoulders made him look smaller than usual. "But it isn't true that we started it, sir. The Earthers were taunting us, sir."

"I expect you to have the self-control not to respond to taunts."

"They said they were going to beat us up, sir!"

"So you decided to start something yourselves."

"No, sir. It wasn't till one of them said—" He choked on his words from sheer fury. "He said, 'Don't bother with them. It's not like they really count as people on Mars. They're just the dogs that do what they're told or get kicked.' Sir." His mouth twisted and he blinked hard. "I couldn't let that stand, sir. You know I couldn't."

Brown rocked back on his heels, staring at the ceiling. Briefly, I sympathized with him. What could he possibly say to reassure the men, after what we'd all been through? What he, specifically, had done?

But the Earthers didn't know what Brown had done. They had an idea of what it was like on Mars, what our class system was like. And I didn't much like the thought of Mars having that kind of reputation. Of course rank was important to us. That didn't mean we thought of commoners as dogs. Everyone had their place, didn't they? I didn't ask to be born how I was, any more than they did.

The whole class system was due for some kind of overhaul, to be sure. I had said so myself more than once. That nobles like me should be foregoing some of our inherited privilege, trying to make Mars more fair. But I hadn't thought it was bad enough that even spacers from another planet had heard of it.

To the chief he said, "Are they free to go?"

"Free to leave the station. Not free to roam around on it anymore. We put them on a list; they'll be turned away at the hatch next time."

Brown nodded sharply. "Come on, men. Let's go."

As we left, I quietly asked Nguyen, "What about Moira Singh? Was she with you?"

He rubbed his scruffy chin. "I think she was…well, I thought she was. She was right before that. But she didn't get picked up with us."

When we reached the dock, the captain was waiting. He ran his eyes over the shuffling, hungover collection of sailors we had brought back. "Is this everyone?"

"Everyone we could find, sir," replied Brown.

The number came up short by three, not counting the six deaths we'd experienced on the way over, or those we'd lost with Vasiliev in the Andromeda's prize crew. We desperately needed more, so the captain authorized a press gang.

I didn't relish the task, going around seizing Martian nationals for our ship. There were plenty around, sailors from merchant vessels mainly, and the Venusians had no objections so long as we left their own people alone. But the impressed men put up no end of fuss and I felt like the villain for selecting them.

All along the concourse, up and down, between the docks and the embassy, I kept my eyes peeled for Moira. Had something happened? Had one of the Earthers dragged her into an alley and stabbed her? Or had she truly lost her mind and forsaken Mars forever?

What could I ever say to her fathers if she had?

Eleven

After leaving Venus, we returned to a three-watch schedule. One of our new crew members was a former merchant captain, and Captain Kim had given her the third watch. Vargas still wasn't an officer, as she wasn't formally sworn to Their Majesty's service, but the captain trusted her far enough to navigate and manage the men.

Not far enough to stand that watch alone, though, and I was moved to her watch. It was a relief not to have Brown breathing down my neck anymore. And Vargas was cordial, though not talkative.

Heading leeward, away from the sun, we kept the sails angled the opposite way as before, to speed up our orbit and move us into a higher one. Each day the captain checked the angle of the sails and the bearing of the ship and had the men make minor corrections. The slightest change in the ship's angle would change the sun's angle as it hit the sails, which could throw us wildly off course. Here, so close to the sun, we were affected by every slight variation in its intensity, which kept rotating the ship out of its proper attitude. One day the mainsails had to be reefed a few meters, the next day let out again. Other times we had to furl the sails to pass through meteor showers.

Despite our efforts, the sails did take occasional damage and required considerable upkeep. I went out with Goldstein more than once, working along the lee side of the sails, to service the hydraulic lines and patch small holes. Even here, the force the sun imparted was so faint that we couldn't afford the slightest decrease in the sails' efficiency.

Maggie's behavior continued to worry me. She had stopped crying, of homesickness or anything else, and started drinking. For a girl of her size, the standard alcohol ration was far too much, and before Venus she had always refused it. Lately, she was stubbornly drinking all of it before going to sleep. At least we now had eight hours between watches instead of only four, and she had never turned up for duty drunk. I was neither her mother nor her captain, and I had no say in what she did, but it concerned me.

I floated on the quarterdeck on watch one day, scanning the stars with my spyglass. Nothing to see; no suspicious shadows. Unsurprising, given Earth space was a good month ahead. But there were always pirates hanging around Venus. I had to stay alert.

It was hard to focus on my duty when I felt this hollow. I had thought I hated Moira. I had certainly never wanted to see her again. Yet now she was gone and I wanted her back. Every day I put back on an old, dirty shirt, and the smell of my own rank sweat wasn't what upset me, it was the loss of that daily reminder that she—well, at least didn't hate me. That she was quietly thinking of me, remembering what was important to me.

But what had *happened?* I thought I knew her so well. Or at least, I once did. I knew the way she twinkled her eyes when she had thought of a dirty joke she couldn't say aloud. I knew the way she leaned low over a horse's neck when leaping a creek and that the only way to tell she was afraid was that she became even more reckless than usual. But I couldn't begin to guess whether she had really deserted.

She must have been a part of the planned mutiny, or she wouldn't have been able to assure me I'd be protected. Even that shocked me. At home she had been reckless, but never rebellious. Always respectful to my parents, quick to finish her work. I would have considered her a loyal person. To betray not only her commanding officers, but Mars itself—how could she do that?

Well. I supposed I hadn't really known her at all. After all, I had never predicted she would let me down the way she did so many years ago, and yet she had. I had thought I could count on her. Every single other person in my life had had to be managed, their reactions predicted, their demands balanced. With her, I just assumed. Of course she would understand; she would adapt to what I needed. She always had before.

My anger came roaring back. Why *wouldn't* she mutiny? Why wouldn't she desert? Maybe that was really who she was. Reckless. Disloyal. Thinking nothing of the future. Only thinking of what she wanted in that moment. If she had thought about consequences, she would never have kissed me that night.

I kicked back and forth across the quarterdeck, the closest I could get to pacing. Off the port side, off the starboard side, back again. Ramesh Singh was never going to see his daughter again. And I was going to have to be the one to tell him that. If she so much as set foot on Phobos Station—which she was just rash enough to do—they'd catch her in a heartbeat, and she'd be dead.

I was so angry about that, I wanted to strangle her myself.

Suddenly I stopped myself with a hand on the astronavigator. I had simultaneously realized three things. First, I was here to watch, not fume, and I was fuming. Second, it had been a long time since I'd scanned the stars.

And third, there was something there.

A cursory glance was enough to tell me there was no time to calculate her speed and trajectory. She was visible with the naked eye and I could see her growing larger. She was *close*.

I kicked off the back window, shouting for Vargas and the captain. The crew sprang to their stations.

Hurrying forward to our berth, I rousted out Maggie. Just as I feared, she hadn't woken at the bosun's whistle. "Get up. We're under attack."

She fought her way out of her sack, squinting at me blearily. I could smell the alcohol on her breath; I could only hope everyone else would be too busy to notice. Pushing her ahead of me, I returned to the quarterdeck to belt on a cutlass and man my station over the gun deck hatch.

I had barely arrived when one of the huge levers that controlled the sails gave a lurch, the free end slamming from the floor to the ceiling.

"What was that?" I asked no one in particular.

"They hit our sails," said the captain calmly. "Avoid the sail deck; they're likely to try the same again."

He was right: the levers jerked and thrashed like living things. The enemy was still too far away to hit a small target like the ship itself, but the sails spread for miles. It was like hitting the broad side of a barn.

We returned fire with the stern chasers and the swivel guns, loaded with chain. If they were trying to kill our acceleration by tearing up our sails, we could do the same to them.

"Mr. Prescott, come up here," called the captain. "Your watch was at the stern window; you'd best stay there to help Mr. Vargas. Mr. Borisov can relay orders on her own."

I chewed my lip. Maybe she couldn't, but I could hardly tell the captain that. "Aye aye, sir."

From the curving glass window, I could see the enemy continuing to approach: a black circle against the stars, behind us and to sunward. Not as close as I had originally thought, because the sails were spread, casting a vast shadow. It was hard to say exactly how close without knowing how large their sails were. Oddly, the black shape was now shrinking instead of growing.

"They're furling their sails now," said Vargas, handing me the glass. "Might be burning emergency fuel to decelerate as well. What do you think?"

I gazed intently at the black circle. It was certainly shrinking, but how much of that was sails, I couldn't say. Handing back the glass, I turned back toward the captain to relay what we had seen.

"We'd best redouble our efforts with the sternchasers," he said. "Their crew will be in among the sails, getting them furled, and a good hit might take out some men."

I returned to Vargas to watch the view. A torpedo streaked by the window and tore into our sails. From here, I could see one of the metal arms buckle and a tear slowly travel along the fabric.

The enemy ship finished furling her sails, narrowing to a tiny cylinder. Still growing, but Vargas was right—they were trying to decelerate to match our speed.

We held our fire until they approached more closely. No point in wasting shot trying to hit a target that tiny. But soon it was close enough to see their forecastle and the shape of someone there, outlined against the light spilling in from the sail deck. On the starboard side, pointed north to face us, I could see her flag: the skull and crossbones.

At last I saw a flash of light, a torpedo igniting and beginning to speed toward the ship, and told the captain.

"All hands, brace for impact!" he shouted.

I was on the quarterdeck, braced against the port wall, when the shot hit. It did no more than wrench my arms, but there was a scream as Maggie launched into the air. She had been improperly braced, holding on with only one hand. Now she hung stranded in the middle of the sail deck, out of reach of the quarterdeck railing.

"Permission to help her, sir?"

I didn't hear the captain's answer, because just then Vargas cried, "They've fired their grapple! Brace for all you're worth!"

The grapple. A dangerous tactic for both ships, but it could work to keep two ships together when their speeds were too different to engage for long. Just as Maxwell had always said, whether fighting or fucking, you have to hold on tight.

The trouble was that it would immediately match the two ship's speeds, with brutal degrees of acceleration. If our speeds were more than a few tenths of a knot different, neither crew would survive it. Even if not, our only hope was being as tightly braced for impact as we could.

And Maggie was hanging helplessly near the ceiling.

Without stopping to think, I lunged at her with all my strength, barreling into her in the air and slamming her into the ceiling. She cried out with pain, but I shoved her arms into the loops up to the shoulders.

I had barely secured my own arms and legs when the grapple hit. Acceleration yanked me hard to port. My head was pointed that way, and all the blood rushed to it, making my vision red and hazy. Maggie's head pointed starboard, so she would have blacked out. I couldn't turn my head to see; I could only hope she was secure enough to stay in place.

I forced myself to think, to figure out what was happening. The grapple must have attached somewhere on the starboard side, so the whole ship was pivoting around that point like a cat being swung by the tail. Or rather two cats, with their tails tied together, because the enemy ship would be caught in the same circle.

As our momentum dropped, the force let up a little, though our swift rotation around the other ship still imparted some. Like two dancers clasping hands through a spin, the two ships were under centrifugal force that pulled us sideways.

The captain's voice called, "Starboard guns, prepare a volley." I repeated the order, because somebody had to. Though how the crews would manage to function under a false gravity that pulled them away from their guns, I wasn't sure.

A low moan from Maggie reassured me that she had made it. Thank the ancestors. With that worry off my mind, I took stock of myself. Down was now to port, so I was hanging head down on the wall. Carefully I crept out of the handholds and climbed along the wall to Maggie. "Are you all right?"

Her face was pale and clammy, but she answered me promptly. "Better than I deserve. I think my arm's broken."

"Stay there," I said. "There will be more shots soon."

I clambered down toward the port gun deck hatch and looked down. It was a mess down there. A torpedo had gotten loose, crashed against the outer hull, and plowed the whole length of the deck. Fortunately, it hadn't yet been armed. But at least one of the men had been in its path. I say at least one because it was not clear, from the remains, exactly how many people it might have been. The rest of the men were getting clear of their restraints and carefully pulling themselves back into position around the guns.

"Never mind these guns," I told them. "The grapple's attached to starboard, so that's where the enemy ship has to be. Come up to assist the starboard gun crew; I have no idea of the situation there."

I climbed back up, this time along what had been the floor. "Sir, I've ordered the port gun crew to come to starboard."

"Good. Get there yourself and assist."

Just then Varga, watching the stern window, shouted, "Their launch is on the way!"

Damn. We could hardly be farther from ready. How could they be on their way so fast?

"All hands, prepare to repel boarders!" called the captain. I called the port gun crew to me, wondering where to expect the enemy. At the port airlock they'd have to climb up into the ship while we were waiting right above, which seemed a fool's errand. But the starboard airlock would open on a forty-foot drop. Either way, impossible conditions to fight under. I divided the men, to be sure, and joined the group at the starboard airlock.

Every time we had drilled, we had arrayed ourselves in a hemispherical cloud around the airlock. That obviously wouldn't work. The best we could do was cling to the walls—the old ceiling and floor—around the airlock. I twisted my left elbow into a strap and dug my feet into two others, to leave my sword arm free.

Thus prepared, I finally had a second to look around the ship. It looked entirely foreign under the new false gravity. The sail deck was now a long, narrow passage with a high ceiling, with the captain tucked into an alcove, hanging sideways in his secure chair. I craned my neck to see it in the old way, but my middle ear wouldn't let me trick myself.

If the boarders came in this way, they'd have to clamber along the same handholds we were, fighting one-handed the same as us. So it was no real disadvantage, and we filled up most of the wall space. They'd have to come through one or two at a time.

At last I heard the soft thump of a launch being fastened to the airlock, and the screech of the outer door being forced. They were coming on this side after all. The inner door rolled open. I drew my sword, craning my neck to see what was happening. Where were the boarders?

All at once, they leaped through with a hair-raising cry. I hung on the wall, gaping, as they plummeted past me, not touching the walls. Surely they would smash to pieces on the bottom?

But no, I realized after a moment they hung from somewhere inside their launch on thin cables. I hacked at one, severing it neatly, but it didn't matter. Already the pirates had reached the quarterdeck railing. Only five of our men were near enough to the captain to do any good, including Vargas, and there were over a dozen pirates.

Wrapping my hands in my coatsleeves, I leaped off the wall and grabbed at a cable to slide down. The friction would destroy my coat, but better than ripping the skin off my palms. I abandoned the cable as it crossed the quarterdeck railing and worked my way along the perpendicular deck, drawing my sword again as I approached the pirates.

I was too late. Vargas tumbled down into the corner just as I got close, and before I could get into sword range, the captain was rendering up his sword.

I hung there on the railing, aghast. It was the shortest battle I'd ever heard of. Where did they come up with tactics like that? And how could we counter them next time?

Stupid thought; there would be no next time. We had been captured by pirates. If we were lucky, we would be prisoners for a long time. The Earthers might be talked into a prisoner exchange, but being pirates, our captors would probably want a ransom. Of course, if we weren't so lucky, we'd be shoved out the nearest airlock.

It took the pirates some time to assemble everyone, during which time they finally released the grapple and the false gravity vanished. One by one, we had to present ourselves to the pirate ship's captain and hand over our swords. I hung back, as if it mattered in what order I accepted my shame and failure. My cutlass was perfectly clean as I held it flat in front of me. I should have been faster. I should have killed at least one of them.

Staring forlornly at the sword, I didn't realize at first that it was my turn. I came forward and released the cutlass so that it floated in front of me. How could this even be happening?

The pirate captain was tall, tan, and curly-haired. He took my sword without comment and turned to the pirate next to him.

"That's the lot," he said in a flat Earth accent. "And all credit to you."

I followed his gaze to the woman beside him and went white hot with rage. Without even thinking, I pushed off toward her, fists at the ready.

It was Moira.

Rough hands dragged me backward before I could reach her. One of the pirates held me with my arms twisted painfully behind my back. Moira looked, for once in her life, surprised.

Then she laughed. "Don't worry about her," she told the pirate captain. "She's not trying to go back on her surrender, she just has a personal grudge against me."

"I hadn't thought of that," the captain replied. "Are you sure you can handle this crew? Given you've got a history with everyone on board."

"I'll be fine," she said. "Do I get to decide what happens with the officers?"

The captain sketched a mock bow. "Whatever you want. You've earned it."

She paused, furrowing her brow. I knew that face; it was the face she made when she'd made up her mind ten minutes ago but wanted you to think she was thinking it over. "The captain and the mate go in the escape pod," she said. "I can't have them on the ship, but the captain at least doesn't deserve airlocking. The midshipmen I want to keep. I've got nobody else who can do navigation."

"They're not going to want to help you."

"That's why I need two of them." She winked at him cheerfully.

Captain Kim was grave as they escorted him into the pod. As well he should be; his odds of getting picked up at all, let alone by a Martian ship, were slim. "If I get home before you," he told me quietly, "I'll tell the Admiralty you didn't stay behind of your own choice."

"Thank you, sir," I said. If I had refused the chance to go into the pod with him, choosing to stay with the pirates, that would be seen as collaboration. I'd be guilty of treason. Though if I had had the choice, it would have been hard to make myself get into that tiny pod, with only days of oxygen.

A spacer stepped up—Gomez. "I want to go with the captain," she said.

Captain Kim frowned at her. "While I would certainly appreciate your presence, no one expects the common spacers to—"

"It's not about expectations, sir," she interrupted. "You're my best bet to get back to Mars *ever*, to see my daughter."

Understanding dawned in his face. "Very well."

The pirates allowed it, and the pod was pushed loose with the three of them in it. The pirate captain took his leave, with several others of the boarding party, leaving Moira in command with a small crew of pirates.

Twelve

Ntumba finished tying Maggie's arm to the splint and said, "Let this be a lesson to you. When they say brace, you stick both arms into the loops, up to the shoulders if you can. Legs too, if you have time. Hanging on with one arm is a recipe for, well." She waved at the splint.

"I know," said Maggie quietly. "I'll be more careful."

"How is the crew?" I asked Ntumba. Maggie and I had been confined to our berth since the attack, and it didn't seem there was any plan to let us out. "Are they resisting Singh's command?"

"No, everyone likes her."

"But it's their *duty*—"

Ntumba gave me a look. "How much duty do you really think this crew feels toward Mars? After all they've been through?"

I fell silent. Why would I assume the crew that had planned a mutiny would balk at working with pirates? Why did I keep assuming any of these people had even basic loyalty?

Ntumba closed her medical kit and moved toward the hatch.

Before she could go, I asked, "Will we be allowed to exercise? The Solar Accord gives prisoners the right to one hour exercise per day."

"They're pirates. They didn't sign that and they don't care."

"Can you at least ask?" I didn't have to remind the surgeon of the necessity of my request. Here in space, our bones and muscles would atrophy without regular, heavy exercise. If it got bad enough, we'd be space-bound—permanently unable to return home. There were machines on one of the upper decks, relying on springs and friction to provide the necessary resistance, but here in our berth there was nothing to exercise with.

"I'll let them know." She nodded sharply and was gone.

I sighed and came back over to Maggie. "How's it feel?"

"Hurts," she said. "Thanks for saving me."

"It was a near thing," I said. I wanted to shout at her, about drinking so much, about her carelessness. But what did it matter now? We weren't going to see combat again.

I curled into a corner, the pressure of the walls the next best thing to gravity. In space, you start to feel starved for heavy pressure, for the feel of a chair under you, for the weight of a blanket.

Mars wouldn't know yet the ship had been taken. By now the *Andromeda* would be almost back, and my share of the prize money would be sent to my family. That was good; I wasn't sure of the exact amount, but it should hold them for months at least. And my pay would continue to be disbursed to them monthly. The first they would hear of my capture would be when ransom was requested. Or, if the pirates decided to keep me, when the *Mariposa* failed to arrive back at Mars when expected. A few months would pass, and then my family would receive my death benefit, the equivalent of six months' pay.

It wasn't enough. It was far from enough, but it should be at least something. If they had any sense, they'd use that money to settle their debts and try to find a small place where they could live with William. But I didn't feel easy in my mind about it. Without me there to bully them into financial responsibility, they'd spend it or simply try to stretch out the clock before foreclosure.

I closed my eyes and pushed the back of my head into the hard wood behind me. This capture had been a personal failure, yes, and probably the end of my career. But that wasn't the worst part. The worst was having undergone so much misery—Brown's bullying, the bad food, the reeking of the suction latrine, the head- aches at night from rebreathing my own air, terror of mutiny, the violence I had witnessed and perpetrated—only to not save my family after all.

Moira sent for me soon enough. I faced her across the cap- tain's cabin, a plush room I'd never had occasion to enter before. Dark blue cloth padded the walls, and the hammock hung in a dedicated alcove.

She herself was almost unfamiliar in her pirate getup: bare feet; loose brown trousers, gathered at the ankles; a red shirt tied beneath her breasts, exposing her midriff and the tiny ruby twin- kling in her navel.

I stood gaping for a minute, and she crossed her arms with a tinge of embarrassment. "I got tired of the old Navy uniform. Bought this stuff on Venus."

Shaking my head to clear it, I forced my eyes back to her face. "Moira, what the hell is going on?"

"I joined the pirates," she said quietly. "After the mutiny failed, I felt there was no hope. No point in being anything other than a rug for the feet of Martian nobles. And then there was that fight in the bar."

"You deserted."

"The Earthers said we were dogs, no good for anything but

kicking. And I thought—that's what I've been." She shook her head. "I couldn't live like that anymore. So yeah, I deserted. If you want to call it that. I freed myself."

"And went straight to them?"

"Where else? You know Venus doesn't take immigrants. Couldn't go home. But the pirates are always hiring. It's a living."

"Better than a living," I spat. "A whole ship all for you, if you told them where to find it and how to take it. That was the deal?"

"It wasn't like that!" she objected. "I wanted to get back here and save everyone else."

"Not all of us wanted to be saved," I said. "Right now the captain is running out of air in that tiny pod because of you. And I don't know how many people died in the attack."

"Four," she said quietly. "I know. I don't like that any more than you do. But it's a warship. Kim would have taken it into battle more times on the way back to Mars anyway. This way they have their freedom. Most of the crew has agreed to stay on after we get to Luna."

"So that's where we're going."

"Yeah. Earth supplies pirate vessels as needed, pays for specific missions."

I scowled. That sort of underhanded dealing was exactly what I expected from Earth. "So what's the plan for me? Keep me for ransom?"

Her lips thinned. "I don't know. I kept you here because I could protect you. After we get there, you're out of my hands."

There was a lot I could say to that. I kept to the most pressing, the thing that had been eating at me since she first started washing my shirts. "And why do you care to protect me? I didn't think you ever wanted to see me again."

"I didn't." She turned away, pretending to study a painting on the wall. "You were pretty nasty, that night. I kept wondering, why didn't you just say you weren't interested? Why did you have to kick me in the teeth like that, with all that talk of class and what sort of person would be good enough for you?"

"That's not—"

She held up a finger. "Then I realized. You *hadn't* said you weren't interested. You could have easily said, 'Moira, I am not in love with you, I am never going to be in love with you, it isn't gonna happen.' But you didn't." She turned to me, smiling broadly. "You didn't because you couldn't. Because you never lie."

I gasped for breath. How could she— "You're grasping at straws, Moira. You're hearing what you wanted to hear."

"So say it," she said, still smiling. "Go ahead. Tell me you didn't feel what I was feeling. Tell me you just weren't that into me."

I ground my teeth. "What I *felt* was irrelevant—"

"See? That's why." Kicking against the wall, she crossed to the other side of the little room. "Don't get me wrong, you were an ass that night and there's no excuse for it. But I decided to forgive you. The plan was not to seek you out, to give you your space. Because the one thing I did hear loud and clear was that you wanted that."

"I did. I do."

"But the universe threw us together. Of all the possible planets, all the possible ships, we ended up in the same place. That feels like fate."

"It's chance."

"Maybe it is. I don't care. I didn't appreciate, before, how lucky I was to know you in the first place. I'm not letting chances slip out of my fingers again. You're here, I'm here, and I'm not going to quietly disappear by night because you can't handle how I feel about you."

She finished her little speech and hung there facing me, eyes darting over my face and away. I took a deep breath, let it out, took another.

"So much for what *you* think," I said. "How *you* feel. But this isn't a one-person venture. Nothing has changed for me since that night— No. That's a lie. I'm angrier at you now than I was then. You betrayed us. You betrayed Mars. I *never* would have thought that of you. I swore to the captain you never would have deserted. I thought of you as a loyal person. It turns out I never knew you at all."

Her eyes flashed. I knew that look. Damn it, I had *liked* that look. "Speaking of thinking you know a person. How do you suppose I felt, watching you drag Maxwell back toward the airlock?"

My face heated. "If I had refused, it wouldn't have saved him."

"I'm sure that's what every other person on the ship thought."

I wanted to keep fighting with her. Because she was wrong, and more, because I missed fighting with her. God, I had forgotten how much we had argued, over the most ridiculous things. And how her eyes sparkled and she talked fast, while I leaned on my back foot and tried to think of citations. A game, then.

But it wasn't a game now, was it? She was a traitor. And, for all her talk of protecting me, my jailor. I couldn't let myself forget that. "Am I free to go?"

The fierceness went out of her face, and for a second I could see her naked disappointment. Then she turned away. "Of course. Marron is waiting to take you back."

Marron was an inverted triangle of a man: broad, Earther shoulders over bandy legs. His brown face was creased, mainly in cheerful patterns, and half-hidden by a wiry beard. He became my escort around the ship. Maggie and I were permitted to exercise and even join the crew for meals and entertainment, provided he had his sharp eyes on us.

Wise of Moira to order it. I absolutely would have sabotaged the Mariposa if I could. Machine oil in the algae tank. A gun hatch wedged open. It was my duty to kill us all rather than let the ship remain in enemy hands. If I ever returned to Mars, I would have to testify that I had done all in my power to hinder enemy operations. But nothing was in my power to do; Moira had been careful of that. She knew me that well.

I sat one evening, watching the men play cards. It was an Earth game I didn't recognize, with complex rules which were never spoken aloud. All I could tell was that the goal was to run out of cards, and infringements of the rules were punished with being given more cards while everyone jeered.

After a hand had ended, Marron looked at me. "Want to play?"

"I can't, I don't know this game."

Everyone hooted. "Fresh blood! Fresh blood!"

"It's more fun when you don't know the rules," said Marron. "I'll deal you in."

I quickly realized it was more fun for them if I didn't know the rules. For me it was just an exercise in trying to hold rapidly increasing numbers of cards. But by the third match I began to get the hang of it. Diamonds went on other diamonds, but spades went on hearts, unless it was a face card, in which case it went on clubs. Clubs had to go on even numbers of any suit. If you played a jack, you had to stick your thumb in your ear while you did it. Other cards had special words that went with them.

"Kilimanjaro," I said, laying my last card down to the cheers of the men.

One of the Earthers slapped my back. "See! You Martians pick this up like lightning."

"Why shouldn't we?" asked Yao softly. She had brightened

some since the pirate takeover, though her eyes still looked sad. "It's like the Navy. Ten million rules and usually you find out when you get punished for not doing them."

I stiffened and handed the deck back to Marron. "I'm done playing."

The others continued the game, while Marron sat on the outskirts with me. He pulled a little bundle out of a locker and started unfolding it. "Sorry somebody had to bring politics into it."

I shrugged. "She has a right to her feelings. I just can't listen to that kind of talk. It's against the regs. Which, I might add, there's an entire book of. That bit is Section 16, paragraph nine, article seven: Duties of Captured Officers."

He stared at me for a few seconds. "So it's true what they say about Martian nobles?"

"Why, what do they say?" The little I'd heard of what Earthers thought of us was bad enough. He wouldn't know about the pressures of our life, the harsh training that had made us what we were. Only that we were the privileged, as our society understood it.

He finished unfolding his bundle, which turned out to be a torn shirt and a needle and thread to mend it with. "That you're all super smart."

Oh, that. My face warmed. "I mean, a little? Mars was originally settled by scientists. They were chosen for being some of the brightest people on the planet. That first five hundred families became the noble class, so ... you do notice some extra scientific ability."

"So that's how you guys can navigate with math alone. In your heads." He tapped his, awed.

I shifted, a little uncomfortably. Noble genetics could be a mixed bag. It wasn't all being good at math. William's condition came to mind. And the intelligence some boasted of was just another thing for commoners to envy.

"It's just trigonometry," I said. "Middle school stuff."

He snorted, licking his thread to stab it through the needle's eye. "Depends on where you went to middle school." A shout went around the circle of card players—Yao had already won the next hand. Marron flicked his eyes from me to Yao and back again. "What is the point of all of it? The fake-feudal thing?"

I bristled. "It isn't fake. It's no different from what our ancestors in Britain and Russia used to do."

"And were done doing since long before they came to Mars. So why resurrect it? Why have an aristocracy at all?"

"Early on, there wasn't one," I said. "The first colonists had their original land claims, but they meant to just let anyone come, have no real government except what each settlement decided. But then more people started coming. And Earth corps, all wanting a cut." I tried and failed to keep the bitterness out of my voice.

"You could have closed immigration, like Venus did."

"I suppose. But we—they wanted more people to come. They just didn't want people to exploit Mars. They had a plan to terraform it, even back then, and they had to put that project in the hands of someone who could carry out generations-long endeavors. A democracy never would have kept the same goal that long. And when land can be bought up by just anyone, it'll be bought by unscrupulous people who just want to mine it."

"But what's to keep you people from being just as bad?"

I turned one hand palm-up. "Investment, I suppose. Knowing we're protecting that land for our children and our great-grandchildren. We received it from our ancestors, it's—" I groped for words, trying to frame something so obvious and deeply-felt, I had never needed to explain it before. "It's a sacred trust," I finally said. "It's the meaning of our lives. Especially after the Singularity. We know how fragile our life on Mars is. Every day the solar wind erodes the atmosphere just a little bit. If we aren't keeping up the project, if we aren't in space bringing gasses back, Mars will die."

He gave a respectful nod. "I do understand that, I guess." With a gesture toward Yao, he added, "But what about everybody else? Are they okay with all this?"

I looked down at the deck. "It's not perfect," I said at last. "Putting all the power in a few hands makes it harder to exploit the planet, but once the power is there, they'll grab even what they don't need. Parliament is only composed of nobles, and of course they aren't always thinking of the common good so much as what's good for them."

There was a lot more I could say to this. Years ago, Moira had been something of a revolutionary, politically. She used to read me bits out of her books, and it had made so much sense. A whole different view on things than I'd learned in school. For a while I had gotten into it myself. I had dreamed of running for Parliament myself, getting reforms passed.

But after Moira had left, I'd never cracked another of those books. I hadn't changed my mind, I'd only lost faith in the idea of reform. How could it ever happen when everyone in the system was trapped in one way or another? I'd never have the money to run for Parliament, that was certain. And Moira's favorite social reform leader had died. Equality for all Martians was a dream that couldn't stand the harsh light of reality. And too many harsh realities had broken in on me, those years.

Marron was smiling to himself. "If I was a Martian, I'd be waving pitchforks by now. Man the barricade! Aux armes, citoyens!" He lifted one muscle-bound arm in a fist over his head.

I couldn't help but crack a smile. "I see why you went in for piracy."

His smile disappeared and he returned to his mending. "I went in for it because it's a living," he said. "Being a pirate is less romantic than you'd think."

"So's being a revolutionary," I countered. "I'm pretty sure."

When I got back to our berth, Maggie was staring out the tiny round window beside the gun port. She turned as I came in. "Do you think we're pointed the right way?"

I came and looked. "More or less. Can't tell better without a sextant. But look, there's Denebola, almost dead ahead. At any rate we're headed downstream and out, like we should be. Why?"

"They want my help with navigation."

I shook my head. "Maggie, you can't. That's treason."

"I don't want to help them get into trouble! I just don't want to be lost in space forever because they don't know where they're going."

"I know, but just think. If they don't get to Luna like they want to, that's one ship that isn't fighting Mars."

She gave me a stricken look. "But I'm twelve. I want to live."

"We might live anyway, and then you'd be exiled for having helped them. Don't you want to get home?"

Her lower lip pouted out. "Not really."

"But you were so homesick!"

"I got over it. I realized, why miss my parents when they're the ones who sent me here? What kind of parents do that? All because I'm the second child and won't have a fortune. But I don't care about any of that! I want to be—I don't know—just a regular person, in a little house, with a job. Why can't I have that?"

I took a slow breath. "Because we were born to something better, you and I. We were born to defend the empire our ancestors built. Think about it. Centuries of terraforming, and just when they were getting close, the Singularity and they had to start over with nothing. You're the descendant of all that. You should be proud." This was the second time in a day I'd had to explain this. It felt flimsier every time.

She turned away to rifle in her bag. "I was proud when I left home. Now I'm embarrassed. I thought we were better than this. Now I think we're garbage." Pulling out a pair of earplugs, she stuffed them in and turned to the wall.

The next day, Marron returned Maggie to our berth after an hour's absence.

"Where have you been?" I asked, somewhat acidly. I was so tired of these six walls. I had already rifled in every locker and sack in the room for anything useful, and tried taking apart the torpedo tube only to find that the ammunition had been removed and the launch mechanism disabled. Somebody was thorough, that was for sure.

She raised her chin. "I was taking a bearing."

"For the enemy?" I shot out of the corner I was nestled in. "How could you, Maggie?"

"I told you all the reasons. I'm just sick of all this and I don't want to die. And we would have, Lucy. We weren't accelerating outward fast enough. They're putting more sail on now so we don't pass Earth before we've gotten far enough out."

I knew I shouldn't ask, but I was burning with curiosity to know if she'd done it right or not. "Can I see your work?"

She handed me her notebook and I flipped it open. Bearings taken off Jupiter, Saturn, and the sun. Simple enough. And she had finally mastered the math involved. So we should be round about—oh dear.

I schooled my face to neutrality, kept my voice casual. "Did you look in the back pages of the chart book?"

"No, I just used the astronavigator and the big chart. Why?"

"No reason." I handed her notebook back. "Good job."

Maggie was clearly too preoccupied to notice anything. But I retreated back to my corner with my mind spinning.

We were heading straight into the Geminids. A common danger of any voyage; comets left trails of debris in many parts of the solar system. On Mars they made meteor showers, but here in space the rocks could be much more damaging.

Especially with the sails out.

At Maggie's advice, they were spreading all the sail we had, and that meant every single mast would be vulnerable. With them tucked tight, we could avoid most of the debris. Or we could steer north or south if there was a big piece in our way. But Moira wouldn't see them until it was too late.

My moment of triumph vanished. Yes, the pirates would be thrown off course at least and perhaps killed. Keeping that information from them was exactly what Their Majesty's government expected of me. One less ship fighting Mars—isn't that what I had said to Maggie? And I was supposed to put my life on the line for the Empire.

But the thought of Moira on the quarterdeck, steering the Mariposa into her doom, was more than I could bear. When the rocks started to hit, it would be too late to try to steer around them. She would watch the sails come loose and blame herself for not knowing. And there would be no more spare masts or sail in the hold, after the damage she'd wreaked on them when she took the Mariposa. It would be just like what had happened to the Valiant, with the same horrible end.

I uncurled from my corner with a sigh. It was the wrong thing to do and I'd feel guilty about it later, but what could I do? I hammered on the door and summoned Marron.

Moira received me in her cabin. Afraid to be seen conversing with me by the crew? Or hoping it was something personal and private?

"Do you have a chart in here?" I asked abruptly when I was ushered in.

Taken aback, she fetched one from a locker. I flipped to the right page. "Maggie found our position here. One-thirty leagues by fifty-three forty degrees by forty-two k north. And this is where we're headed." I pointed to the speckle of dots just downstream of our position.

She frowned. "I don't know what that is."

"The Geminids. Meteor trail. You've got to take the sails in and take us north, oh, ten thousand k. Do you have enough emergency fuel left, after setting this course?"

"We should have." She stared at the chart. "Maggie didn't find this. You did."

"I wasn't supposed to tell you. It's treason."

Somehow saying the word aloud brought it home to me. How many days of captivity had it taken me to betray Mars? Six?

"I won't tell anyone it was you." Her eyes were dark and earnest.

"Yeah, but they'll just ask me. At the court martial. Did you aid the pirates in any way during your captivity? And I'll say—"

"You'll say no. You didn't aid the pirates. You gave personal advice to a personal friend for personal reasons."

I opened my mouth. Shut it. "You're not a friend," I said at last. "And it wasn't a personal reason. I just don't want my ship scuffed up, is all."

She grinned. "Right."

"I mean it, Moira. We're not friends. We're not ever going to be friends anymore."

"I know." Her smile didn't fade.

All I wanted was to stomp out of the room. I had to settle for floating. But dammit, I was about done with her attitude.

Thirteen

When we reached Earth space, Goldstein went out with one of the pirates and painted over the Martian flags on the outside of the ship. That was a pang. One thing I had said to Moira was true: I still felt the Mariposa was my ship. A Mars ship. Seeing her dressed down and decorated with the skull and crossbones was like seeing my mother stripped naked and painted, like one of the Aphrodite dancers.

But it was necessary, because the space around Earth was swarming with ships. Most docked at the orbital station which housed Earth's space elevator, but we bypassed it and orbited Luna instead.

"Why don't you go to Earth?" I asked Moira, over dinner. She had begun inviting Maggie and me, along with a few of her senior crew, to dinner in the officer's mess every evening. It was strange seeing that formal dining room, where manners had been so strict, taken over by pirates who ate with their hands and burped at the table.

"Out of consideration for the pirates," Moira answered. "Earth always meets contractors on Luna because a lot of them are space-bound."

I blinked, startled. All the Earth pirates who had joined the crew seemed hearty enough. I never would have guessed they couldn't take Earth's full gravity. I could, at least in theory. In the exercise room, I commonly cranked the dials to an equivalent of one hundred eighty pounds, about what I would weigh on Earth. But I'd never felt a whole Earth gravity; even Aphrodite Station was only half.

No Imperial Navy officers ever get space-bound. Exercise is mandatory and shore leave is an inalienable right. Did the pirates just not have the discipline to exercise when they were in space? Or were they failing to get regular planetside time at least yearly? It didn't make sense; they were free agents and should be able to take leave whenever they wanted.

Moira bid me a private goodbye before leaving on the launch to dock at Luna Station. "I don't know yet what's to become of you," she said. "I might be able to get you home, if there's a prisoner exchange planned. If so, I'll send for you. Otherwise I won't tell them you're here, and you'll stay on the Mariposa longer."

I shrugged. Of course I wanted to get home, though I wasn't sure how I'd fare once I got there. But that was a bridge to cross if the Earthers agreed to release me. "And Maggie?"

"I've asked her. She doesn't want to go back."

My heart sank. Not that it was any surprise. But it hurt, watching her give up a duty to our ancestors we both shared.

The launch returned several hours later with Marron, who came to claim me. "Cap'n says you're to be handed over," he said.

"For release?" I asked.

"I assume so."

Luna Base was a cheerless place, with weak gravity and blank gray walls. Moira sat in a drab lounge at her best pirate ease:

sprawled across three chairs, her bare feet tucked under the arm of the last one to keep herself in place. She was wearing the red cropped shirt again, the one that made me stare.

I perched on the edge of the next chair over. "Am I really going home?"

"Soon, I hope. They have no exchanges planned, so they have agreed to hold you for ransom. Which should come as soon as a message can go back and forth, don't you think?"

My face fell. "Moira, you idiot. You should have asked me."

She jerked upright, gripping the armrest to keep from flying off. "What's wrong?"

"My family has no money." I could barely say the words, so long had I kept them secret. "That's why I came to space. Did you think I wanted to be out here? Even if they could scrape together the money, I wouldn't want it. They need it more. They're going to lose the house."

She stared at me in shock. "What about my dads?"

My lips twitched and I swallowed hard. "Already left, when the horses were sold. You hadn't had a letter?"

She shook her head. "Probably been one waiting for me at Phobos these six months."

"You can't let them ask my parents for money. You can't."

Glancing at the clock at the far side of the lounge, she frowned. "I'm meeting with them in five minutes. I don't have time to get you back to the launch. Come with me."

She pulled me into the bathroom adjoining the lounge. It smelled of disinfectant and old urine. The metal stall doors all swung wide: no one here but us.

"I want to pass you off as a pirate, but you'll never do it in that uniform," she said, by way of explanation. "Give me that jacket."

Reluctantly I pulled off my dark blue coat. It had cost thirty pounds, new. Now it was tattered at the cuffs and had dark stains here and there if you looked close, but it still bespoke authority and dignity.

Moira folded it and tucked it between the sanitizer dispenser and the counter, along with my buff waistcoat. Then she demanded my shirt. "Sorry," she said, before ripping out the stitching on the ruffled collar. "I know how you feel about your shirts."

I took a deep breath. She was carefully not looking at me in my stays. I didn't know what that meant. "Do what you must."

She dressed me back in it, using my cravat as a belt, so it hung like a tunic. Her hands were quick and deft, never touching my skin as she worked. I took off my boots and stockings and put them with the rest.

"Not the boots," she said. "Those would be a shame to lose if the cleaners come in here. I'll keep them for you. A pirate captain might have boots." She slipped them on her own feet. A perfect fit, as always. She was several inches taller, but I had large feet for my height. I had given her my cast-off shoes for years.

I surveyed myself in the mirror. The knee-breeches were rolled up into shorts; my shirt sleeves folded up to the elbow. I felt naked.

"The braid won't do," she said at last. "It looks much too Navy." Her nimble fingers undid it, combed it instead into two French braids on either side of my head. Once, she accidentally brushed my neck, and I shivered. I remembered, those last years together, how careful I had been not to touch her. How afraid I had been that the least touch would start something I wouldn't be able to stop. And I remembered every single time I accidentally had.

"There," she said with satisfaction, completely unconscious of anything amiss. "You could be anybody. Certainly not a Martian officer."

"Coming from you, I suppose that's meant to be a compliment," I said tartly, following her out of the bathroom.

The meeting with Earth representatives was nothing like I had imagined a military briefing would be. Instead it was a great deal more like a meeting with my parents' creditors. A great deal was said about "achievement of fiscal goals" and "mutual profitability" and "win/win scenarios." I realized, at last, that they were trying to sell Moira on a long-term contract. What she had won from her battle with us was the Mariposa itself, which established her as an independent agent. It was up to her what to do with that.

"Of course you could simply work a trade route," the head Earth agent, Ms. Knauss, said. "And there's profit there, depending on how many cargoes you could deliver in a year. We have routes to Venus and Halfpoint Station, and hopefully will have more stations around the solar system soon. But you wouldn't really be encountering any less risk than you would as a privateer. Mars ships will still see you as a hostile, and you'll be wanted on any station where Mars operates. So for the same amount of risk, you could be turning over much larger profits. Here's what a comparable ship earned this Earth year." She sailed a sheet of paper across the table. "That's at least double what any of our trade ships made."

Moira frowned, staring at the number. I wanted to argue against Ms. Knauss that the risk wasn't comparable because pirates seek out engagements and trade ships avoid them. That deliberately going after Martian vessels was a much bigger act of treachery than mere desertion; that the penalties from Mars might be the same, but didn't she want to sleep at night?

But I was supposed to be there as some kind of clerk, so I wrote some squiggles in a notebook and waited for what Moira would say.

At last she sighed and put the paper aside. "All right," she said. "I'll try one contract. Then we'll see how the crew feels about continuing."

Ms. Knauss beamed. "Welcome aboard, Captain Singh. It

turns out we have a very special contract we're looking to complete, and you're ideal for it, as you're newly enough out of the Navy that the word won't have reached Mars yet. It'll be a challenge, but I think you're equal to it. And, of course, the completion bonus will be very generous."

Around the glowing verbiage, she sketched out her plan. Earth didn't want a prisoner exchange with Mars; they were aware of Mars' officer shortage and wanted to keep it that way. But there had recently been an important prisoner taken by Mars, an intelligence officer whose information would be extremely useful to have. They were currently housed at Deimos Prison, in Mars orbit.

"Deimos?" Moira exclaimed. "We're never sneaking a prisoner out of Deimos unnoticed. It's locked up tight as—well, on Mars we say 'as tight as Deimos.' It's completely secure; nobody's ever escaped from there."

"No one said anything about sneaking, Captain Singh. You're in command of a Martian vessel. Since you came straight here, it won't even be reported missing yet. Your ship's known identification should be enough to get you close, but once you're ready to extract our operative, you're welcome to make as much noise as you want. Ideally you would remove the entire population of the prison, but if that's impossible, get as many as you can."

Moira still looked reluctant. "I don't know ..."

Another paper came sailing her way. "As you see, we have detailed layouts, recent passcodes, plenty to help you carry it out with minimal risk. The bonus we're willing to pay is at the bottom."

She stared at the number for a long time. At last she said, "Done. I'll do it."

The Earth agent was all smiles and congratulations. Then she said, "Oh, you were asking about prisoners of your own, weren't you? We'll be happy to take them and undergo negotiations for ransom on your behalf. Seventy-five percent of the profits are yours to keep."

Moira shook her head. "Oh, it turns out there wasn't anyone who wanted to go home. I must be a good captain or something, everyone signed on permanently as crew."

Ms. Knauss hid her disappointment well. "Ah, well, keep it in mind for next time. Most of our contractors rely on us for prisoner ransom services, and you'll find they're highly satisfied with the results."

"I certainly will." Moira rose from the table, clutching her papers.

❧

Back in her cabin, I gave Moira a piece of my mind. "You could have gone back to your old job!" I said. "Didn't you like shipping cargos?"

"It was all right," she said. "But the Earthers are right, the pay isn't comparable."

"Of course it's not comparable! People are willing to do it for a lot less because you're less likely to get killed."

"Is that the part that bothers you?" Moira pulled her foot up to untie my boots. "I thought it was the treason part."

"That too. But you don't care about that."

"No." She lobbed the first boot at me and started on the other. "God fuck the Emprex, that's what we always said. I love Mars, the place, and Mars, the people. But Mars, the government? Fuck 'em."

I hugged my boot to my chest, shocked. "How can you talk that way?"

She only looked tired. "Mars didn't treat me like it treated you. For you it was balls, and boarding school, and a New Oxford education. For me it was a future of stepping into my father's shoes or being homeless. My class doesn't get a platter full of opportunities. We get what's left."

"You could have taken the university exam."

"Competing against Founders who have been cramming in private schools since they were five? Don't make me laugh."

I sighed. She wasn't wrong, and hadn't I deplored our stratified society in the past? "I always hoped someday things would be better. Remember I was going to go for Parliament? See if I could make a change for the better. You can't change anything by leaving and shooting at Martian ships."

She tossed me the second boot. "You may remember," she said hotly, "leaving isn't my choice anymore. By now, if Mars would let me, I'd be in Landing, taking my dads around the museums. Instead I'm never allowed to go home again, and if I show my face on Phobos they'll cut my head off. The one thing I can do for my family anymore is send money. So I'm going to do that. I'm going to send as much as I damn well can, and if I send enough maybe my dads can leave Mars too."

"And go where?"

"Earth. Or Luna, if Earth's too heavy for them. On Earth Ramesh wouldn't have to kiss your father's boots to have a job. On Earth there isn't a class system. Nobody would have ever told you that you couldn't ever be with—" She cut off. "Anyone you chose. None of this would have happened."

She was wrong on so many levels, I wasn't sure which to argue about. My father's friendship with Ramesh being a real thing independent of their social class? Ramesh never agreeing to live on a bare rock with no horses?

Or the fact that my family had never told me I couldn't be with a commoner. That that was all my own decision?

"Fine," I spat. "I know my place. I'm a prisoner. You're the captain now."

Marron escorted me away from Moira's cabin. "Too bad you didn't get handed over," he said with a wink. "I was thinking I was finally done babysitting you."

I sighed, in too foul of a mood to join with his teasing. "Can I stay with you for a while? I can't bear the thought of being stuck in my berth again. I'll stay out of the way."

"If you feel like watching me service the number six gun, sure."

He got his toolcase from the gun room and we went to the gun deck. The number six was already gaping open.

"Misfired in the last drill," he said. "I had Foulet try to fix it, but she couldn't figure it out."

I perched on the number four, hooking my feet beneath it to keep myself in place. "Are your Earth guns much different?"

"They don't look much different. But that doesn't mean it won't be a bitch to fix." He took out a screwdriver and started tinkering with the innards of the gun. "So," he said, voice echoing inside the hollow tube, "since you're not going back, but you're still not joining the crew, I thought maybe that meant you and Moira got together. But by the looks on your faces when you came out of that cabin, I'm thinking no."

I startled so hard I lost my grip on the number four gun and flew backward. Recovering, I pushed back to my seat. "What makes you think we would ever be…'together'?"

"The way she flirts with you," he answered, unperturbed. "Can you hand me the bigger screwdriver?"

"That would be aiding and abetting the enemy," I answered. "Get it yourself. Did it ever occur to you she flirts with me just to annoy me?"

He pulled his head out of the tube and got the tool himself.

"But if it really annoyed you, you wouldn't spend so much time talking to her."

I cringed. He had a fair point. I should stop torturing myself and stay away. "I'll make a note. More time staring at the six walls of my berth."

"Besides, don't you know each other from before? She talks like she knows you."

Damn it, she would tell everyone everything, wouldn't she? I glanced around. No one on the gun deck at this moment but us. "We grew up together," I said at last. "We were best friends."

He pulled his head out, mouth in an O of surprise. "Friends? You don't act like it."

I shook my head. "We're not any more. She . . ." It was so hard to explain. Especially to an Earther. "She said she loved me."

"And you didn't love her?"

"It's not *that*," I said. "It's that I couldn't have ever been with her, and she ought to have known that."

He sniffed, head back inside the gun. "Is that how things are on Mars? Commoners aren't even allowed to look at you?"

"No! I mean, sure, it would have been a big scandal, but those things happen. My parents might have supported me. It's just…" I didn't want to say it. It made me sound mercenary; of all things, I had learned never to sound like I wanted money. The only respectable thing was to already have it. "My family is poor," I said at last, quietly. "I had to make a good connection, to keep my family out of poverty."

The sounds of tinkering inside the gun paused, but he carefully didn't look at me. "I see."

"It's all very well for you to be judgmental," I said. "You don't know how it is on Mars."

"It's true. I don't." He pulled his head out. "Everything is fine in here. It should have worked."

"Maybe Foulet just doesn't know how to operate it."

He touched his forehead and pointed at me. "I should have started there, shouldn't I?" He closed the gun up and began the firing drill. "Open. Place shot inside."

The shot was mimed, as we rarely used live ammunition for drills. It was heavy and hauling extra for drills would weigh down the ship unacceptably.

"Attach ignition switch. Set timer. Close. Aim." He peered out the little radiation-glass porthole. "Pull vent handle—"

"No," I burst in, without thinking. "Push firing release switch."

He looked up at me. "The what?"

I sighed. I had just helped the enemy, again. Yet another reason to stop all this fraternizing. But no point trying to confuse him now. "The one on the top."

He pushed it. "Why the extra step?"

"Because this way the gun is disabled till you want to enable it. No accidental venting of atmosphere. And you can permanently disable the whole gun by taking the firing mechanism out. The whole thing's locked up. You can't get the outer port open no matter what you do." As I well knew, having been locked in a berth with a disabled gun the entire time. Which gave me an idea.

He pulled the vent handle and the port gave its characteristic whoosh. "Torpedo away. If there were one. No wonder the gun drills were such a disaster. We should have had the Martian crew show the rest of us."

While his back was still turned, I slipped my hand into his bag and took a screwdriver. It went up my shirtsleeve. "You should have been doing them before now," I said. "What if you'd come upon an enemy and half your crew didn't know how to fire the guns?"

"Moira wants us doing them every watch from now on." He swept the rest of his tools out of the air and shoved them inside his bag.

I fought a pang of disappointment. Finally someone I could talk to about the thing that was eating me most, and the conversation would be over. Back to my box.

But instead, he perched on the number six, bearded chin on his hands. "I don't get it," he said. "Why were you so angry at her for asking? I mean, it does no harm for her to just ask."

"It ruined everything," I said. "As long as nobody said anything, it wasn't real."

"Sounds like it was real," he said. "On both sides."

"But if neither of us *knew* ..." I trailed off, frustrated. "I had my life all planned out. I was going to marry somebody, like I had to. But she and I always would have been best friends. We could have ridden out together every day, just like before. Nothing had to change if only nobody had said anything. I'd decided that years before, just never say a word and she would never know, and that way I knew I'd never do anything."

He eyed me skeptically. "Yeah, but you would have sooner or later."

"I wouldn't! I take things like promises very seriously. I never would have been unfaithful to whoever I married."

"Uh-huh. You really think you could keep that shit up for fifty years or however long it was? You gotta be more realistic. You're a person, not a saint. Either the secret was eventually going to come out and you guys would have given in, or the pressure would have been so impossible to bear that you would have had some ridiculous fight and parted ways. Trust me." He tapped his broad chest. "I've been around a few times."

I considered that. Of course I had imagined a thousand ways that it could have come out. Perhaps we would be riding far out by the fjords, and stop for a break. Lying in the long grass, watching the clouds sail by, like we did so often. And one of us would hitch up on our elbow, look down at the other, and be drawn to her lips like a magnet. I had lain awake many nights with thoughts like that. But I had never intended to put them into action. And hadn't I managed years of keeping the secret, after I fell for her?

"The pressure was already impossible to bear," I said at last. "I felt a little angry with her all the time. Like she was making it hard for me on purpose, even though she didn't know."

"So when she made her move, that all came out."

When she had kissed me, I had had to jerk back, to jump to my feet, to start a fight. If I hadn't, if I had delayed a single second, I wouldn't have been able to stop. That had been clear to me in a flash. I would have kissed back, buried my fingers in her hair, and—well, never mind the rest. I had thought through that idea enough times, as I lay awake the entire night, haunted by the ghost of that truncated kiss.

"We'd fought before," I said. "I thought maybe she'd apologize in the morning. And then I could take back what I'd said."

"She doesn't owe you an apology for liking you."

I folded my lips together. "She didn't have to leave the whole planet to get away from me."

"It sounds to me like she did." He pushed off the gun, took his bag, and headed forward. "Nothing had changed. She still loved you. You still loved her, which she might have guessed. Either you were going to get together or she was going to leave, and you didn't want to get together. So she left you the whole planet to yourself." He shook his head as he reached the hatch of my berth. "I like you, Lucy. Pure Martian class. But you do *not* deserve that woman."

On the way to Deimos, Moira closeted herself with her best officers, trying to work out a plan. Maggie had moved out of our berth to sleep between the guns with the others, so I spent a great deal of time alone, pushing back and forth along the walls. I watched the planets crawl across the constellations of the zodiac, day by day; memorized more astronomical tables; wrote letters home.

The last was the most difficult. I wrote them up in my notebook, scratched lines out. Who knew when I would have any chance to mail them, or what information I could safely give them. I had a draft from months ago, which I hadn't bothered mailing at Aphrodite Station, since radio rates were so expensive and paper mail so slow. "I was surprised to see Moira Singh is a member of the crew as well. You may tell her parents she appears to be in good health." It was true, so far as that went, but I couldn't very well ever send it. What would I write now? "You may tell her parents she is a traitor to the Empire and is never coming home"? I wrote the words anyway, just to scratch them out again.

Maggie's absence also left me time to consider my options for escape or sabotage. I inspected every inch of our berth for possible weapons or a way out. I had Marron's screwdriver, but my first idea, attempting to repair the bowchaser in our room, proved impossible. The whole firing mechanism was gone, and without it, I couldn't so much as open up the tube.

I could, however, unscrew any panel I wanted in the walls. Each wall, except the metal of the outer hull, was the same densified wood—thin but strong, and lighter than metal would have been.

The decks above and below were the same. Wood panels, about a foot and a half square, secured at the four corners with screws. Going up, I ruled out immediately. Above me was the sail deck, right where the forecastle began. Someone was always there, without fail. The walls weren't much better; they opened on the gun deck where the men slept and messed and played cards, when they weren't exercising the guns. But below was only the store level. Hopefully there wouldn't be anyone in the different storerooms.

Twenty minutes of careful unscrewing later, I eased one edge of the panel upward. It was dim down there; that was promising. I put one eye to the crack and peered down.

Below was the gun room, where the gunner was stationed during a battle, ready with repair tools. The room aft of it held all the ammunition, where it could be passed up the hatch right outside my berth.

Either room would be perfect for my purposes. In the gun room, I could find the necessary tools to fix the bowchaser in my room. Or I could go through it to the ammunition room, strike a spark, and blow the ship to pieces.

It was hard to force myself to keep moving after that thought. I didn't want to die. I didn't want Moira to die. But I had a duty, so I slid the panel a little farther open.

And stopped. Because now I could see a shape against the port wall, and another on the forward wall. A lumpy shadow as long as a man.

I held my breath and listened. I heard the faint whooshing of a crank fan, the kind every berth has, to keep the air circulating so the carbon dioxide won't pool around our heads as we sleep. And under that sound, very faint, I heard a snore.

I eased back the panel, heart pounding, and screwed it in. If the gun room had been taken over for a berth, there went any hope of a stealthy exit from my prison. I supposed the pirates didn't like the Navy notion of berthing all the men in rows, between the guns. They'd want to spread out, take their privacy, and why not in the gun room when no one was using it?

After I stowed my screwdriver out of sight, I turned slowly, heels over head, and let myself drift with my feet toward the sun. I should be disappointed. I should be eagerly searching for a new plan, a way to redeem myself after my craven betrayal when I corrected Maggie's navigation error. Instead I felt only relief.

Then anger rushed in after it, turning my stomach hot and

my limbs ice cold. I knew why I had turned traitor over the navigation, and why I was tempted to give up now. Moira was why. Because she had turned traitor first, and because she was influencing me. I kept trying to remind her—and myself—that we were enemies. But she was getting in my head, and I hated her for it.

Fourteen

The mood on the ship as we approached Deimos was cheerful. Nobody slacked in their work, despite an end to floggings. They all had their share of the future profits calculated to the last decimal point, and a plan for how to spend it. Some would go a circuitous route from Earth Force's bankers, through independent bankers at Halfpoint Station, to discreet contacts on Mars who could deliver it to loved ones, along with letters. The rest the sailors would keep, though I wasn't entirely sure when or where they'd get a chance to spend it. Perhaps a blowout weekend on Luna when all this was through.

I caught snatches of their plan, as they worked on costumes and makeshift weapons. Moira was going to put on the captain's uniform and epaulets, passing herself off as "Captain Wang-Hawking." Maggie had supplied the name; a family connection of hers whom she was quite sure had never gone to space. A real noble name was essential; no one could fool Martian nobility by referencing nonexistent Houses.

Moira had Captain Kim's code book also. It was a captain's duty to destroy it before surrendering, but the pirates' attack had been so rapid that he hadn't had a chance. Between that and the ship itself, freshly repainted with the Martian rust, green, and blue, we would have no trouble getting close.

Getting out was the more difficult part. The crew prepared makeshift grenades full of shrapnel to clear out rooms of guards. The team would fight their way to a service airlock intended for waste removal, where (with luck) the launch would be waiting. Then the *Mariposa* would ignite our emergency fuel and make our escape, hopefully long before another ship could get after us.

It sounded simple enough when they explained it. Privately, I thought there were far too many points where it could go wrong. But of course I wasn't going to try to think of a better one for them. Best if it went wrong, preferably in a way I got to survive.

We approached Mars with the sails reversed, to catch the braking laser from Phobos Station, which they obligingly fired. As we drew closer, Moira took to standing on the quarterdeck in her captain's uniform, Maggie by her side, so that any glimpse from outside would show a proper Martian display.

The snowy neckcloth set off her dark skin beautifully, and the coat hung well on her angular figure. But, much as I loved the Navy uniform, I didn't care for it on her. The pirate get-up suited her better.

"A braid," said Maggie immediately, looking her up and down. "The officers never have short hair."

"Shit," she said, trying to pull her cropped hair around to the back. It made a tight pigtail, no more. "Anyone have any spare black hair?"

One of the men donated his long, dark beard to the cause. It was wiry and not quite the right shade, but braided tightly and smeared with black machine oil, it looked close enough.

A day closer, they switched on the radio. Phobos requested

passwords; Moira read them out in her most cultured accent. We were allowed to proceed.

"I didn't know you could talk like that," I told Moira.

"You were the main person I talked to growing up. Of course I can."

We slid into orbit not far from Deimos and obtained radio clearance to approach. I swallowed hard as Moira and her chosen team boarded the launch.

"Aren't you going to wish me luck?" Moira asked me.

I stammered, at a loss. Of course I didn't want her to succeed; that would be disastrous for Mars. But even I wasn't so heartless I could actually say such a thing.

"It isn't too late to back out," I said at last.

"Chin up," she said. "I'll be back soon."

When the airlock shut behind them, Marron gave me a nod. "Time to shut you up. I can't watch the radio and you."

I preceded him forward to my berth, weighing the risks of attacking him. On the one hand, he was unarmed and had stopped taking his escorting duties very seriously, since I always obeyed him meekly. On the other, he had shoulders like an ox. In an un-armed fight, he was more than a match for me. And there were still a dozen men left behind on the ship. Even if I could overpower Marron, there wasn't much I could do before one of them caught up to me.

No. This wasn't my moment. But in my room, I still had the screwdriver I had palmed when I was watching Marron fix the guns. I was never going to have a more perfect diversion. Half the crew was off the ship, and the rest would be standing by to make a quick escape. And right here in Mars orbit, I didn't have to destroy the *Mariposa*. All I had to do was somehow disable it, or send out a signal.

I waited till Marron would be out of earshot before getting

out my screwdriver. Then I crept to the panel I'd opened before. I had it off and was down in the gun room in under a minute.

As I'd hoped, no one was down there. I uncovered the fiber-optic light, letting the sunlight in. Everything I needed to fix the gun in my berth would be here. I rifled through lockers while turning over plans in my mind. What could I do with that gun? Fire it for a signal, at least. But for that I'd need some kind of signal flare, and there was nothing like that in here. Probably in the ammunition room next door.

But among the supplies, I spotted something much simpler. Every gun had an ignition switch, and there were any number of spares here. I grabbed one, a round disk the size of my palm, and put it in my pocket. A packet of explosive powder, too, and some tape. That was enough to make a bomb adequate for anything I might want.

I listened at the door before slipping out. As I'd hoped, there didn't seem to be anyone on this level. This was simple stores: crates of the officers' food packets, barrels of beans and of rice. Rum stores. The doors of all those rooms would be locked against theft, but I didn't need any of that. I dived down a hatch to the level below.

It was cold down here, so far from the sunward side of the ship, and cramped. This was where the fuel was kept, both rocket fuel and thruster propellant. Toward the aft were the engines. I didn't want to go too far that way; if I were the pirates, I'd have a man ready at the engines right now, preparing for a quick escape.

But I had an idea in mind now, so I squeezed between the fuel tank and the outer hull, then headed aft. About two-thirds of the way down, there was a valve that connected the tank to the engine. When it was time to move, someone would need to crank the wheel and let the fuel pour into the engine before igniting.

I knew the system's workings. It had been my duty to know the function and maintenance of every part of the ship. Here was the wheel. But here, behind it, was the actual piece that stopped the fuel from entering the engine when the valve was shut.

I could, of course, just turn the wheel, letting the fuel into the engine. Without ignition, it would bleed out into space. But someone would surely notice before too much had gone, and come back here to crank the valve shut again. I had to blow the whole mechanism.

The packet of explosive powder was far too much for what I wanted. I didn't want to ignite the tank itself; that would likely destroy the ship. I suppressed a small shudder; I wanted to live. And I wanted, somehow, for Moira to live too. Her odds weren't good if captured either, but I shut down that line of reasoning. I had to do my duty, didn't I? And if Moira's mission succeeded, that meant dangerous prisoners and Earth spies would be set loose. Spies with information that would harm the Empire. I couldn't allow that.

I carefully shook the amount I wanted onto a piece of tape, waving the tape through the air to catch loose crumbs. Then I pressed the tape onto the back side of the ignition switch. A tiny little bomb, just like that. Wasn't there a poem about a battle lost for a horseshoe nail? This was hardly bigger.

I cranked the dial as far as it would go, which was twenty minutes. Normally they only needed about ten seconds, to give the gun crew time to shove the torpedo out of the hatch. Once it was in space, the spring would wind down and a flint would strike, lighting the fuel inside the torpedo and sending it toward the enemy. The bigger explosion would come when it hit its target—a contact charge set that one off. But occasionally a longer timer was needed, for when we let loose a broadside meant for a ship that was far behind.

Twenty minutes was plenty of time to get back to my berth. I started to move through the narrow crawl space, but I was stopped by a shout. "Hey! Who's there?"

I turned. It was Maggie.

While I was sneaking out of my berth, Moira was drinking the health of the warden, a stout sad-eyed captain named Blake. "It's really very kind of you to bring this, Captain Wang," Blake said, not for the first time, as he brought the bulb to his lips. "If you don't mind my saying so, you don't look much like a Wang-Hawking."

She drew up her head with a fine, noble air and said, "I do mind your saying so, as it happens." No wasting her time explaining or making excuses for her dark skin. Why should she? Plenty of nobles didn't look like their Chinese, English, or Russian Founder ancestors by now. "Are these the sort of manners that are acceptable here?"

Blake got flustered and dropped his brandy. Swiping it back out of the air, he said, "No, no, I do apologize. It's rare enough I get the chance of a decent conversation, and there I go spoiling it."

Hausmann, one of the *Mariposa*'s original crew, loomed behind Moira in a spacer's uniform. She was a big woman, who had been there to manhandle the prisoner on board. Not that the prisoner, a slight, dark Earther named Foulet, had put up any real protest. She was supposed to be dejected, having no real hope of overpowering Hausmann.

Now Foulet was being led by two guards deeper inside Deimos, her tattered clothes and fake manacles a pitiful sight. The rest of the crew remained behind on the launch, packed in like sardines, waiting for their moment.

It came soon enough. Blake paused in the middle of the sad story of how he had lost his first command and been sent here, surely the worst posting in the entire Navy and the most thankless, and gave Moira a bleary look. "That stuff you brought is…"

His eyes unfocused, refocused, lost it again. "Much stronger than …" He trailed off.

His lieutenant, hanging near his elbow with a drink of her own, might have been alarmed if Blake had slumped to the floor. Without gravity to pull him down, he only hung there, glassy-eyed and beginning to drool, as the concoction in his drink began to take hold. The lieutenant saw his drink bulb beginning to float out of his hand and ventured, "Cap'n, your drink …" before she too succumbed.

Moira met eyes with Hausmann, and they let a few seconds slip by to be sure. Then they tied and gagged the officers before giving the signal to the crew.

Foulet, meanwhile, had let herself be taken deep into the heart of the moon. Here, there were no windows or fiber-optic lights. Deimos was sometimes in the shadow of Mars; sunlight wasn't always reliable. Instead, dim green chemical lights lit the rough stone tunnel.

Handrails on either side of the tunnel allowed the guards to hand themselves along, while keeping Foulet between them, out of reach of the walls. The only way for her to move was to let them drag her. They passed turnoffs for low-security cell blocks, for kitchens, for waste disposal. All as the map had predicted. At last, they reached the massive metal grate before the high security cells.

As one guard turned to unlock the gate, Foulet slipped out of her fake cuffs and went for one of the knives under her shirt. Without gravity to pull the cuffs to the ground, the action was almost soundless, so the second guard didn't notice what was happening until she saw the knife.

She let out a single shout, cut off when the knife connected with her windpipe. The other guard turned, gripping the grate in readiness to push off. His massive body, propelled at that speed, would have slammed her clear down the corridor. But Foulet already had a second knife in her hand, which she threw at him. It got him in the side of the neck. Messy, but quick. Foulet didn't like wasting time.

She grabbed the female guard's ankle, dragging the still-twitching body close and then kicking it away. That gave her enough thrust to reach the grate. She brushed away floating globules of blood and hooked the male guard's key ring.

After that it was easy. There were more guards inside the cell block, but a needle grenade took care of them all in one shot. Foulet smiled to herself as she came around the corner and saw the lacerated bodies. The Martians hated this sort of thing. Not sporting. Not gentlemanly. Somehow they thought it was more honorable to hack a person apart at closer range.

Rules for keeping at arm's length what you were doing, was how Foulet always put it. Pretending that you were better than any other butcher. Better to own that it was brutal and terrible and get it done as fast as you could.

Back near the entrance, Moira sent the boarding party down the corridors, securing one room at a time. The kitchen and waste workers were civilians and meekly let themselves be restrained. The barracks would be full of guards, so Moira blocked off the door. All she needed was to stall them long enough to get away with the prisoner.

Moira and Hausmann took the radio room. The ceiling was one large skylight, showing a field of stars and the long radio antenna. A lieutenant sat there, boredom on his face, doodling with a pencil in his notebook. He looked up in surprise.

"What are you doing in here, sir?" he asked. "The airlock is that way."

Moira ran him through. Hausmann stared at her in shock. "You just killed an *officer*," she managed.

"What did you think we were here for, playing pattycake?" Moira slammed her cutlass back into its scabbard.

"I know, I just…" She gulped. "I know we all agreed to this. But it feels wrong."

Moira turned to look her in the eye, voice softening. "I hear you, I do. We weren't given ten million choices, here. You know he wouldn't have spared us if he knew what we were here to do. You know he'd call for help the first chance he got."

Before Hausmann could say anything to that, the radio started squawking. "Deimos Prison, this is the *Relentless*, approaching for prisoner transfer. Please respond."

They exchanged a panicked look. Moira launched herself at the radio and grabbed the receiver. "*Relentless*, this is Deimos Prison. Do you, ah, do you need a brake?" She glanced up at the window. Not in sight yet.

"No sir, we are approaching in Mars orbit from Phobos."

Moira frantically hunted through the notebook for a list of radio procedures. Or were those all stored in the lieutenant's head? Founders were notorious for never writing things down. What had the station said when the *Mariposa* was approaching?

"*Relentless*, I'm, ah, going to need your authorization code."

"Code? Oh the passphrase. Yes, sir. Violet Rubicon albedo caryatid."

"Very good, *Relentless*. Please, ah, continue to approach."

Engrossed in the radio and her hunt through the notebook, Moira hadn't glanced up in some time. And, of course, there is no sound of footsteps in space. The first she heard was a strangled gasp from Hausmann.

She slammed the receiver down and lunged toward Hausmann. It was too late; the Martian sailor behind her had neatly cut her throat. Moira caught herself against the wall beside the door, where she could see Hausmann's attacker. Just a common spacer, bald and dark-skinned.

She hesitated. This was different—a comrade, not a noble. She began moving again in a few heartbeats, but by then the man had launched himself at the radio. He had heard the message from the *Relentless*. He would want to warn them off. But if they knew what was going on, they'd attack the *Mariposa*, and Moira and the rest might be stranded here.

A second's calculation. If she lunged after the man, she'd reach him after he already had the radio. Small chance she could grapple it away before he'd said at least something. So she aimed to the side a little, where the cord of the radio came up from the desk and into the ceiling, where the antenna would be. One slash of her sword cut it through, just as the man was drawing breath to shout his warning.

She hung in the air a moment, waiting for the man to come at her, but instead he darted into the hall. She followed him a few body-lengths behind. He went straight for the main office, where Moira had met with the warden.

What could he possibly want there? Did he know the captain and lieutenant were still alive, shoved under a desk? Or was it a detour on the way to the airlock, to get to the launch? There were still three men guarding the launch; it couldn't be taken so easily—she hoped.

The main office had two doors, one here and one a few yards down the hall. Moira waited outside the first and watched the other. If it was a trick, the man would emerge from the other and head for the launch. But he failed to come out. With a grimace, she grabbed a handhold next to the doorframe and kicked the door in.

The man hadn't bothered to block the door. He hadn't needed to. She found him floating by the ceiling, against the large skylight, with something in his hand, flashing between his fingers. A mirror. The *Relentless* was in a line of sight from here, and he was flashing a warning.

She shot upward toward him, knocking the mirror out of his

hand. He had sheathed his knife to take out the mirror. A brave serviceman, thinking only of getting a warning out and nothing of his own safety. But she killed him too, because she was only one person. Impossible to be sure you could subdue someone if you don't have them outnumbered.

Coming out of the room, she called after the rest of the boarding party. "Everyone, out, now! If you don't have the prisoners, leave them!"

❧

Maggie dragged me upstairs by the elbow. I went along quietly. I'd done my duty; soon enough we'd be back in Martian hands. Perhaps the pirates would kill me first. I couldn't be sure.

Nguyen was at the stern window with a spyglass. "There's definitely something coming," he said.

"We'll just have to sit tight," said Marron. "Our cover isn't blown yet. And they're at least ten minutes away."

Maggie interrupted, "I found the prisoner down by the engines."

Marron raised his eyebrows. "She has a name, you know." He looked over at me. "I could have sworn I locked you up."

I just stared back at him. I could lie, but I was bad enough at it that I'd probably give more information away than if I kept my mouth shut.

"Did she do anything down there?" he asked Maggie.

"Not that I saw. Should I check?"

"Do that. We might need to make a quick getaway when it comes time for it."

He made me stay on the quarterdeck, where he could keep an eye on me, and borrowed Nguyen's spyglass for his own look at the approaching ship. The radio crackled with the *Relentless'* hail, and Moira's response. At the sound of her voice, something in me softened and began to melt, like the snow when the long Martian winter finally begins to break. I pressed my lips together. None of this weakness. I was surely not the first Imperial officer to be tempted to betray my duty for a woman. I couldn't give in.

I watched the surface of Deimos, lumpy and patched with occasional windows. Inside, Moira would be—what? Scrambling to make her escape? Still trying to reach the prisoners? She'd be a fool to try to reach the prisoners now, if she hadn't already. Minutes were ticking away, as the *Relentless* drew closer. She didn't have much time for an escape.

Then I remembered minutes were ticking away in a completely different way. It didn't matter if she got here fast or slow, did it? In…seven minutes, now, the little bomb would go off and there would be no clean escape even if she did get here.

My stomach was caught in a vice. I wanted to throw up. I bit my knuckle instead, worrying it in my teeth. Why had she gone out there? Why had she taken this bloody mission? This mess was her fault.

But it was also mine.

A stray flash gleamed from one of the windows. A light-signal, not aimed at us. I couldn't see any of the message, but I could guess. Someone was signaling to the *Relentless*.

My eyes flicked to the pirates. If they didn't see it, I couldn't warn them. But Nguyen did, and gave a shout.

"That's it, that's our cue," said Marron. "I make them ten minutes out at best. If our men aren't back in eight, we're leaving."

"You can't!" I cried.

He shot me a glare. "You're not a member of this crew. What a time to decide you care what happens to her!"

I strained my eyes toward Deimos. If Moira didn't come back, it didn't matter. Whatever I'd done down below wouldn't hurt her, only win back the *Mariposa* for the Empire. Which of course was what I wanted. I chewed harder on my knuckle.

At last I saw the little rectangle of the launch detach from Deimos. A cheer went up from the pirates on the quarterdeck. No one was looking at me.

I flung myself over the rail and down the hatch. No time to look at my watch, and it didn't even matter. If I'd had ten seconds to do it in, I still would have tried.

When I reached my makeshift bomb, the timer was on the last minute. I grabbed the spring and clicked the release that let me wind it back to the start. The tension left my body, and I clung to the fuel valve, panting.

I shouldn't have done that. I should have left it as it was. I had betrayed the Empire a second time in failing to sabotage the ship when it had been in my power to do.

And yet, I couldn't make myself reach back up and set the timer again. I was too weak. I was strong about everything else in the world, but I couldn't be strong about her.

Slowly I propelled myself back up the hatches, meeting Maggie on her way around the engine. "Down here *again*?" she asked, narrowing her eyes. "What did you do?"

I shook my head and brushed past her. She let me go and went back to looking over the engines. I didn't think she'd find what I'd done. Not that it mattered.

When I reached the sail deck, Nguyen was cranking open the airlock. The away party spilled out of the airlock, all talking at once.

"Battle stations," Moira declared, leaping to the quarterdeck. "You can tell your friends later how it went. Yao, Foulet, McDougal, get the prisoners secure somewhere."

The prisoners came out of the airlock, supported by sailors. I stared at them in shock. They were pale, filthy, dressed in rags, with atrophied limbs. "Spacebound," I whispered to myself.

"Surprised?" asked Moira, from above me.

I joined her on the quarterdeck. "Of course I'm surprised. The Solar Convention—"

"Is something they only follow when people are looking." She threw herself into the captain's chair. "These people were never meant to be free again, so what does it matter how they treat them?"

I stared after the prisoners as they drifted up to the housekeeping decks. Moira raised her voice. "All hands, secure for acceleration. Stand by to burn emergency fuel on my mark." Buckling herself into the captain's chair, she waited for me to secure myself beside her. "Mark!"

There was a dull roar that seemed to come from all around. At first, we didn't seem to move. Then I felt the thrust pushing me gently aft, as Deimos slowly shrank behind us.

We weren't moving fast, but we were accelerating a good deal faster than the Martian ships were likely to. We held no cargo and the fuel tanks were completely full. Thanks to my treachery.

The *Relentless* turned side-on to train her guns on us. Not fast enough to catch us, but close enough for one good broadside before we got out of her range.

"Stand by, port gun crews!" cried Moira.

I watched her command the ship through her first battle, trying to hide my admiration. I expected Captain Kim to be able to do this; he'd had an entire career of training. I did not expect it of Moira, whose entire Navy training consisted of one voyage and two battles, one of which was entirely spent below decks, loading torpedoes into tubes. But she had trained with the gun crews daily, just as Kim had, and she had them responding to her commands like clockwork.

The Martian ship's broadside shook us up, but that was all. We accelerated past them and away.

On the upper deck, Yao and Ntumba were checking over the prisoners. They made a ragged line, over a dozen of them, floating vacantly while they were examined. Each had long, scraggly, matted hair, and I could smell them as soon as I came through the hatch.

"They weren't even given water to wash with," Ntumba said to me in a low voice. "Food seems to have been passable, at least. No signs of scurvy."

"What can I do?"

She shot me a look. "I thought you didn't do anything."

"I want to help with this." I didn't feel like explaining any more. I didn't have any more answer than that. I only felt sorry for these poor souls. I couldn't understand why they had met with this illegal neglect from Mars, but I thought they deserved the right kind of treatment from a Martian. The treatment the Empire promised.

She gave me a pair of shears, and I went to each one, cutting their hair. The first I approached was clearly the Earth spy; she hadn't been in long. Her hair was matted, but only down to her shoulders.

"How much of this do you want to keep?" I asked.

"None of it," she said, surprising me with a fluid Martian accent. "Go ahead and cut it close."

"I thought you were the Earth agent we'd been sent to extract," I said, gathering the clumps of hair in one hand as I took them off.

"I am," she said. "That is, I work for Earth."

A traitor, then. I tried to keep my face expressionless. After all, more than half the crew was Martian, and I had gotten used to their defection. I threw the matted hair away and brought her a damp cloth. "Best we can do without gravity."

She smiled. "It'll have to do for now. But your surgeon says I should be able to return to gravity in time, since I was imprisoned only six months."

"I'm glad to hear it," I said, and moved on to the next. He was so shaggy I could see little of him but a pair of bright eyes. "May I?" I asked, and he silently inclined his head.

It took much longer to return him to a civilized appearance, but at last his hair and beard were cropped as short as the shears could do. I moved back to survey my work—and gasped. I recognized this man, or I thought I did. I'd seen his picture in the papers, years ago. That jutting jaw, the heavy brows in a dark face...

"Are you Alexei Khan?"

He raised his eyes to my face in surprise. "People still remember me?"

"How could anyone forget? After the time you chained yourself to the doors of Parliament, nobody could talk about anything else for weeks!"

"You were a supporter?"

Now that was something I would never have admitted in the drawing rooms of Mars. "Well, I mean, I've never seen myself as a radical, but my—this friend of mine liked you, and she would read me your writings. You made a great deal of sense. Like colonists being allowed to serve on juries, even for nobles. Because we ought to be peers even if we aren't at present. It certainly would be a step in the right direction."

He nodded. I could see how he had gained such a following; his every gesture seemed weighted with purpose. "What happened? We were planning for a march in Landing and a general strike—it was going to be the biggest thing for the social-reform movement that had ever happened. We had so much support. And then they came knocking on the door..." His eyes were pained.

"The newspapers all printed that you had died. Massive heart attack. Mourned by all who knew you."

He gripped my arm. "And did the march still go on? The strike?"

I shook my head slowly. "No. People said it was too soon, that we had to mourn, and yet somehow it never actually got rescheduled."

He dropped my arm, grimacing. "Of course it didn't. Of course. That was the whole point, I imagine. Cut off the head and the beast dies. Some people were deeply threatened by my reforms."

"But your reforms wouldn't have taken anything away from the nobility! At least, I never saw anything that would."

"They believed it wasn't going to stop with jury duty and a house of commons. We were going to get greedy and want more. Perhaps to chop off all your heads!" His head shot forward to stare right into my face.

I moved backward a touch. "You weren't, though, really?" My voice betrayed me and made it a question instead of a statement.

He laughed. "Not the chopping off heads part. Further reforms, yes. It was all in my books. You should have read more of them for yourself."

Yao appeared at my elbow. "You're still talking to your second customer and I've finished with all the rest," she said. "I'm going to go assign them all berths."

"Do you know who this is?" I asked her. "This is Alexei Khan!"

She stared back blankly. "I'm sorry, I don't know him."

As she led them off, I stared after her in dismay. So the government's ploy had worked. Arrest the man, get him out of the papers, and watch him be forgotten.

It was hard to believe all this of Their Majesty's government.

Fifteen

That evening after dinner, I hung back when the others left the officers' mess. I had a decision to make, one which would hopefully remove me from further temptation like the one I'd just experienced.

"I would like to offer my parole," I told Moira. It was perfectly legal for me to do. While ideally I would be attempting sabotage, the Navy recognized that it wasn't usually possible. And if I could say I was paroled, it meant I no longer had to keep trying and failing.

"What, you've lost interest in blowing us all up?" Her eyes twinkled at me over her drink bulb.

"Still interested. But you've made it as good as impossible, so why not admit defeat?"

She gave me a narrow look. "Not so impossible. Marron told me you got out of your berth somehow while I was gone. That's why you were on the sail deck when I got back."

I opened my mouth to answer her, but couldn't speak. There

was nothing in all of it I wasn't ashamed of. Ashamed I'd tried to get her caught by the Empire; ashamed I had backed down at the last minute. No matter which way you looked at it, I didn't come off looking good.

"Just tell me," she said, leaning in and holding my gaze. "Did you hurt my ship? Is there anything down there set to go off? Are we going to be eating vacuum sometime because of something you did?"

I blinked and swallowed. "No."

"That's all right, then." She moved back with a sigh. "I wish I could tell you about it all. It was hard, being over there. Being on the other side now. And Hausmann getting killed…"

Dangerous. I was already too compromised with her. "All I'm offering is my parole. I'm still your enemy."

She shrugged, forcing disappointment off her face with a sardonic grin. "Fine. Parole accepted."

"Don't I have to swear on something?"

"Do you want to?"

"Not especially."

"That's fine then. I trust you."

"You shouldn't trust me! I'm your enemy!"

"Uh-huh. Then I'm the enemy that knows your weakness. Your weakness is that having implied a promise, you're going to keep it even if it's absolutely disastrous for you. So why bother swearing? Nothing you could swear on would make you more obsessive about keeping your word than you are now." She finished off her drink and stowed the bulb in the dish caddy. "Now I'd love to keep flirting with you, but duty calls."

"This wasn't flirting!" I protested, following her out of the officer's mess.

"You weren't," she said over her shoulder. "I was."

❧

The first thing I did with my newfound liberty was seek out Alexei Khan. How could I not take my chance to speak with a great man?

I found him in the weight room, elastic bands clipped to a harness over his shoulders holding him against the treadmill. His wasted legs trembled as he struggled to put one in front of the other.

"Sir," I said, "not like that. Not when you're just beginning. Use these." I handed him the half-strength elastics.

He bowed his head and took them. "It's my barber from earlier. Now I owe you two favors, not counting the rescue."

"It's Prescott, and you owe me nothing. I don't … actually work here."

He looked up from fastening the elastics onto the treadmill. "Except giving haircuts?"

"I'm a prisoner, technically. A Martian officer. I suppose that means you hate me."

"Why, because of what they did to me back there?" He gestured astern with his chin. "I hate no one, Prescott. That's an important part of my message, that anyone can be part of the change."

"I wanted to be part of the change," I said, drifting past him to the next treadmill and fastening myself on. "First on Mars. I was going to run for Parliament, but then we didn't have money and I had to do this. And then in the Navy, there was so much I could see wasn't right, but I didn't have power to fix anything. The Navy's been running the way it has for centuries and it's not going to change for one person. You can't take a ship hurtling at forty knots and change its course by spitting out the airlock."

"A ship going forty knots, a tiny bit off its course, will soon end up somewhere entirely different. Isn't that true?"

"I felt …" I started running, the awkward lope permitted by

the elastic. "I felt that the Navy was changing me a lot more than I was changing the Navy."

"It does that," said Khan, his voice a little breathless from the effort to keep his feet carefully stepping forward. "I had my beginning as a policeman, you might know. I thought it was a way to do some good, keep the crime out of the neighborhoods so people could live peacefully. Of course I found it much the same as you found the Navy. A giant machine, plowing forward at its own rate. Crushing people beneath its wheels. We spent all our time catching petty thieves and never did make the poor neighborhoods safe.

"So I told myself, 'Just keep your head down. Do what you're told to do, and someday, you can become the police chief, and you can change all this. You can choose to make the police department a different place.'" He stopped walking and wiped the sweat from his forehead.

"I know you didn't become the police chief," I said. "What changed?"

"One day I was patrolling on my own and caught a boy selling candy without a license. A stupid law, which the candy makers had gotten passed so they didn't have the competition. The boy needed the money and had thought he could get away with it. I knew it—I knew all that. But on its own, my arm just flew up and—" He mimed holding a club in the air. "I had been there so long that it was changing me. A person isn't their inmost thoughts, a person is their habits, and the department had shaped mine.

"I realized that I was never going to make it to being the police chief unless I allowed myself to be transformed. Because the machine propagates itself; it doesn't allow anyone at the controls who hasn't been completely made over into its image." He carefully unclipped the elastics, allowing his withered legs to coil back up underneath him.

"The Navy is the same," I said, slowing to a stop. "They were training me to be like them. I didn't feel like I was, inside. But you're right, I acted as if I was."

I thought of the moment when I chased down Maxwell, watched him wrestled into the airlock. Moira had been disappointed in me. I was a little disappointed in myself, too—not that I'd had no choice, but that I had not even questioned whether I'd had a choice.

He glanced at me sharply. "Are you still loyal to them?"

"I—" I looked away, confused. "To *them*, no. Not to the officers who acted like that. But to Mars, yes."

"Who is Mars, Prescott?"

That, I knew well from his pamphlets. "The planet and the people," I said, as if reciting a catechism. "Not the Emprex. But isn't it all the same, up here? If we don't defend Mars from Earth, Earth will take everything, destroy planet and people. That's why I can't help the pirates."

He blinked. "I never suggested you should help the pirates. I am asking who you are loyal to, because you don't seem to know. Are you out here to keep Earth landers off Mars, or because you're still trying to follow the rules?"

I unclipped myself from the harness, mainly to give myself something to do besides look him in the eyes. "I can't seem to do either," I said, in a choked voice. "I am *trying* to be a good officer, and I'm just too weak."

"The Navy will never change, Prescott," he said, his voice gentle. "It will never pat you on the head and say, 'Good job. You've done enough.' It will push and push and make you hate yourself, because the more you hate yourself, the harder you'll work, and the less you'll be able to notice the wrong it does. If you don't want that, it's time to make a different choice."

"It's not my choice to make," I said, moving toward the door. "I made an *oath*. I said I would serve Mars at the pleasure of the

Emprex. My word is everything to me. If I could break an oath like that, how could I claim to be a good person ever again?"

"Maybe," said Khan, "you should worry less about being a good person. Mars is full of good people and it hasn't helped yet."

The rendezvous point was a few degrees downstream from Mars; far enough to be out of the usual trade routes, but close enough we arrived within a few days. Several other pirate ships cruised beside the huge Earth ship.

"Funny," said Moira. "Ms. Knauss didn't say anything about anyone else being here."

I watched the ships thoughtfully. "What happens now?"

"We hand over the prisoners, get our payout. See about the next contract. I'm sure she has more work for us." She chewed her lip. "What's next for *you*, I don't know. I hadn't thought that far through, when I kept you on the ship. All I knew was I couldn't set you adrift with Kim. You might have died out there."

"I suppose you want thanks for that."

"Not especially. I didn't do it for you. I did it for me, because I didn't want to lose you. I knew you wouldn't be grateful."

"I *am* grateful," I said, because the reflex to be polite was too strong to resist. "And for not giving me up for ransom on Luna. But I've got to get back somehow."

She shook her head, frowning. "I'm sorry for that, I really am. But you can't get back to Mars from here. If I give you up to Knauss, she'll want ransom. She's not going to give you a lift without looking into who you are. And I doubt she's headed that way, in any event. Downstream of Mars like this, it'll take her ages to get anywhere but Halfpoint Station."

"I can't stay with you forever," I insisted. "The longer I stay, the more time I have to account for to the Navy, when I get back. And the harder it is to have a good story for them, where I really did all I could. You know how I am about lying."

She turned to face me, looking me up and down. "But you haven't done anything to lie about. I think you must be the most loyal officer they've ever had."

I opened my mouth, thinking of how I'd warned her about the meteor trail. A personal favor, she'd said. But what about the bomb I hadn't set off? She didn't know about that. I certainly wasn't going to tell her.

Or that she was getting to me more than I had let on. That I was afraid her influence would make me betray the Empire, sooner or later.

"I certainly hope not," I said at last. "They should all be doing the same."

"They aren't," she said shortly. "They want you to be loyal, because it makes you easier to control. Once they get to the top, they don't bother."

I chewed on that for a while, increasingly uncomfortable. "You think I'm some kind of sucker?"

She turned to face me. "No," she said, her smile fond for once instead of teasing. "I think you're too good for them, and they're taking advantage. If they were all like you, I'd still be a loyal spacer."

"And you think Earth is better?"

"I don't know," she said. "But I do know what the choices are. It's them or Mars, and I know I can't stomach Mars. Maybe you can."

I gazed back toward Mars, shrunken to a tiny violet button. Could I? I believed in Mars, I did. Believed in the dream of terraforming, which had become a reality. Believed in the sacred duty of the Founders to keep planting the grass and replenishing the atmosphere against the solar wind that eroded it.

But Khan was right. None of that was the same as the Empire, let alone the Navy. The Empire had imprisoned Khan, thrown Maxwell out an airlock, let Brown off a rape charge with a slap on the wrist. Or people within the Empire, at least. It was a massive, complicated machine, but at least some of the people at the controls were evil.

Khan, according to his pamphlets, had handed in his badge and nightstick the same day he'd had his revelation. No backup plan, no dreams of revolution. He had simply decided he couldn't be a part of the system any more and had opted out. For over a year, he had lived in a crumbling tenement and worked on a factory line. In his words, "I had decided it was better to be crushed between the wheels of the machine than to be one of the men turning them."

I couldn't say he was wrong, but I couldn't just opt out the way he had. Not when my family back home was living on my pay. If I died out here, at the pirates' hands or from my clumsy sabotage, they'd at least have my death benefit. Perhaps that was the best thing. It might be enough for them to buy a little house somewhere for William, if they had the sense to do it.

If I turned traitor, my family could never have that. They could never even speak my name in company again, for the shame they would feel. Not that they would ever have a chance to appear in polite company again.

"I can't stomach the alternative," I said. "I suppose you think me a coward."

She turned back toward the window, so all I could see of her face was the blank curve of her cheek. "It's never been my place to accuse you of anything."

I wondered, as I made my way back to my berth, if she had sharpened that statement to hurt me as carefully as I had sharpened so many of mine. Either way, it lodged deep.

Moira returned from her meeting with Ms. Knauss in a white rage. She shot in from the airlock like the launch was on fire, vaulted over the quarterdeck railing, and kicked a crate of oxygen masks. It was too securely attached to fly loose, which only made her angrier.

I pushed up from the sail deck to join her. "What happened?"

"What fucking happened? They're thieves and swindlers, that's what happened."

I waited. She fumed for another minute, staring out at the massive Earth ship. At last she sighed. "The pay isn't as good as expected. Look." She handed me a thin sheet.

"It looks very—oh." I read the rest of the items underneath "bounty." "They charged you for the supplies we took on at Luna?"

"They said they would provide it at cost because of our special business relationship with them. Does that look like fucking cost to you? Cost to Earth, which has more oxygen and hydrogen than they know what to do with?"

"I don't understand," I said. "How can they possibly do business like this?"

"Because they're the only game in town. I could ship cargoes, but I'm not going to get a rate better than that elsewhere. Venus has a markup too, even though they can't get rid of their gasses fast enough. Mars won't sell, obviously. So I can go private and buy from some other Earther, but the price will be even worse. I know how it goes. The merchant ship I was on before the *Mariposa* was practically bankrupt. Cap'n offered me part owner, and I turned it down because I was better off just pulling wages."

"At least you came out in the black?"

"For a mission they knew was dangerous, which they said was a *big* payout. I shudder to think of what a small payout would be." She snatched the paper back and shoved it into her back pocket. "And then I asked about death benefits. Hausmann *died* out there and I know that's the risk we all took, but it meant something to us. We're not a bunch of numbers to wager and lose." She shook her head slowly. "There's nothing. We're 'private contractors,' we don't get a death benefit. The fucking *Martian Navy* does better for their men than Earth will do for Hausmann."

I chewed my lip, unsure of what to say. Of course everyone knew that Earth was shamelessly corporate; that was the whole reason Mars had wanted its independence in the first place. Mars wasn't perfect, but I would have never dreamed of merely shrugging when a tenant or employee of mine died. I would have been over there with a basket of food the next day, and with a fund for the children by the end of the week. We took our responsibilities as landowners seriously. Most people I knew did, or tried to. Tenants were neighbors, almost friends. They weren't people we could easily ignore, living right on our land as they did.

I had a guilty moment of gratification. Here, at least, was one thing Mars did better. But I couldn't say I had told her so, that that should show her for trusting Earthers. It was far too late for her to backtrack, and I still wasn't sure she had even chosen the worst of bad options. With her spirit, wouldn't she have sooner or later found herself out an airlock like Maxwell?

Instead I said, "Do you have a fresh contract?"

"She wouldn't talk about it yet. Earth has a big plan, apparently, to share with all of the captains of the ships here. I'll have to go back in the afternoon watch."

"Let me come with you."

She spun around. "What? How does that make sense?"

"Ms. Knauss thinks I'm your clerk, right? She's met me. She won't go telling the Admiralty I'm helping you. She doesn't even know I'm an officer. I just want to be there so I can be sure you're not getting sold a raw deal. Not that you don't know how to do business but—well—moral support."

She raised an eyebrow. "Why moral-support me in a task you think is immoral in the first place?"

My face warmed. "You let me worry about my own morals. You need to be worrying about Earth Force swindling you."

Moira wasn't the only pirate captain to bring a plus one. At least a dozen people sat around the long table on the Earth ship, with Ms. Knauss and a clerk of her own at the head.

"I'm sure you're all wondering why you're here," she said. "But before I tell you, I need everyone to sign this nondisclosure agreement."

One of the other captains looked at the sheet, as it came around the table to him, like a fanged snake. "If you don't trust us to keep Earth's secrets, you shouldn't be working with us at all," he said angrily.

"I do, I do," she soothed. "But the lawyers, they insist on this kind of thing."

Once everyone had signed—myself with a deliberately unreadable scrawl—I saw why Ms. Knauss was so concerned about secrecy. She rose from the table, unveiling an easel with an unmistakable drawing on it. "Mars's new mining station," she said, as if anyone in the system needed an explanation.

A buzz went around the table. I only stared at the wheel-shaped sketch. That station was the pride of Mars right now. It would make Mars truly independent of Earth and its corps and its crippling prices. With a place to refuel and to send ships home with thrust lasers, Mars could finally exploit the asteroid belt. Ice, gasses, whatever anybody could want, all free for the price of digging them out.

Of course Earth wanted to destroy it. Of course. But I felt sick at the very idea.

One pirate spoke up. "If you're planning an attack on the station, why bring us into it? Isn't this a job for Earth Force?"

"We want to be able to deny knowledge and involvement," said Knauss. "Of course Mars will suspect we were behind it, but they'll have an easier time accepting a ceasefire if there's room for them to believe it was rogue actors. If anyone is uncomfortable with the idea of keeping our relationship completely secret, now would be a good time to leave."

No one budged, and the talk went on to money. Here, at least, I could be of some use. I raised my hand politely. "Sorry, may I draw your attention to item six on this list you've passed out? Munitions, it says, are to be provided at cost. Which is a good price, but it seems to me that since all munitions are to be fired at the station, that cost should be fronted by Earth Force in full."

I gave a sunny smile. I knew how to work this angle, the "I'm not poor, I'm entitled, and thus you should cut me a deal so I don't walk" angle. It didn't matter if I was bargaining the price down to the single shilling in my purse, I never dropped a sign that that was what I was doing.

Once I'd spoken, the other pirates chimed in. Couldn't they have fuel funded at fifty percent for the same reason? After all, normally contracts went to pirates over Earth Force to save money, but now Earth *needed* pirates for this specific job.

"I can't imagine this is the only job you ever want to do for Earth Force," said Ms. Knauss tightly. "You don't want to get a reputation of being difficult to do business with."

The pirates hesitated. Earth could live without us; we couldn't live without Earth. Or, well, the pirates couldn't.

But I pressed the issue. "Not being difficult at all," I said sunnily. "But we do know our value. Certainly there are private actors around the system who would be interested in hiring us for some work. And even Mars might..." I let the sentence dangle. Mars would never hire pirates—I didn't think. Even if they could get around the questionable ethics of hiring pirates, the Admiralty didn't have the kind of cash Earth did.

Several pirates shot me dirty looks. After all, everyone in the room was either an Earther or a Martian defector. The looks clearly read: *we're not working for Mars, no matter what they offer.*

But Ms. Knauss bought it. "Well. Perhaps the munitions, at least, we could cover. Fuel…hmm. Perhaps the first thousand kilos? You shouldn't really need more than that to brake when you arrive."

Moira was smiling again when we came out of the conference room. "God, you were amazing in there. You made it sound like we had all these choices, that we could do whatever we wanted."

"I'm an old hand at that trick," I said. "My parents are too proud to pay under the asking price for anything, but I always do. I just make it sound like I'm only entitled, not desperate."

She cast me a sidelong grin. "I never thought I'd look up to you for poor-people tips."

In the hall outside, I saw Alexei Khan. We had handed him over earlier, along with the other prisoners. "Captain Singh, Miss Prescott," he said warmly. "I had hoped I would have a chance to say goodbye."

Moira clasped his hand briefly. "Where are you going to go now? Earth?"

He shook his head solemnly. "They will be leaving me at Halfpoint. I've heard there are people there who can provide me with a new identity and smuggle me back to Mars."

"You're going back?" I protested. "After all they did to you? You'll be in a wheelchair at best. Next time they'll kill you!"

"I have to do it," he said. "You see how badly the reform movement has struggled in my absence. With what I've suffered,

I only have more credibility to lead the movement. Change is not optional, Prescott. It's coming, and all I have ever wanted in my life is to pave its way."

Moira gave him a tearful hug. I shook his hand more stoically. I had little doubt it would be the last I saw of him. He couldn't lead a movement without revealing his presence, and when the Imperial Police found him, they wouldn't be as merciful as before.

I watched him go, my chest aching for more than one reason. I mourned for him, yes, but I also envied him. What must it be, feeling so certain of his moral course that he was willing to die for it? All I felt about mine was turmoil. I had failed to serve Mars the way I had sworn to. I felt, more and more, that I couldn't. But could I seal its fate as a mere colonial power, strangled by the Earth corps, either? To say nothing of my family.

The smart thing, of course, would be to do what anyone else would have done. Do what kept me safe at the moment, or whatever felt right. Then when I finally got back, lie at my court martial, make it look like I had been what they wanted. Keep my head down for the rest of my service and get out when the war was over. Surely the Navy was full of people doing just that.

But to accept that level of secrecy and underhanded dealing didn't sit right with me. I was never any good at lying, of splitting myself in two: the self that was supposed to exist, and the self that did. It felt like the last years with Moira had felt, playing a part every day of the girl who wasn't in love with her friend, not at all, knowing it was a fake but unable to do any different.

I wasn't, really, all that bad at lying. I had tells, sure, but people weren't generally looking. I'd gotten away with it so many times. The reason I tried so hard not to was that it hurt me so badly. I felt no longer myself, like I didn't know who I was. Was the real me the lie or the secret?

When I was a midshipman, my identity was clear—it was handed to me in a package, just like the uniform. *This is who you* are, who you should be, who you look up to, what your values are. My uniform coat lay on a bathroom counter on Luna now. I had to somehow find out who I was without all that. Without the identity of gentlewoman or midshipman or prisoner.

Moira gave me a funny look, as we passed down the narrow corridor. "You all right?"

I shook my head to clear it and gave a bland smile. "Of course."

"I have to stop off here." She gestured at a hatch labeled "bursar." "Apparently they'll send our bounty wherever we want. The bank on Halfpoint releases it, they'll change it into Martian pounds, and then it'll be smuggled through Phobos and sent to my dads. Or, you know, whoever."

The man behind the desk smiled blandly at us. "Captain Singh, yes? You'll want to direct how you want your pay disbursed."

He handed us a stack of forms. Moira pulled out her own notes, percentages of the money owed each crew member and what they wanted done with it. With a sigh, she picked up her pencil. "I hate math."

"That's why you hired a clerk," I pointed out. "Give."

Soon I had the numbers straight for her. Everyone had earned at least the Earth dollar equivalent of fifty Martian pounds. Not too shabby, really, though small compared to what Moira had expected. Together we filled out a transfer form for each one. I noticed she sent twenty pounds of her own share to Hausmann's family. I smiled to myself as I filled out forms. Earth might fail her crew, but Moira herself never would.

"You can also send letters," Moira said as she started on the last form.

I thought about that. What if I never went back? I didn't *want* to go back. Ancestors, how little I wanted to go back and face my court-martial. There was so much to lie about already. All the more, if I did what Khan might suggest and stopped trying to be loyal to the Navy.

And I had a rare chance here. Moira had been marked as a deserter because the Navy knew where she was supposed to be, and she hadn't arrived. I, however, was a captive. If Captain Kim ever got back to Mars, he would testify to that. If not, I was probably assumed dead when the *Mariposa* had reappeared at Deimos, crewed by pirates. No one had been offered for ransom. Wouldn't they assume I'd been shoved out an airlock?

I hung there, blinking, staring at the sheaf of papers clipped to the desk in front of me. Had I had my freedom all this time and hadn't noticed? All I had to do was never go back. I'd be declared dead, my family would get the money they needed, and I could be free.

The thought gave me a little peace. I would figure something out, sooner or later. Maybe I could get onto a civilian Earth ship, work my way to Luna or somewhere. Disappear. Opt out. And so long as no one ever found me, my family would be safe. Safe, if not prospering. Maybe that was the most I could give them.

The only hard part was knowing they would think I was dead. I wanted so much to tell them otherwise. But could they really keep that secret? My mother certainly couldn't. And I wasn't at all sure of the security of the mail.

At last I took a sheet, addressed it to William, and sketched a series of concentric circles, hoping he would remember that time at the shore, the circles of stones we had made together. Him, at least, I could spare that sorrow.

SIXTEEN

I watched from the quarterdeck as the pirate ships spread their sails. It was a glorious sight, seldom seen from such a vantage point. They had spread out, miles apart, to leave room for the massive sails, and then, almost in unison, the huge masts began to unfold, the fabric rippling and flashing with light as it smoothed out.

Watching the fleet, I felt awed, almost proud. No dread for what the mission would entail. No judgment of the crews of these ships. Would Khan be proud of me, no longer thinking as the Navy wanted me to?

Since I had lost my officer's coat, I'd gone around the ship in only shirtsleeves and my spare blue waistcoat. It made me feel smaller, without the extra space my trailing coattails had taken up. Less important. And yet, without noticing it, I'd stopped minding. I took up the same amount of space on this ship as everyone else.

Maggie floated next to me, in a sailor's shirt and trousers. She'd gone further down that road that I had. Further than I wanted to. But I found I wasn't angry at her anymore. She had to make her choices, same as the rest of us. There wasn't a right one.

She goggled openmouthed at the array of shimmering sails. "Now this," she said, "is better than anything we saw in the Navy." Her eyes slid over to me. "What? No judgmental comment?"

I lifted one shoulder a fraction. "Not today."

When the sails were fully unfurled and we had matched acceleration as best as we could, launches began buzzing among the ships. The different captains wanted to talk. Moira invited them all to dinner on the *Mariposa*, as it had the largest captain's mess.

"And you're going to be there too," she said, nabbing me by the elbow before I could surreptitiously float away.

"Why me?"

"Because you helped so much at that meeting. They know you now and might want to say thank you for your help."

She wasn't wrong. As soon as the food was cleared away, Coelho, the burly, bearded captain of the *Estrela*, proposed a toast. "To Singh's girlfriend, a bargaining goddess, who got us the kind of deal we never get from Earth."

"I'm not—"

"She's a wonder," Moira interrupted smoothly, nudging her shoulder against mine. "Don't be too humble, officer. You really put the screws to Knauss."

I was left redfaced and spluttering. On the one hand, how dare she? We weren't together, had never been together. On the other, perhaps she was only being diplomatic. It wouldn't be easy to explain who I was and how I had been admitted to their number if she tried arguing that point.

In any event, the conversation had moved on to strategy. "With six ships, why do we need to worry about stealth?" asked Coelho. "We're almost a fleet. Let's just hammer it with broadsides till it blows."

"You're an idiot," said Hussein, a small stout woman with

flashing dark eyes and a red hijab. "It'll have layers of radiation plating, being out there permanently like that. We'd need better guns than we have to go at it like that."

"We have to think of the ships that may be nearby," said Moira. "There's likely some there to defend it, and who knows how many ships will be fueling and loading there."

"Well those, at least, we can just attack," he said.

"Anyone know what defenses the station itself has?"

Moira shook her head, unclamping the caddy from the middle of the table to make room for the drawing of the station. It was a giant wheel in space, like Aphrodite Station but larger, complete with artificial gravity, an aeroponic farm, massive thrust lasers. Everyone knew that much. But what weapons it might have couldn't be seen in the picture.

"This is all we have," Moira said. "Captured from flybys. Earth has no spies there."

Hussein shook her head. "They couldn't have waited to do this when they had better information?"

"This is their long shot," said Moira. "Enormous coup if it works. And if we all get killed? They don't pay a dime."

"Shit," said Coelho. "I wish we could have talked it over among ourselves without *her* there. Hell, I wouldn't have been paying so much for fuel from them all these years if I'd had all of you in the same room with me to bargain together."

"It's by design," said Moira flatly. "Divide and conquer. Deal with each of us separately and she's always got the upper hand. But she's brought us together for this, and by the time we get back, we'll have hashed out some things, I think."

Hussein looked nervous. "So you all think this is a mistake?"

Moira shook her head. "No. We can do this. But we have to be smarter than they are. We can't just fly in, guns blazing. We need a plan."

I scanned the faces of the assembled pirate captains. Some

stared blankly at Moira; others furrowed their brows as if to force an idea to materialize.

Deftly Moira snatched the map and rolled it up. "Sleep on it," she said. "We'll meet again here tomorrow. Bring any and all ideas."

The next morning found me in the forecastle, taking a bearing. Moira came in and then stopped dead. "What are you doing here?"

I held up the sextant. "Checking Maggie's work."

She gave me a long, appraising look. "Dare I ask how much I can expect you to do on this ship?"

I raised the sextant back to my eyes, mainly to hide my face. "It's just, I'm probably never going home. I've accepted that."

Or I thought I had. Just saying those words made memories come thick and fast: riding horses beside Hellas Basin, Olympus Mons towering high over the plains, the deep blue sea that flows in the Valles Marineris. My parents. William.

Jupiter smeared into a bright blob, and I blinked hard trying to bring it back into focus. "So I thought, if I'm not worried about the court martial, what would I be doing to pay my way around here? And this is something I can do that I feel all right about."

"Even though you're navigating us toward the station?"

I lowered the sextant to glare at her. "Are you *trying* to make this more difficult?"

"Just trying to get a bead on what's going on in your head. I remember thinking we two understood each other better than anybody in the world. And then realizing, all at once, that I didn't know what you actually thought about anything. Hadn't known in years."

"I felt like you understood me pretty well most of the time."

"Apparently not," she said bitterly. "Maybe I understood you about as well as you understood yourself. Which wasn't a lot. Maybe still isn't a lot."

I suppressed a grimace. For someone who supposedly didn't understand me, she sure could cut to the quick of what I was struggling with. "We can't all size up a situation on a dime and know exactly what to do. Some of us have to think about it first."

It had been meant as an expression of envy, how I wished I had her sureness in herself that made her instantly able to weigh the choices available against her values. But as the words left my mouth, I realized she wouldn't hear them that way.

She drew herself up a little, eyes flashing. "Well we can't all be Founders, *officer*," she spat. "Not all of our brains are quite up to your standard." She shot out of the room like a cat with its tail on fire.

I turned back to the stars, kicking myself internally. We seemed doomed to forever be at cross purposes.

The ship rang with song as we passed out of Mars's orbit and arced toward the asteroid belt. Navy regs allowed singing only off duty, except for the tuneless chants the men used as they hoisted and lowered the sails. Now the crew sang like canaries as they went about their work—some like canaries, that is, and some more like crows.

Nguyen was the most enthusiastic singer. He constantly changed up the words of the old songs, making parodies about anyone and everyone. There was even a bawdy one about the sexual hangups of the nobility, though they politely stopped singing it whenever I came on deck. On his off-watches, Nguyen sang plaintively about home to a large audience that gathered on the sun deck.

The *Mariposa* wasn't as shining clean as it had been in Captain Kim's day. Back then, every inch had been polished daily, mainly to keep the men busy, and now the rigging in the sail room was dim with grime. But the crew was happier. They did what actually needed to be done, and as for the rest, they didn't bother. So long as the algae got stirred, the laundry done, the oxygen levels tested and corrected every day, what did it matter?

I remembered Kim and Brown, how they had insisted our direction and discipline was the only thing keeping this ship from disaster. That no one would ever work without us making them; that they needed us as much as we needed them. I shouldn't be so surprised to find that was a lie, after everything else that had happened, but somehow I was.

I started lending a hand around the ship, pretty much at random. My old job of standing over people, frightening them into working harder, was gone now and I didn't miss it. But I had been trained in most ship systems, so each day I picked a team that looked stressed and helped them out. I wanted to pay my way somehow.

I was working in wastewater one day, clearing a blockage on my own. It didn't smell any better than before, but I was better used to it now. And at least I knew what I was doing.

"Excuse me, sir," said a voice behind me, and I turned around. It was a youngish man with dark skin and a short beard—Doubek, one of the original crew.

"I'm not an officer anymore," I said. "Or not on this ship, anyway."

"Yeah, but I figured you might know what's up. Can you look?"

I followed him into the atmosphere control room. It was a

cramped cubby, little more than a broom closet, with a number of tests running on the dark wooden shelves.

"See, the oxidation test is fine," he said, gesturing to a row of test tubes. "And I just did the CO_2 test; it's fine too." He showed me the little syringe, showing the reactant was the correct pale blue.

"But?"

"But the combustion test isn't right." That was a simple enough test: trap a set volume of the ship's air in a jar, create a spark on some cotton wool inside, and time how long it took the fire to go out.

"How long did it take?"

He held out his pocket watch. "Twenty-five seconds."

I grimaced. It should have been at least thirty. "What's the barometer say?"

"The what?"

Rubbing my forehead with one hand, I said, "That's the fourth test. You check the barometer every watch. Should be the very first thing you check!"

He looked abashed. "I'm sorry—it was Hausmann's job. I was learning the different tests when she ... But I thought I had learned them all."

"You must not have noticed her doing the barometer check because it takes two seconds. It's all right." I moved over to check the dial. "Well. We clearly have a problem. I'm glad you asked me about it."

He stared at me in a panic. "A problem? How bad of a problem?"

I could see my deliberate calm had done nothing to soothe him. "We have a breach. Probably have had for some time. Give me the log."

I flipped the pages. Up until Deimos the numbers were all good, written in Hausmann's careful hand. She had been life-support mate, under Sato, but Sato had died in the attack by Moira's crew. So she had stepped up and had been trying to train Doubek as her mate, but it was clear it had gotten ahead of her and she'd run out of time.

On a fresh page, Doubek's observations began: messy, and not in the right columns. But this was where the problem had started. The time for the combustion test had slowly decreased: twenty-nine seconds, twenty-eight, twenty-seven...

"It's a slow leak, for sure," I said. "We'd have noticed a fast one. But we have to inform the captain and begin a search."

Moira took the news gravely and mustered all available crew to run airflow tests. The basic test was simple: fill the air with a fine dust (rice flour was the handiest choice), shine a light through it, and watch the eddies. We had to shut off all the fans that circulated air between decks, because those created so much movement we couldn't see anything else.

I was on the gun deck, shining a light along the row of torpedo tubes, when I spotted it. Dust motes swirling toward the number eight tube, and never swirling back. "Got it!" I called.

The crew cranked up the fans again and I headed up to the sail deck. I found Goldstein by the airlock, already suiting up.

"It's the number eight starboard," I said. "Want me to come?"

He grunted agreement, and I got into a suit, assisted by the Earther who was his current mate.

Once we reached the gun port, the problem was obvious. A shot that would have been harmless on the thick radiation plating had hit a port dead-on, wedging it slightly open when it should have been sealed except when firing.

Goldstein sighed and clamped his legs to the hull. "We'll be here a while."

"You have everything you need?"

"Mm." He opened his case, exposing shining rows of tools, all meticulously fastened in place, and handed it to me. "Nine mil."

I selected the appropriate one and passed it over, still trailing its safety cord. "I'm surprised nobody inspected all this after Deimos."

"Nobody ordered it," said Goldstein.

"Things have been a little chaotic," I admitted. "We've gone through two life support masters in the past months and Doubek didn't seem to know who he was supposed to report to."

"Marron said we should all be taking our own *initiative*," Goldstein said sourly. "Which seems like an easy way to say, he wants us to do our job but he won't do his. Cutter."

I passed it to him, waiting to release it till I saw his gauntlets close around it. "You don't like the way the pirates do things?"

"You see how well it works. We've been leaking air for days and nobody noticed." He pulled free the deformed plate and handed it to me. "Don't suppose you've thought of a way to botch it out here that won't kill us all."

I stared at him in shock. Somehow I had assumed all the men were happy to be pirates now. Many certainly were, and loudly. But Goldstein had defended the Navy's ways to me before.

He had paused in his work, watching me.

"No, I don't," I said at last. "I'm sorry, you took me by surprise. I thought everyone was happy under the new command."

He grunted. "I was." He took a fresh plate from me and slotted it into place. "But going after the station, that's different. It means everything to the folks at home. I might be working for Moira now, but I still care about them."

"I know how you feel."

He looked up sharply. "Of course you do," he said. "You're a loyal officer. Not one of us. There's no conflict for you."

His words stung me. Loyal officer? I still felt guilty for not being one. As evidenced by my telling no one but Moira that I wasn't going back. I knew I didn't want to go back. And I knew I didn't want to do anything that would hurt Mars. But what did that leave for me? How would I know what I *should* do? What should I spend my life on besides hiding?

Moira had an inner loyalty; a clear sighting on her guiding star that she always knew how to follow. She didn't have to be loyal *to* anything, any more than the *Mariposa* had to follow another ship to know where it was going. Why didn't I have that? Was it simply a matter of deciding?

When we came inside the airlock at last, reeking with sweat and groggy from stale air, I was still wondering. Where could I find a star of my own I could feel confident following?

Seventeen

From then on, I noticed a tenser atmosphere on the ship. The easy camaraderie we'd had since the pirates had taken over was gone, replaced with—nervousness? Quiet? At first I thought everyone was simply anxious over the near-disaster. It was certainly true what Goldstein had said, that such a thing would never have happened on a properly-managed Navy vessel. Moira had gotten more careful about checking on the various masters and mates, but perhaps the crew had lost some confidence in her.

But it was more than that. Moira continued to exchange dinners with the other captains, but when she left to visit another, the launch she took was almost empty. Everyone somehow had something else to do. Everyone except the small crew of pirates she had returned to the *Mariposa* with.

A separation had somehow happened between the Martians and the Earthers, who had previously messed together as a single crew. The sailors returned to their old cliques from before the takeover, and if an Earther wanted to join them, there somehow never happened to be room.

I had the fortune of being above the conflict, since I ate in the officer's mess with Moira, but I caught several meaningful nods in my direction from the Martian crew when they were at liberty, clustered in tight little knots.

Finally I surrendered to curiosity and joined them one dog-watch. "Trying to get my attention, Nguyen?"

Nguyen nodded and looked at Goldstein, who seemed to be the center of this little group. "He thought we should bring you in on this."

"Turns out I wasn't the only one with a problem attacking the station," said Goldstein. "The lot of us have decided we won't have any part of it." The others looked back at me with grim agreement.

A shiver ran up my back. And why not? They had planned a mutiny before; they weren't afraid of it. It would only be easier this time, with the weapons chest sitting open and unguarded all day. Moira had tried trusting the men; easier by far than beating the men, but would it have any better result? I flashed back to those tense days when the cutlasses were missing, watching my back, trusting no one. But this time it wouldn't be me in the center of the waiting vultures. It would be Moira.

"I can't help you mutiny," I said quickly. "I gave my parole, and I take that very—"

"Mutiny?" broke in Nguyen. "No! Why would we have to mutiny against *her*? She's one of us."

The warmth seeped back into my bones. Of course not, they loved Moira. "Then what's the plan? She agreed to attack the station."

"We're going to confront her," Goldstein said. "We'll tell her we're not doing this."

I tilted my head skeptically. I had never been able to change her mind on anything once she had begun doing it. And here we were, leagues from anywhere, accompanied by five pirate ships bristling with arms. But they had to try, didn't they?

"All right," I said. "For all the good it'll do."

"Thanks for doing this," said Yao warmly. "I know how you hate her."

I just blinked. "Hate her?"

"Well, I mean, you tried to strangle her with your bare hands when she came back on the ship."

Oh. That. "Well, that was a while ago," I said. "And she doesn't seem to hold it against me."

A glance passed between a few of them. "We think having you on our side will help our case," Nguyen said. Of course, that had been the subject of all their whispers and glances. Would I help them, and would it help or hurt them if I did? They'd have picked apart all of Moira's winks, her teasing comments, and asked themselves if she liked me or was only trying to make me uncomfortable.

Even I couldn't answer that question. Pressed, I would probably say both.

They confronted her during the morning watch, approaching the rail of the quarterdeck in a mass. The Earth pirates thought nothing of vaulting the rail, but the Martians still held some lingering respect for what had once been an officers-only space.

Moira came to the rail and looked over. "What's this, men?"

"We want to talk to you," said Goldstein. His eyes fixed on Marron, floating beside her. "Martians only."

Marron narrowed his eyes. "Cap'n, I don't know if that's wise."

She shrugged him off. "These are my people, Marron. I'm safe."

He searched the crowd of two dozen Martians, spotting me beside the rail. Swinging over, he passed by me with a questioning glance. I read his question: can I trust her safety to you?

He knew me well. No matter my opinions on anything, I would keep her safe. I gave a tight nod and clambered up the rail, perching on it so as to stand between Moira and the men: not abandoning them to join her, but not letting any of them closer to her than I was, either.

"It's like this," said Goldstein. "You never asked us if we wanted to destroy the station. We're on board with piracy, but it's a bad contract to take."

Moira scanned the faces. "You all agree?"

"It's one thing to be picking off Martian ships, freeing prisoners," put in Nguyen. "That's Navy. I'll fight the Navy any day of the week. But the station isn't just for the Navy, it's for all of Mars."

"It's run by the Navy," she said.

"But think about it," Nguyen said. "Since Mars got our—its independence, Earth has been trying to take it back. The corps don't like Mars being for the Martians, being terraformed when they wanted to mine it. We beat them in the war, so they tried to starve us out. Embargo us, hike the prices, so we couldn't get gasses without agreeing to their terms. They were making us mine *ourselves*, just to pay for the terraforming project. And in the end, they never would have settled for minerals. They wanted us to let the corps operate freely on Mars. And they would have gotten it sooner or later, without the station. Strip-mined Mars, torn up the grasses and let them rot their carbon back out, poison the water. You know they would have."

I regarded him, impressed by his concise summary of the situation. I hadn't even known the common spacer understood what they were fighting for. I had assumed the mutiny proved they didn't; that, not knowing the stakes, they had chosen their own comfort.

"The station changed that, and that's why Earth wants it gone. Mars can get gasses from the asteroids now; it don't need Earth. But Earth is going to keep fighting till they get rid of that station."

"If the station's gone, the war ends," said Moira. "Mars will have to make terms."

"But we don't want that," said Nguyen. "Earth is trying to make us kill the cow we're milking. No war, then what do we do for a living? Mars nor Earth owe us nothing if we're not killing each other for them."

I cringed internally. He was right. War was bad for both planets, but good for the crew. They were exiles of two planets, those with a death sentence waiting on Mars and those who had left Earth for one good reason or another. Their only hope of making a living was in space, but with nowhere to set their feet, they needed a planet to pay them. Shipping cargoes would never be profitable enough.

Moira nodded slowly. She saw it too. "Earth didn't offer us any other contract," she said. "They pushed us hard at this one."

"Of course they did," said Nguyen. Goldstein had settled down toward the deck, letting the more voluble younger man do the talking. "They want it bad and they don't care if it don't work. They'll send the next batch of pirates to do the same. It hurts them nothing so long as they don't get caught doing it."

Moira bowed her head, hands gripping the rail. At last she shook her head. "I don't know what you want me to do. I took this contract so we could get fuel and air to keep flying. It was the only choice I had, and Earth did all it could to screw us on the deal. And now we're more stuck than we were. There's one of us and five other ships, and not one of them cares at all what comes of Mars."

"Do *you* care?" Yao called out.

Her head snapped up so hard she almost lost hold of the rail. "Of course I fucking care. My family's there, same as all of yours. But I just don't see another choice we have. If we refuse to fight, we don't get air again. How long you think we can live on algae and yeast and the oh-two canisters? Six months? And that's if the other ships even let us go in peace instead of attacking. We can't fight off all five."

There was silence among the men. I watched them chew over the math, math I'd already considered. I hated what Moira had agreed to, but I couldn't see what choice she had. I was a prisoner, but I was freer than her in that sense. I could simply refuse to be a part of what they were doing. The station would fall or not fall, and either way, it wasn't on my conscience. I could hide in my room the whole time, let the whole thing fall out the way it was going to.

But the consequences would be the same. I saw them in my mind's eye, the same as they did: Earth ships docking at Phobos, Earth machines tearing up the ground. Everything that had taken my family so many generations to build, destroyed. Because corps saw only one metric in anything: the number of dollars of value they could ship back to Earth. You can't ship a beautiful pebbly beach. But you can crush it up, melt it down, dump the slag in the sea, and ship back iron ore and magnesium salts.

And I knew every man there had a place they were thinking of, a place they'd never see again, but which somehow was still the ground of their heart. They had betrayed Mars, meaning Their Majesty's Government. They had never, not in their heart of hearts, betrayed Mars, the green and growing land broken with jagged red ridges. And now they were going to have to. Their feet had been floating all this time, but now their hearts would be cut loose from their gravity too.

One by one, I saw them accept it. There were murmurs as

they worked it out among themselves. Goldstein spoke for them all. "At least we can't just destroy it outright," he said. "There are good people there. Some we know, maybe. We've got to leave them a chance to evacuate. Can you make sure of that?"

Moira chewed her lip, thinking. "I don't know," she said. "We still haven't got a plan for how we're going to pull this off at all. That thing is massive and we're only six ships. But I'll talk to the other captains."

The captains were still meeting every night, trying to hash out a plan. I didn't usually attend, but this time I joined Moira at the airlock without being asked. She shot me a thankful glance.

This dinner was at Coelho's ship, whose cramped conference room couldn't pretend to the grandeur of a proper officer's mess. On Earth ships, everyone messed together, captain down to cabin boy. This room was meant more for meetings, and the walls were hung with charts.

Coelho sat at the head, glaring down at Moira. "What do you mean, your men have *concerns*? You promised they were on our side now. What do they care what happens to Mars?"

"Some of them may have loved ones on the station," she answered. "They want to be sure we're not just charging in to explode the whole thing."

Coelho sneered. "You think Mars would give us that consideration?"

"The laws of war—"

"Mars doesn't give a damn about the laws of war when they can get away with it," he said. "You know that. And we're pirates. Nobody even expects it."

"I want to be better than them," she said quietly. "What was the point of leaving if I can't be better than them?"

Hussein grimaced slightly. "We're hardly in a position to be choosy," she pointed out. "If we can do it at all, we'll have to take whatever plan will work. Fast or slow. If we can't get it done, there's no payout from Earth and no more fuel or air."

Victory or death, was what it came to. No one was giving away air and water for free. I didn't envy any of them the moral conundrum.

"I still think we should strike hard and fast," said Coelho. "And the hell with anybody who's not on our side."

"I'm still not happy with that plan though," said Hussein. "We have no idea what defenses the station itself will have inside. And now if we've got to worry about Moira's crew turning on us—"

"I never said they would—"

"Clearly we need more information," broke in Coelho, with a look to Hussein I couldn't read. "Why don't the rest of us start our deceleration now, to let the *Mariposa* get ahead? You can still pass as Martian, if you repaint. You can take stock of the situation and flash us back the intelligence when we pull into range, a day or so later."

Moira cast a suspicious glance around the table, but in the end she nodded. "The more we know, the better the chance we can pull this off the way we want to."

That's how I ended up, with Marron assisting me, back on the hull. We were painting yet again. Beside the Martian flag, which we hadn't yet removed, we added the colors of a well-known mining company.

Before the station had been in operation, the ships of Tharsis Enterprises had gone on years-long missions to the asteroid belt, digging out what they could before coming back. My wager was that the same company still operated in the area and would now frequent the station.

The rest of the ships in our flotilla had furled their sails, giving us time to get ahead and reach the station first. A few of the crew could go aboard, hopefully get a look around, and have something to tell the others when they arrived.

I probably shouldn't have volunteered for the job. After all, it was helping the pirates fool Ares Station, the last thing I wanted to do. But on the other hand, if I hadn't done it, someone else would, and I was in the mood for a spacewalk. The ship felt a little claustrophobic sometimes.

"I hope the cap'n isn't too disappointed in Earth, with this mission they're sending us on," said Marron as he carefully applied the viscous glop. Paint that worked in space, without the liquid freezing or boiling off, wasn't exactly easy to use. "She had it in her head that Mars was bad but Earth would be better, and I don't know how to tell her every planet's got its problems."

I sighed and smeared some on. "She's mad about them not paying death benefits, but that doesn't ruin it for her," I said at last. "She wants a place away from our class system. She thinks it's why it didn't work out for her and me."

He chuckled, and I turned toward him in surprise. "But that's true as far as that goes, right? There's no class system on Earth."

"Oh, no legally-enforced one," he said. "None you'd admit to in public, ever. On Earth nobody would say you couldn't get together because you were rich and she was poor. You wouldn't even have *met*."

I furrowed my brow. "So people aren't allowed to—"

"They're allowed to live wherever they want, in theory. In practice, she couldn't have afforded to live in the same town. Maybe not even the same continent. The top one percent of people on Earth are … well, fuck, I don't know what they're like. I've never met 'em. I'd never in a million years get the chance to meet 'em.

If I were lucky I might be, like, the gardener of the hairdresser of the personal assistant of one of 'em. Lucky because, that would be a job and on Earth it's damn hard to get one."

My heart sank. Of course it all had to be too good to be true. Somehow every place was broken. "So is that why you went to space? No jobs on Earth?"

He gave a snort. "Nah, I left Earth to get away from my mother. She's gone now, but, well."

"You visit home much?"

"Never." He cleared his throat. "Been out here so long, you know. Can't take the gravity."

I was silent for some time, smearing the paint on and wishing I hadn't asked. Surely if he'd wanted me to know he was space-bound, he'd have brought it up before on his own. Or perhaps pirates thought nothing of it.

Marron cleared his throat again, gruffly, and gave a sharp sniff. "Go on, I know you're curious. You're sitting there, half sorry you asked, half wondering if you can get away with more questions."

"It's none of my business."

"Don't you want to know? Don't you want to maybe tell me it's my own fault because I didn't put in the exercise time? I get that a lot when they wheel me off the ship at Halfpoint. It's seventy-five percent Earth-standard there and I still can't take it. Broke a bone last time I tried." His voice held a bitterness I'd never heard in it before.

"Look, I'm not half sorry I asked, I'm *all* sorry I asked. I've been in space barely over a year. I don't know anything."

He drew a long edge line and began filling it in. "Y'see, when you've got an independent ship, it's hard to make the books balance," he said, more softly. "I was shipping cargoes at first. Moira might've told you about that; it's the same whoever you work for. The price of the cargo only barely covers the cost of the voyage.

Fuel is expensive, food, air, water, and that's if nothing breaks and you don't have to go in the hole for the repair supplies. It's always something. We cut a lot of corners. Half the crew you need so everyone works double shifts. Shitty exercise equipment. Sure as hell no time to take your six weeks ashore before you go out again. Maybe you're lucky and you get to go down every other year. And then one time you do and the doctor says, 'You're done. Don't go back up, 'cause if you do, you can't ever come back.'"

No wonder Moira hadn't wanted to ship cargoes. I had judged her so hard for that, but I couldn't now. "Why'd you go back up then?"

Marron breathed a long, slow sigh. "I love it out here. I do. Once you're used to the big dark, Earth feels like a rabbit warren. People on top of people. Here you have room to *breathe*. Which is ironic given there's no air."

I laughed, relieved that he didn't seem to be angry anymore, and went out on my tether for a better view.

"It looks good." From here I could read the *Mariposa*'s new name, *Melpomene*. It had the advantage of using the same first letter and saving some paint. "We'll need to do something about the aft window, though. The quarterdecks on merchant ships are nowhere near that wide."

"Moira said the same. They'll be putting up plating to cover the sides." He edged carefully back to the airlock with me close behind. "I can tell you never told Moira how you felt. She's walking around all day like she's got fleas."

"Telling her's not going to do anything," I said. "Pretty sure our problems run deeper than that."

Still, she was there when I came out of the airlock, where the EVA mate should have been. "What are you doing here?" I asked, as she popped the seals on my helmet and guided it off my head.

"Hard to get good help these days," she said cryptically. By which she meant, if I wasn't mistaken, that she didn't quite trust Goldstein after the confrontation the other day.

And she did trust me? That was a cheerful thought, as I squirmed my way out of the suit. I stowed the pieces in the correct lockers and headed down to my berth to change my shirt. The spacewalk had been short enough that it wasn't disgusting, but I still felt the need for a fresh one.

Only as I reached the door of my berth did I notice Moira trailing me. "Can we talk?" she asked when I turned. "Privately."

She waited, arms folded, for me to shut the door. Her face was strangely blank. "I found something in the engines," she said evenly. She held it out in front of her. "Did you do this?"

It was my ignition switch, that I'd never removed from the fuel valve. I stared at it, knowing my face was giving me away, but unable to do a thing about it. "Moira, I—"

"How could you?" she cried. "After you *promised*. I thought you were on our side now. Or at least halfway so. Maybe I was just hearing what I wanted to hear."

"I didn't break my promise," I insisted. "That was before."

"You were always watched before."

"It was at Deimos."

She regarded me, the ignition switch still drifting in front of her. "I don't know whether to believe you."

That hurt more than anything else she could say. "I thought you always knew you could believe me."

"You're smarter than that," she said, dark eyes snapping. "You don't lie, but you're not so bad at choosing what to leave out."

"Fine," I said. "Ask me anything. I'll answer."

"Why did you put it there and not set it?"

"I did set it," I said, cheeks burning. "Then I got worried you were going to get left behind, and that made me think you would surely be caught if I let it go off, so I ducked back below and un-set it."

A smile started to rise on her lips, and she jerked it down. "How is that being a loyal officer?"

"It wasn't. I failed. I—well, you know I've given up on that now. I'm not going back. I decided."

"But you still won't join my crew."

"No. I don't believe in the Navy anymore. It must have been good at one time, but it's too far gone now. That doesn't mean I believe in what you're doing. And anyway, it's not safe for me to join you. Sooner or later, your names and faces will get on a wanted list on Mars—those that aren't already. I can't let them find out I deserted."

"You're still trying to protect your reputation?" She raised an eyebrow. "But you said you didn't think you could get back."

"Not for me!" I said quickly. "For my family."

"You don't want them to be embarrassed by you?"

"Moira! You said you wanted the whole truth. Can you quit guessing for five seconds and let me try to tell it?"

She held up her hands. "Okay. Okay. Try."

"As long as I'm missing, my family gets my pay. Right?" She nodded. "And if I'm declared dead, they get my death benefit. Which is a lot. Might be enough for them to keep the house. At least pay off enough of the interest that they can get ahead of it, maybe make some kind of income off whatever land they can keep."

She shook her head in frustration. "It's always money with you. Would it be so bad for your family to have to live like the rest of us do? Working in a factory or on a farm isn't a death sentence, Lucy!"

"You thought that's what it was? You thought I was just afraid to be poor?"

"Isn't that why you—" Her voice cracked, as though not

wanting to repeat any of what I had said that time, not wanting to remember that awful argument. "Why you wanted to marry some rich woman?"

I stared at the floor. Of course that's what she had thought. I hadn't said.

"It's William," I said quietly, eyes fixed on my hands. "His care isn't cheap. His companion gets three hundred a year. And if we lose the house at the seaside, I don't know how he'd cope. He's always lived in that house. Being near the water makes a big difference for him. The thought of making him live with me in some garret—"

"I'm sorry," she said softly. "I didn't realize. You never explained."

"You never gave me a chance. You left without talking to me again."

She gave a low, humorless chuckle. "Well, you didn't seem to want any more of me."

I shot her a quick look. "You'd never let that stop you before. I thought for sure, if you felt that way, you'd be throwing rocks at my window within a day or two. I thought—" A lump swelled in my throat. "I thought you'd fight harder for me." Tears glazed my eyes, a thick bubble distorting my sight, with no gravity to make them fall.

Her hand was under my chin, forcing me to look up at her. I blinked hard, trying to hide the tears. "In fairness to me," she said softly, "have I made that mistake since?"

I opened my mouth, wanting to answer, but my throat felt choked. I should be backing off, leaving the room, finding a way to make some kind of distance. Like I always did. Instead I could only feel happy that she was finally here, listening, understanding, not angry at me.

She moved closer, brushing my mouth with hers. The breath went out of me. Abruptly I remembered that kiss so long ago.

How much I wanted it then. How much more I had wanted it once I had stopped it.

Reaching out, I slid one hand into her hair—that thick, black hair, which always used to work out of anything she used to fasten it, to leave that one strand always brushing her cheek. I cupped the back of her head.

"Not going to run away this time, officer?" she murmured, her breath tickling my lips.

I pulled hard, bringing my lips firmly against hers. Yes. Like this. It had tasted like this, felt like this, made my body grow warm like this. But no, I wasn't going to run away. Not ever.

She drew a shuddering breath between kisses. "My god, Lucy, do you know how bad I—"

"Yes," I gasped, pressing my lips to her throat and my palm to her bare belly, where I'd been staring since she'd started wearing that distracting cropped shirt. "You really think I haven't been— with you wearing *that?*"

"I wanted to get your attention." Her hand ran over my left breast, and the tight binding of my stays did nothing to muffle the exact moment she brushed the nipple.

"Mission accomplished," I gasped, untying the knot in her shirt.

We should talk first, I kept thinking, there are things we should be working out ... but I couldn't stop, now that we'd started. Now that the several feet of cool air I'd always tried to keep between us was gone.

She finished undoing my buttons and pulled my shirt off, flicking it off to the side with a decided snap. Soon we hung in a cloud of discarded clothing, clinging to each other, bare skin drawing heat from bare skin.

No more words were said. Was it because we knew each other so well nothing needed to be said, or because we were afraid of breaking the spell?

She spun me slowly around her, and I felt myself falling, bound by her gravity. I couldn't escape; I couldn't even want to. I wanted to fall toward her forever.

Later, we hung together in midair, our legs tangled together and her face snuggled into my neck. I took a deep breath and let it slowly out. Now would be the time to say something. To define what this was all about.

It hadn't been a decision, that I was sure of. I hadn't thought it over and decided to sleep with Moira any more than I had decided to betray Mars. I had slowly slid into these things, helpless to resist.

She was always my weakness. I knew at eighteen years old that I couldn't resist her. That I had to push her away because if I didn't, sooner or later I was going to have to give in. And somehow I had been too slow this time, gotten caught.

Khan's advice was useless to me here. Stop driving the machine: done. And then what? Sleep with the enemy of the Martian people? I couldn't even think of her as that, even though I knew she was. I was compromised much too deeply, with her dark hair tickling my neck and her lean body stretched out against mine. In bed with the enemy.

I tried to weigh my passion for her against all of Mars and I couldn't. My brain simply refused to admit that there could be conflict. Moira: good. Mars: good. Moira headed to Ares Station, to destroy Mars' independence: impossible.

Moira probably thought this was all a set of decisions. That I had decided to be her lover now, that I had decided to join her crew. I should set her straight. It was a kind of dishonesty to let her go on believing this was anything other than a moment of weakness on my part.

"You're quiet," she said sleepily. "What are you thinking?"

My breath caught. I wanted to say, and I didn't want to. How do you tell someone they're your weakness?

"Nothing," I said at last. *Let it lie. Let me pretend. Let me have this moment with my best friend, with my lover, just this once.* I fumbled for a new topic to forestall any more questions. "I didn't know you had tattoos."

"I didn't, last time you saw me naked. When was that, even?"

"Founders' Day, when you—"

"When I pushed you in the lake, right." She gave a low chuckle, her breath tickling my neck. "And jumped in after you, and we both had to take off our clothes and dry them by the bonfire. How old were we?"

"Twelve," I said. I had been so embarrassed when I saw my body had changed so much and hers hadn't yet. I had felt indecent, standing out in the sun with my growing breasts and a patch of down between my legs, where there had been none last summer. And there she was, still lean and brown and unashamed. And beautiful. The only thing that embarrassed me more than my own body was how much I wanted to look at hers.

"The horse, I understand," I said, brushing my fingers along her back, where it stretched from one shoulderblade to the other. "Is it Orbit?"

"Of course," she said. "I loved him more than any of the others. Is he still—"

"He went to Lord Liu-Kuznetsov's near Schaeberle, to be a stud there. It seemed a good place for him." The next tattoo, on her bicep, was a familiar shape: a circle, marked with a diagonal gash and three dots in a line. Mars, with the Marineris and the three Tharsis volcanoes. Underneath were the letters MPP. "What's MPP?"

"Mars is the planet and people," she said. "When I left, I hated Mars so much. Hated everything about it. The stupid class system, and how it came between you and me. How impossible it was to change anything. But I was homesick, too. I missed riding, and my dads, and sitting on the beach at night. So I got that one to remind me, Mars isn't the Empire. It isn't only the things I hate. I love the planet and the people; I always will."

I put my palm over the tattoo and squeezed her more tightly against me. How could I ever have thought of her as a traitor?

"I'm so sorry you can't go back."

I felt her swallow hard, and she tucked her face closer against my neck. It was damp. "So am I," she said huskily.

I was quiet for a while. There was nothing I could say to that. I, too, planned never to go back to Mars, but I hadn't had enough time away from it to feel it the way she did. And could I ever feel the way she did, when she'd had such a love affair with the outdoors, with a horse that ran so fast it was like flying?

But I was curious about the last one, so I slid my hand down to the crease between her hip and her thigh. "And this one? LPC?" I couldn't think of a Khan slogan for that one. "Let the people … command?"

She burst out into peals of laughter, pulling her face out of my neck and wiping her nose. "Lucy, you absolute idiot. You beautiful dunce. Are you hypoxic? It's embroidered on your fucking handkerchiefs."

The blood rushed to my face. Of course it was. Of course. I laughed with her, laughed at my own stupidity, laughed for sheer joy of being here with her and able to laugh. And because she had loved me enough to tattoo my initials on her groin, while I was still busy fuming and resenting and blaming everyone but myself. Marron was right. I didn't deserve this woman.

Eventually she peeled herself away from me and gathered up

her clothes. "We'll be reaching the station soon," she said, pulling her trousers over her hips.

"I want to go with you," I said abruptly, surprising myself.

"You do? I thought you didn't believe in what we were doing."

I moved over to her and ran one finger down her spine, from the nape of her neck down to the small of her back. "I don't even know anymore. Sometimes I think, maybe I just don't have a conscience like you have."

"How can you say that? You're the most conscientious person I've ever met."

"I follow rules. Out here I'm far out of my depth. I don't know what's right. I don't know if it's right to help you, or if I should be stopping you. But I …" I slid my palm back up, circled around her shoulderblade, and back to her hair. "I just want to be with you."

After she'd unlocked the hatch and left again, I hung in the air a while longer, thinking. I wanted to believe I was finally being brave, finally making a decision for myself. But instead I felt like I had thrown my hands in the air and made no choice at all. Had I given in to the inevitable, or only given up?

And yet I felt oddly comfortable hanging here, without my uniform to hide behind, my hair unbraided and circling my head like a starburst. I was so tired of feeling conflicted. Hadn't I fought long enough?

All I wanted, now that I had given in once, was to keep giving in. Just dive headlong after her and not think. Not because I thought it was right, but because I was exhausted with trying to chart a moral course.

In orbit, you aren't really floating. You're falling all the time, but falling forward so fast you never hit the ground. That was all I wanted to do from now on. Fall forward and hope Moira's gravity would swing me around.

I closed my eyes and watched cosmic rays trace their faint flashes under my lids. No more of this agonizing. No thinking at all. Just Moira.

Eighteen

The braking laser shut off, and the crew leapt to furl the sails. Ares Station hung in space like a massive wheel, spinning rapidly. Several ships hung nearby—I counted five, all Navy vessels. We shouldn't be out of place, then.

"Ares Station, this is privately owned vessel *Melpomene*, of Tharsis Enterprises," said Moira on the radio. "We are requesting permission to dock."

"I don't know you, *Melpomene*," said the fuzzy voice on the other end. "You file a flight plan?"

Moira leaned closer to the radio, eyes flicking around wildly. "No ma'am, didn't realize I had to. Is there somebody I should do that with?"

"Next time, file it at Phobos. They radio it ahead. With the war on, can't be too careful."

There was a long pause. "Are they turning us away?" I hissed.

"I was sort of counting on being able to take on gases here," said Moira, her peasant accent deliberately broad. "Can we make an exception this time?"

"Hm," said the voice. "You sure do sound Martian. Hey, how about this. Remember the Nepenthe Cup two years ago?"

"How could I forget? I had five bob on Fraction of C. Took the missus to Gagaringrad."

There was a staticky burst of laughter. "Lucky you. I put a tenner on Olympian Sunrise and lost it all. Pull to three hundred meters and we'll expect your launch."

The launch held only Martians, and only those Moira felt she could trust—a dozen men in all, and all our empty gas canisters. That part of our cover story wasn't a lie—we had used a lot of oxygen restoring proper pressure after the leak.

We docked on the sunward face of the wheel, near the rim, where all the airlocks were placed so that passengers could stroll out easily under the local gravity. The moment we locked on, the floor seemed to come up from below. The gravity felt right in my bones. Exactly Mars normal.

As I came out of the launch, I stopped and stared. This place was nothing like Aphrodite. Aphrodite was a commercial station, filled with flashing lights and businesses. This…this was a garden in space. The whole wall at my back blazed with sunlight, and the curving concourse was a riot of shades of green.

"Eighteen inches thick," said the woman who met us at the airlock, seeing me staring at the window. "So you're in no danger from radiation, even long term."

I eyed the window respectfully. We certainly didn't have any kind of armament that could get through eighteen inches of radiation plating. And with the size of the thing, a blast would barely jostle anyone inside. We would have to think of something else.

On the way to the station, I had cherished the private hope that we would somehow be able to infiltrate it in one go and have the whole job finished by the time the others got there. But it was soon clear that wasn't possible. Our escort ushered us along a carefully determined path, and we passed quite a few red-coated marines at attention along the concourse. Mars had spent years building this station and rested in it all their hopes for full economic independence. They weren't going to leave their jewel lying around unguarded.

The woman led us to a pleasant food court. "Please do make yourselves at ease," she said. "I've booked you with the docks master in an hour to discuss your gas needs. Just follow that sign."

I ordered a pot of tea. Hot food was difficult to handle aboard ship, and in any event, tea out of a pouch wasn't the same. This tea came in a china pot, actually steaming, with two cups and a little pitcher of milk—reconstituted, surely, but milk!

Moira had dressed conservatively, for once: dark trousers and a berry-red coat, her white neckcloth spilling over the collar. It reminded me of the riding clothes she used to wear, back on Mars. And how I had wanted to unbutton that coat. I poured her tea with a practiced hand.

"You've got to ask them if the station has engines," I said. "Milk?"

She gave a startled little jerk. "What?"

"What's distracting you?"

"Look around," she said quietly. "Look at all the people."

I scanned the crowd. Was something wrong? And then I saw it. Martians, dressed in the clothes I remembered, with the soft accents of Hellas and Aeolia and Xanthe. The scent of the tea rose to my nose, bringing with it still more nostalgia.

"It's just like home," she whispered. "It's probably the closest to home we'll ever be again."

I looked back at her, stricken. She was right. I poured milk into my tea and watched it bloom into a pale cloud. I hadn't bargained on feeling this homesick, here leagues from home in the black. Just as they had done with Mars itself, my people had come upon barrenness and left it flowering. They didn't mind hacking their freedom out of cold space any more than barren rock.

Had I been too cavalier about leaving home forever? Here I was on Martian territory again. All I had to do was tell that nice woman the truth. With a few strategic omissions of how I'd collaborated with the pirates. I could be home free, and nothing would happen to this beautiful station.

Moira drank her tea, oblivious to the conflict inside me. She wouldn't have this trouble. She knew what she wanted, what she had to do, and what she was sacrificing. Nostalgia could be a simple thing for her—just sadness, not temptation.

The other afternoon had been straightforward for her. She'd been trying to get back with me for so long, and had finally gotten what she wanted. What she had chosen for herself. I had gotten myself so conflicted in conscience that I couldn't choose at all. I had simply let it happen—let my deprived heart and body have what they wanted at last, because I couldn't come up with a good reason to deny them anymore. But I couldn't deceive myself; it wasn't really an answer.

I looked at her, where her dusky throat stood out against the white of her neckcloth, and the dark hair hung over her face the way I remembered. Nothing had changed, had it? Everything was still a mess; nothing was going to be simple. So it was best to stay on plan. Don't think. Don't decide. Just keep falling forward.

"I'm going to go over to the information desk over there," Moira said, throwing back the last of her tea. "See if they have maps or anything."

I sat alone with my tea, pouring a fresh cup just so I could watch the milk swirl again. William had loved to watch it. If you poured a cup without calling him over to look, he'd snub you all afternoon.

A shadow fell across my teacup. "Prescott, of all the people!"

I jumped to my feet, tension crackling through my body. We hadn't brought weapons, for fear of a search at the airlock, but perhaps if I got the first punch in … My brain registered the lanky body, orange hair, acne. "Bing?"

He grasped my hand firmly. "Well, I'll be. How did you get here?"

"I might ask the same of you!"

"Oh, after we brought the *Andromeda* in—good prize out of that, by the way, our shares were one hundred ten pounds each—I got assigned here. It's a cush assignment, let me tell you. Gravity everywhere but the hub, and I don't have to go to the hub much."

As he talked, I kept half my mind on his words. He was a veritable fountain of information about this station, and information was what I needed. With the rest, I tried to work out a cover story.

"But you!" he was saying. "After Captain Kim got rescued without you, I thought you were a goner. Especially as neither you nor Maggie showed up in the hostage lists."

"I ended up having to find another way home," I said. "Without Maggie, I'm afraid. I'm not sure where she is right now. I got free of the pirates and worked my passage on a merchant vessel. I assume from here I should be able to get home well enough."

He cast me an admiring look. "I should say so! The hero's welcome, after all that."

Out of the corner of my eye, I saw Moira coming back from the information kiosk, then spotting me and veering away. I longed to give her just one look, somehow send her a message with my eyes, but if I looked, Bing would look, and he knew Moira.

"Come on," I said. "I haven't had the tour. You have to show me *everything*."

He cheerfully complied with my request, leading me the whole long walk around the rim, past concourses lined with trees and through greenhouses where beans grew up the leeward wall in the blazing sunlight from the opposite side. There was even a whole sector just for water processing: open sewage tanks, settling tanks, algae tanks. "Funny to see those standing open, when on a ship everything has to be covered," I said. "If the station ever stops spinning, that water will go everywhere."

"It's never going to. It took ten ships loaded with fuel to spin it up in the first place. Would take the same amount to stop it."

"So it doesn't have engines of its own?"

"No. Can't, really. Trying to keep them pointed the right way while the whole thing is spinning would be almost impossible. No, if an asteroid crosses our path, we have ships tow us out of the way."

I frowned. "Wouldn't that be just as bad? Where do they attach their grapples without getting swung around by them?"

He waved his hands in the air vaguely. "Imagine a bicycle wheel, spinning. Where could you grab it without hurting yourself?"

I ran my tongue around my teeth, thinking. "Only by the axle. But you can't have an axle here. Nothing can rotate freely while passing through the hull without letting the air out in the gap. To stop the air you'd have to weld it and then you wouldn't exactly have an axle."

He shrugged. "All right, not an axle, exactly. Two spindles. They're in a socket sort of thing on the outside, on ball bearings. They don't spin, and the ships grapple onto that."

I tried to picture it. Was there some way we could use this to control the station? Swoop in, grapple the spindle and drag it around like Moira's crew had done to the *Mariposa*? I didn't think so, not given the relative mass of the station and any of our ships.

"That must be a massive load to pull," I said. "What would you say its mass is, total?"

"Gross? About ten million tons, give or take. Net is exactly eight million, but I don't know the exact amount of cargo on it right now."

I filed the information away. "Mostly just from the mining operations, right?"

"Yeah, you want to see?"

He brought me to a doorway that unlocked with a key (a problem, I noted) and up a long ladder. As we rose, the illusion of gravity fell away and was replaced by a spinning sensation.

"Sorry," he said, as I clung to the ladder to keep it from sliding away sideways. "It even gives me a funny stomach."

"I'll be all right," I said, and kept climbing.

We came out on an open concourse, like the one below, but with a much tighter curve. The ceiling here was low and connected to the floor by a network of struts. "To keep the wheel attached to the hub?" I asked, gesturing to them.

"And to hang onto. Look." Bing stepped off the ladder and staggered sideways, grabbing at a strut. I followed him, off-balance from the motion. A memory flickered into my mind: the day William and I rode a carousel in Landing, back when our family still tried to winter together in the city. He had been eager to sit on the unicorn till the ride had started, but the second it began moving up and down, he had panicked and begun to scream. I clambered off my bay horse, which was across the carousel from him, and tried to walk across the empty center to get to him. I must have been five or six, and had thought I could simply walk in a straight line. But the motion of the ride had confused my steps, left me staggering sideways when I tried to beeline to my brother.

I hadn't thought of that day in years, but the spinning station gave just the same sensation in my rubbery legs and my inner ear. I could walk, sort of, barely held down by the centrifugal force, but not at all in a straight line.

"You all right there?" Bing had gained his footing, strut still in hand to steady him.

"I think so." Using the struts, I picked my way over to him. The ceiling was so low I could reach out and touch it with my free hand. Bing was ducking slightly to keep from cracking his head. "What's above us here? Why doesn't the ladder go any further?"

"That's all storage. The wheel wobbles less the more mass is at the hub, but it's almost impossible to *do* anything up there with the changing vectors, so they just put in these big tanks. Over our heads here is oxygen. Then over there a little is rocket fuel. Water is the other way."

He pointed out a pipe, leading out of the tank and down the spoke, alongside the ladder. "It's filled and dispensed down below. Much safer to have the refineries all on the rim, where nothing can fly into the air. We bring in the crushed rock and ice through the leeward airlocks, melt it down, and process it. We bottle a thousand tanks of oxygen a week, and more than that of hydrogen fuel. Of course some water gets tanked as-is, too. And the metals get kept, too, if they're useful. We're shipping back materials every month for the war effort."

"Truly astounding," I said, and meant it. This was everything Mars had ever wanted: gasses to replenish the atmosphere; metals for ships; fuel. Everything it had struggled to produce on its own.

We started back downward, past the dizzy spinning and into the false gravity. "Have you reported to the commandant yet?" asked Bing.

"Not yet."

"I'll bring you—the offices are right by here."

My knuckles whitened on the ladder rungs. "Do you get many merchant ships here? Besides the government shipping?"

"Not many. The one that just docked is the only one I've seen all week."

So no chance of passing myself off as having come from somewhere else. "The *Melpomene*," I said helpfully.

"So where did you meet up with it?"

Good question, I thought. Where in the system could a Martian ship want to stop before the asteroid belt, besides Mars? But just then, we reached the main offices.

Bing's cheery deference got me through the layers of clerks in the outer offices, and I was finally ushered into the commandant's presence. She was a formidable presence: stocky and broad, with sharp black eyes and iron-gray hair. "Captain, may I present Midshipman Lucy Prescott-Chin. Mister Prescott, Captain Li-Popov."

I saluted. "Reporting for duty, sir."

"I remember seeing your name on the missing list, Mister Prescott. From the *Mariposa*?"

"Yes, sir."

"The pirates released Captain Kim and Lieutenant Brown, but kept the two midshipmen," put in Bing. "She found her way back on her own."

"Mr. Abington, I do not appreciate interruptions. You are dismissed."

Bing shut his mouth and saluted sharply before turning around.

"I'm sure the Admiralty will question you left, right, and backwards before allowing you to return to duty," she said. "My own duty is only to ship you back there at the nearest possible opportunity. Luckily the *Destiny* is departing at nineteen-hundred hours, so you won't need to spend a single day here."

I curled my toes inside my boots. Nineteen hundred hours?

At best the rest of the pirate fleet wouldn't arrive till tomorrow. "Yes, sir. Am I at liberty until then?"

She nodded and scribbled out a chit to hand to me. "While you have time, find yourself a proper uniform. They have shops in the market quadrant."

I stumbled out of the office, clutching the credit chit. It could have gone worse. There could have been a more serious interrogation; I would have had to work out some barely-plausible route for the imaginary *Melpomene* and hope they never checked with Moira. But it also could have gone better. Now I had only a few hours to somehow get out of going back to Mars.

Because it was clear that was what I had to do. For a moment I had been entranced by the green leaves, the splashing fountains, the way strangers nodded politely as they passed. I had forgotten the beatings, the airlocking, the rape. I missed Mars; I didn't miss the Imperial Navy.

Soon there would be a battle, and good people like Bing might not survive it. I wasn't happy about that. But there were good people on the ships heading this way too, and they had to carry out this mission to live.

Don't think, I reminded myself. *Keep falling forward. None of this really relies on you.*

I hurried back to the food court where I had parted from Moira—what, an hour ago? She wasn't there. Of course she had her meeting with the station master; I wasn't sure how long that was supposed to take. I headed back toward the airlock, only to find my way blocked by frowning marines. Right, I was dressed in civilian clothes and no longer had an escort.

Past the food court was the market district where I managed to buy a dress jacket. My breeches and waistcoat would do. Though considerably worn, they had been my original uniform ones. A hat finished the picture. The cost recorded by the shopkeeper made me cringe. Money my family wouldn't get to see, deducted from my account with the Admiralty.

I wondered, briefly, how often the station radioed Mars. Would my parents find out I was alive by my appearance here? Or would the station be destroyed before word got back?

Would I be exposed as a traitor when the mission ultimately failed?

Now in proper uniform, I returned to the corridor and was saluted by the marines. That simple, eh? Though I supposed the shops wouldn't have sold a uniform without the commandant's note to identify me. At last I reached the proper airlock.

The launch was gone.

Two marines stood beside it, swords at their sides. "Wasn't there a launch here recently?" I asked.

"It left, sir," said the senior of the two. "They seemed in an almighty hurry."

I chewed my lip. A hurry because they'd been found out? No, they would never have been allowed to leave if they had. Perhaps because Moira meant to leave me on purpose. I took a deep, shuddering breath. Of course she thought I'd betrayed her. I hadn't even known for sure I wouldn't until after the fact.

I walked on, past the airlock, past an area of ore processing— whole rooms full of large tanks. Which ones were splitting water into hydrogen and oxygen, or making rocket fuel? A well-placed bomb here might about do the trick, if the rooms weren't locked and if I had had anything like a bomb. I kept going till I reached one of the agricultural sectors.

This one was arranged to be parklike, with a pond and fountain in the middle and walkways passing among the plants. More importantly, no one was here. I went to the sunward wall, the one that was all one thick glass window, and gazed out.

With no air to defuse the light, the stars were clearly in view, as long as I covered the sun with my hand. And there, in black against the stars, was the *Mariposa*, false name clearly visible on the side.

I rummaged in my pockets and pulled out my tiny hand mirror. It was in the regs to always keep one, since radios couldn't be relied on, and so it had ridden in my breeches pocket since I'd left Mars. I carefully aimed it at the *Mariposa*, moving the mirror slowly to track along with it. No one anywhere else would see the bright flash.

PRESCOTT REPORTING IN, I flashed out in Morse code.

There was a long pause. Then GOD LUCY WHAT THE FUCK

GOT RECOGNIZED, HAD NO CHOICE, I flashed. DID NOT BLOW YR COVER.

Again a pause. I imagined Moira rifling through the possible replies. "Sorry I left without you"? "Will you be there when we attack?"

I decided to bail her out. THEY SHIP ME HOME TO-NIGHT. WILL TRY TO GET AS MUCH INTEL AS POSS BEFORE THEN.

How to say, *this is goodbye forever?* How to say, *I hope they don't hang me when they figure out my story doesn't add up?* How to say, *this wasn't what I would have chosen?*

There was no way, so I started on the intel. GAS STORES IN HUB. COMMAND CENTER 6 DEGREES SPINWARD OF MY LOC. RADIO PROB CNTRLD FROM THERE. AIR-LOCKS SPACED 15 DEG APART THROUGHOUT. EACH GUARDED 2 MARINES. TOTAL MASS OF STATION TEN MIL TONS.

I waited. THANK YOU. BE SAFE OFFICER, she flashed back.

I turned away, tears swimming in my eyes. Then I turned back, realizing there was something I hadn't said. Something I had never said.

I LOVE YOU, I flashed.

There was a longer pause, then the *Mariposa* flashed back. CAPN CRYING TOO HARD TO RESPOND. THIS IS MARRON. SHE LOVES YOU TOO. GET MOVING BEFORE SOMEONE SPOTS YOU.

NINETEEN

I kept moving anti-spinward, past the garden and through a place like a factory floor where people packaged metal ore into crates. It seemed there were three types of places on this station: places of no possible use to me, places that were full of people, and places that were locked.

My first mission ought to be finding a weapon. Ideally a sword, but I'd accept a kitchen knife or a blowtorch at this point. But I could hardly walk up to the marines' armory and request one. Even on the *Mariposa*, access to weapons was at need only. Here, where civilians were all over the place, it would be even harder to find one.

I turned around, made it back to the food court, and ordered dinner from the nicest restaurant on the arcade. May as well fall back on some of the old, aristocratic skills. My meal, a sort of knobbly pasta with beans, was flawless, but I called the waiter back over regardless.

"I hate to complain," I said, with the tone of a person who

actually likes nothing better. "But I really don't think this could be described as *al dente*."

The waiter stammered. "Well, I could have the chef remake it . . ."

"I'm afraid it would end up the same as before, don't you think? Insanity is doing the same thing over and expecting different results. Can I speak to the chef? I want to *see* how they're making this."

Eventually the waiter, realizing I couldn't be mollified any other way, escorted me into the kitchen. "I'm sorry, boss," the man said, as he preceded me inside. "She insisted."

The chef, flushed with repressed frustration, endured my questions about the water temperature, the salt, the semolina content of the noodles. "We're under very difficult conditions here, as you can see!" she protested. "No meat at all, milk only reconstituted, salt rationed, air pressure too low to make a proper boil, and despite all that, I've produced a really acceptable pasta!"

"I think *I* could do better," I said archly.

"Fine!" cried the chef. "Be my guest! Don't let me stop you!"

I tinkered with the heat on the stove, added more salt to the water, and dumped in the pasta. I was going to utterly ruin it, but it didn't matter. While we had been arguing, I had slipped a chef's knife into my coat.

When the mess was done—or rather, severely underdone—I tasted it, pronounced it more to my liking, and marched off with the air of someone who has shown up all the experts. I crunched my way through the pasta, wrote a large tip on the bill, and made my way out.

First goal: accomplished. Now all I needed was to find some way to smooth a path for the boarding parties, when they arrived tomorrow. Unlocking the airlocks would help, but I couldn't get past two marines with one knife, and someone would surely lock them again. Some kind of bomb? It had to go off near when they'd arrive, not now.

No. What I needed next was a set of keys. And I knew someone who had them.

I found Bing rushing out of the main offices and toward one of the stairwells. "So did you get orders home?" he asked, as I walked alongside him.

"Yes, I leave tonight. But I'm at loose ends right now. Can I help you?"

"Oh, ancestors, can you ever. We're scheduled for gun drills first thing tomorrow, but I've only checked the first bank of guns. I have to get them all done before I can go off duty."

"I can do that," I offered cheerfully. I certainly knew how to service torpedo tubes; it was something we had to do incessantly on the *Mariposa*. But I felt a sinking sensation. We had calculated on the ships parked around the station. But I hadn't told Moira the station itself was armed. I hoped I would get a chance to.

When we reached the second level, up a locked staircase, I stood stock-still. I had imagined perhaps five or ten guns. This was thirty, all in a row, long tubes poking through the radiation glass. And not the standard size, either—at least double the size of the *Mariposa*'s guns.

I made the appropriate impressed noises, making Bing flush with pride, and set to work. Every tube needed to be opened, unloaded, inspected, dry fired to test the mechanism, and finally reloaded with a thoroughly inspected new torpedo. That had been easy on the *Mariposa*, where there was no gravity to worry about and the mass of the torpedoes was only fifty pounds in the first place. Here the torpedoes were one hundred pounds, unwieldy even in the slightly lower gravity of the second level.

An Earther could have done it, I scolded myself. One hundred pounds in less than a third gravity? They could carry more than that in a backpack. I carefully maneuvered the first torpedo out of its tube, bending my knees to avoid straining my back. It was all right, really, like swinging bales of hay in the stables with Moira.

Instinctively I shied away from the memory. But no, I didn't have to do that anymore. I could remember those times now. I could remember everything, treasure everything, even keep the fights and the broken hearts as parts of a larger story.

I smiled, laid the bulky cylinder beside the tube, and went on with my work more cheerfully.

Bing had started at the other end, and when we met in the middle, he straightened up with a smile. "Shame you'll be gone before we do the drill," he said. "It's a thing to see."

"Doesn't the station's spin make them hard to aim?"

"Incredibly hard," he said. "We put out targets to practice on, sometimes. It doesn't waste the torpedoes, because we can go out and collect them after. You just learn to account for the way we're moving." He put a hand to the aiming crank. "See, imagine Capella there was an enemy. I can keep a steady aim on it by slowly turning the crank, right? That accounts for our motion. But I don't want to do that, I want to aim a few degrees left of it—anti-spinward—so that when the torpedo leaves the tube and drifts spinward, it'll still hit."

"And the men can do it?"

"At least sixty percent of the time, now. Hoping for sixty-five tomorrow. We get an extra rum ration if we do."

Back downstairs, Bing took his leave and went back to the offices to report. His keys safe in my pocket, I hurried the other way. It wouldn't take him long to realize he'd mislaid them. But given his trust in me, he'd probably check everywhere he'd been before he considered I might have them. I swallowed hard to clear the sour taste of guilt.

And by the time he started looking for me, he wouldn't be the only one. My ship departed in twenty minutes. If I wasn't on it, I'd be absent without leave. I wasn't sure how much time or energy they'd spend searching for me, but I had to assume they'd be on the lookout.

I had implied to Moira that I would be on that departing ship. It was clear by now that I couldn't possibly do that. There was too much at stake. If she attacked tomorrow with the others, with those huge guns trained on her, she didn't stand a chance. I had to find more ways to help her from here. Still, better that Moira didn't spend a second worrying about whether I'd be caught in the crossfire of her attack on the station.

That meant I'd have to find a place to hide until the shift change, which would happen soon if they kept a regular watch rotation. Once the commandant and Bing were off duty, and the ship detailed to return me had left, there would be no one on the station who knew my face. I just needed to lie low for a few hours.

I took a flight of stairs to the upper level. Up here, a little way spinward of the guns, were barracks for the marines and sailors. Further on was a hotel district, above the food court: also no good. Finally I found a storage closet that opened to my key. It held mops and buckets. I curled up in a corner to wait.

I woke a few hours later to the clangor of an alarm bell. I tried to spring away from the wall, only to collapse onto the floor. Gravity. I had forgotten. My back and shoulders were knotted with pain from how I'd slept.

More carefully, I rose to my feet and stretched. How long had I been sleeping? I hadn't meant to sleep at all.

On the mezzanine outside, a company of marines quick-marched past. I leaned over the railing and looked down. People were rushing around in all directions, and the soft murmur of conversation had been replaced with a hubbub loud enough to be heard over the continuing clang of the alarm. Some stood in bunches, staring out the window to sunward.

I squinted toward the window, but could see nothing but stars from here. The *Mariposa* hung where it had before, and a few Navy ships. I had to get downstairs, where I could get up to the window for a better view.

The stairs were a crush of people, some struggling up, others down. From the gabble, it was clear they had no idea what was going on either. I made it downstairs and elbowed my way between two clusters of gawkers.

Without a glass, I couldn't guess much better than they could what we might be looking for. Moira would have one, but I didn't dare try to flicker a light at her with so many people around and staring out. They would pick up her answer the same as I could.

Shaping my hands into a makeshift telescope, I scanned the stars. Nothing, nothing, nothing. Wait. One of the stars in Gemini was occluded. Something was there. Without a glass, I couldn't say what.

A tap on my shoulder made me jerk guiltily. "Prescott!" said Bing. "I thought you'd've been gone by now."

Close to the truth would make the best lie. "I fell asleep," I said with an embarrassed grimace. "Meant to take a little rest while I waited for the launch to depart, and when I woke up it was gone."

"It's just as well," he said, pulling his glass out of his pocket. "Take a look, out by—"

"Gemini," I finished. "I can see something." I turned it toward the missing star and gazed. "Wait, that's—" I stopped. I sounded surprised. I shouldn't sound like I had expected an attack fleet instead. "Is it an asteroid?"

He took the glass back and stuffed it into his pocket. "Can't be anything else. But it's strange. We weren't expecting anything from that direction tonight. Normally we come upon them from downstream, as we pass comet trails. This one's coming from upstream and sunward. Must be pretty eccentric. Not mapped or anything, but then, it's not very large."

I followed him through the concourse. "How big do they think it is?"

"Big enough still to do some damage. Maybe half a k across? If it hits us, and they think it's on a course to, it could plow right through us. So we're putting together an emergency plan."

"Where ships pull you out of its course, like you told me?"

"Yes. Trouble is, the ships don't have enough emergency fuel to do it on hand, so the first task is to shuttle fuel from there to here. Hey! That's something you could do for me. The ship you came on, the *Melpomene*, is still here. Can you hail the captain?"

I pulled out my mirror. "Aye aye."

He hung over my shoulder as I stood at the window across from the naval offices. Carefully I began with, CAPTAIN RAJASTHAN, Moira's alias. Then STATION REQUESTS ASSISTANCE. CAN YOU AND SMALL TEAM COME ON LAUNCH?

I held my breath, waiting for a reply. Surely they would understand I was being watched. HAPPY TO ASSIST. WILL BE THERE SHORTLY. I let my breath out.

I relayed the airlock number Bing gave me and turned away. Moira would be here. Good. At least, I thought so. I wanted to see her. Though with all these people around, and the façade of helping move the station, I wouldn't be able to pull her into my arms like I wanted to. But I could breathe the air she was breathing. That suddenly mattered so much.

We could also talk about what was happening. Did she know? Was this somehow the plan? But it hadn't been the plan when we had left the fleet, and we had kept radio silence since then. But what were the odds it was some rogue asteroid, coming from that direction, at this exact moment?

"We'll need all the help we can get," said Bing, leading me toward the offices. "With a surprise like this, there's not much time to work with. The commandant is trying to decide whether to evacuate non-essential personnel, to be safe."

"I would," I said without thinking, and then more carefully, "I mean, if nothing else, it would get them out of the way."

He laughed, pulling open the door to the naval offices. "Very fair point. These civilians are gunk in the gears today for certain."

Everyone inside was clustered around a large telescope, much bigger than the one Bing had lent me. A midshipman slowly turned a crank to keep it aligned against the station's rotation. The commandant took her eye away from it, a grim look on her face.

"I think you're right," she was telling someone beside her. "Those aren't craters."

One by one everyone had to have a look. I took mine last. The asteroid was a dark, irregular spot against the stars. From here the sun was almost behind it, so we could see few of its features. But within the dark patch were five tiny specks. Specks that glinted.

Ships.

"They're closer to us than it is," said the commandant. "I can't say how much. They've gotten ahead of it to conceal their approach, and will arrive in the middle of our operation."

"Should we belay the operation then?" said another officer.

"Belay it? And get crushed by the asteroid? As near as I can tell, it will hit us near dead center. No. We simply have to get it underway as fast as we can. And reserve some ships to defend us while it's in progress. How many do we have?

"Only four at the moment, sir…"

"Damn it all!" she shouted, kicking at a wastebasket, which overturned. "Well, load up two for the operation and leave two for defense. Best we can do. But better yet is to have the operation complete by the time that force arrives." There was a frightened silence. "So *move!*" she barked.

Twenty

Moira stepped lightly out of the airlock, still wearing the same conservative suit as before. I had convinced Bing I could handle managing the civilian crew myself, and he had left me with a small company of marines. It wasn't ideal, but at least I could keep Moira out of his sight.

It was hard, standing this near her, not to go over, stand close, maybe slip a hand into hers. Instead I hung back with the marines, my tone cordial but not intimate. "I do appreciate your help in this matter, Captain Rajasthan. You've seen the asteroid?"

She nodded. "Is this station able to move out of the way?"

"Not on its own, and that's why we need your help." I explained as I led her and her band of Martian pirates along toward the spot on the rim where fuel tanks sat in rows. Station workers were filling them from pipes leading down from the hub so they could be ferried to the ships.

"The *Melpomene* itself could help move the station," she

offered, her tone innocent. "Wouldn't that free up a ship for defense?"

"I suggested as much to the commandant, since I thought you'd offer. She prefers to keep that job only to the ships that have been trained to do it. Not that they don't trust you," I added hastily. That was what my persona would say, the loyal naval officer concerned with placating a near-stranger. "But it really isn't *necessary*. We've got the entire operation well in hand."

She caught my eye and nodded sagely. "Yes, it does seem things are being managed adequately." Translation: even without sabotaging the operation, things look good for our side.

Once the fuel tanks were strapped snugly inside the launch, we made our way toward the *Nemesis*, the ship we were assigned to fuel. It was a man-of-war, longer than the *Mariposa* and almost twice as broad. The sort of ship that relied often on burning fuel; its engines were surely adequate for the task ahead of it.

The marines hung behind the cargo, trying to stay out of the way, and Moira and I could speak at last. "Did you know this was going to happen?" I murmured.

"Of course not. Do you think I wouldn't have told you? They must have had the idea after we left them."

"Or perhaps left us out of it on purpose," I said darkly. "I don't think Coelho fully trusts you."

Her chin went up. "Maybe I should be the one not to trust him. He can defect to Mars whenever he wants, but if I try it they'll have my head."

I sighed. "Anyway, they must have caught it with their grapples, used it to kill some of their velocity, and brought it along. I can't imagine the calculations it would have taken to be sure it wouldn't kill them all."

"Would've been a hell of a jolt, anyway." She stared out the window, watching the *Nemesis* grow larger. "Five sec decel burn…mark." Maggie, on forward thrusters, made the burn.

"So what are we supposed to do now?" Moira asked. "I thought if you were asking us to help, we'd have a chance to actually do it."

"I had hoped they'd let us ferry the fuel on our own," I admitted. "But they said the marines could handle the barrels, and there was no polite way to get out of it."

"That's how they get you. They won't say they don't trust you, but you find there's no way to get out of being watched." She rubbed the side of her chin. "There are swords in the oxygen mask locker. Best I could do, knowing we might have company."

I sized up the distance between us and the locker amidships, between us and the marines. There were six of us and four of them; those, at least, were good odds. Bing had been counting me with Mars and trying to keep things even. But they were closer to the locker than we were, and already armed.

"I don't think we can take them all out," I said at last. "They're armed and trained. And if we try, we blow our cover when we could save it for a better opportunity, once the fighting has already begun."

She nodded slowly, letting out her breath. "You're right, of course." But I could see it, by the tension in her shoulders. She had been dying to make a move. To get in there, shed some blood.

For my part, I would be happy to delay it forever. To somehow stay out of the way until it was all over.

The ship loomed large in our window, blotting out the stars. Moira took a hesitant breath, let it out. Then— "About your message earlier..."

Maggie cut in. "Shouldn't I be doing another decel burn by now?"

"Shit," said Moira. "Yes." She was caught in careful piloting of the launch to avoid a collision until the airlock thunked into place. The marines floated forward, reaching for the canisters. She stabbed a finger at me. "Don't think this lets you off the hook, officer. We *will* talk."

My stomach fluttered despite myself. Talk? So she could say for herself that she loved me too? There had been plenty of time to say three words. Maybe it was something else. Like, *it was a mistake.* Or, *just because we gave in, one time, doesn't mean we're together now.* Or, *I've changed more than you thought, I'm no longer that person who wanted to be with you.*

But I swallowed and faced the hatch at attention. I was in command of the launch, as the officer who had commandeered it.

A ship's boy cranked the inner lock open, and I handed myself gently through. "Permission to come aboard, sir!" I called to the quarterdeck.

"That'll be the fuel, yes?" came a familiar voice. A shiver went up my spine. No. Not here, of all places. Not now.

He peered at me over the railing. Lieutenant Brown. He had survived the escape pod, been picked up, and managed to make his way back here. And, it seemed, been given a command! Sometimes the wheels of the Admiralty did manage to grind fast, it seemed. Only when I didn't want them to.

"Yes, sir!" I said snappily, eyes front. Perhaps he wouldn't recognize me. Behind me, one by one, the marines passed through the door and started handing the fuel canisters along.

Today I couldn't possibly be that fortunate. Brown swung himself over the railing and hung directly in front of me. "Mr. Prescott! Well, I'll be damned. I had heard you'd made it to the station. How you got there must be quite a tale."

"Yes, sir." No need to make up excuses with this man. He wouldn't have let me speak anyway.

"I also heard you failed to report to the *Destiny* as ordered."

"Yes, sir."

"The commandant worried that you'd overslept. Asked me to take you back, if you ever surfaced. To which I readily agreed. The Admiralty certainly needs to hear your story. It's sure to be interesting *and* creative."

I hesitated, letting my mouth tighten, as if I were furious at his false assumptions. It had suddenly become so easy, keeping the old me as a screen over … whatever I was now. The fetus of the new me, perhaps. But I did, at least, have a guiding star: Moira. I had to help Moira destroy the station, because if I didn't, Moira would have nothing.

"Come, Prescott," said Brown, pulling himself downward a touch to intersect my gaze. "Aren't you going to favor me with the story?"

I looked into his eyes, which were small and blue, and something broke on my understanding. He was just a sadist in a uniform. I had dreaded him so long, fought hard to keep in his favor, and why? Because he was the face of the Navy to me? I had betrayed the Navy already. I wasn't afraid of him anymore.

No, I hated him now. I hated him, not for Maxwell, not for Trask, but for how he'd made me complicit in all of it. How he'd made me bully the men and apprehend Maxwell. All because I had been so wrapped up in the mass delusion of the Navy that I had thought I had had no power. Which was exactly the intent of everything. You punish the men, not to stop them from mutiny, but to make them feel and believe that they are utterly powerless. To make them too afraid of the next beating to think past it to freedom.

"No, sir," I said at last, my voice startling me with its perfect calm.

"Why not, midshipman?"

"Because you wouldn't believe it, sir," I said.

He stared at me, perhaps as startled by my insubordination as I was. Then he shook his head ruefully and turned over his shoulder to order some of his men, "Search the launch. I don't trust this officer."

Cold fear returned to soak my bones. Moira was waiting in

the launch. He knew her for a pirate. That would be the end of everything, at least for us. For her.

Darting to the side, I seized one of the canisters as it sailed through the air from one marine to the next. It was heavy enough to carry me sideways. Reaching for the top, I wrenched open the valve at the neck. Fuel began spilling out, clear blobs clinging around the neck of the canister.

Letting go, I kicked one corner of the canister hard, sending it into a spin and me heading back toward the airlock. The rotation flung blobs of the corrosive fluid across the sail deck. The crew stood gawking at it for a moment before lunging into action. We all knew the same thing: if you smelled ammonia, it had already started to poison you. I felt its acrid stench in my nostrils and held my breath.

The crew was well-trained and moved toward the mess to contain it. Whatever threat I posed, it couldn't be as great as the huge blobs of fuel splattering out all over the sail deck.

The marines, however, were just as well trained. Their orders were always to ignore ship operations and deal with hostiles and prisoners. They let go of their canisters and darted into my path.

I dodged the first neatly enough; he had aimed across my original trajectory and it was easy to pivot off a ceiling strap and change it after he had left his handhold. The second, though, had been waiting for such a move. She hung directly in my path, saber at the ready.

She wasn't expecting to have to use it, though, and I could see her main focus was on her left hand, which she had ready for a grab. After all, I didn't have a sword.

Reaching inside my coat, I got my knife out and stabbed at her left arm. Blood flowed over her arm, crawling along the skin, and she gawked for a second, startled. It was enough to get by her.

By then the pirates were coming through the airlock, fighting off the remaining marines. I swung on Maggie's offered arm and tumbled into the launch. The rest of the pirates followed me a moment after, and our airlock slammed shut.

"My god, Lucy, what happened?" Moira demanded, as soon as we were well away. She piloted straight toward the station, trusting the *Nemesis* would hold her fire for fear of a miss hitting it.

"Brown is on that ship," I said, pulling a rag from a locker and wiping off my chef's knife. "I got recognized."

"Do you think I can get back to the *Mariposa*?"

I gauged the distance to where it hung, sunward and downstream of the station by about half a mile. "No. Not if the station knows who we are, and we can assume it will by the time we get there. Brown will be signaling them as soon as he can. As soon as we move out of the line between it and the *Nemesis*, it'll fire on us."

"But if we go to the station, they'll capture us just as quick!"

"Of the two, I prefer capture." I checked my pocket watch. "And if we pick the nearest airlock, they might not have alerted the marines there by the time we dock."

Twenty-One

The *Nemesis* was prompt with its cleanup. As we drew into a tangent with the station's rim, preparing to lock on, a message light began flickering from the ship's quarterdeck. It was a broad beam, so it could reach the whole station. While Moira carefully made the connection, I spelled out the code. I had to know what the station would know when we arrived.

The airlock thunked and the launch's floor jerked upward toward me. I staggered with the sudden renewal of gravity. Moira steadied me with one hand. "What did it say?"

"Still going. 'Treachery' was all I got before we got turned the wrong way."

Behind us, the other pirates distributed swords. I reached for one.

"No," said Moira. "If we get seen, you're our prisoner."

"I don't care what the Navy thinks of me now," I said carelessly. A part of me muttered that I did, that there were reasons, and I quashed that part without mercy. I couldn't think of that, because if I did, I'd be paralyzed again. Forward momentum was all that mattered—charging after Moira without a thought. I'd worry about what happened after when it was all over.

"Don't be an idiot," she said shortly. "If we get captured, we still need one person free on the station. That's you."

"What do I do then?"

"I dunno. Use your imagination. Break something." She put her hand to the airlock crank and glanced back at the men. "Now."

They rushed through the lock in a body; the two marines guarding the door didn't get a chance to shout. I tagged behind them, feeling awkward and useless without a sword. Perhaps with a sword in my hand, I could have attacked one of the marines before I thought about it. Just like I'd killed people in the past; I hadn't had to think about it then because the decisions had been made for me. Shouldn't it be the same now?

We split up, the rest of the crew hurrying spinward while I followed Moira to the right, toward the main office. We had come onboard at an empty hallway, not much cover to speak of, but not far ahead would be stairs. That might lead to somewhere we could hide.

Instead, when the hall broadened out into a wider concourse, we heard running feet. An entire company of marines were upon us in an instant. In command was a lieutenant I didn't know. But he'd have had the message from the *Nemesis*. If my name or description had been in it, I was a dead woman.

Moira, quicker-thinking than I, grabbed me from behind. I stood passively, unsure what she was trying to do. Then my breath caught as cold steel touched my throat.

"Not so fast, Mister Navy man," she taunted. "I have your friend. I used her to get on the *Nemesis* and I'm not going to let her go unless you agree to let me go back to my ship."

The lieutenant hesitated. So no. My description couldn't have been in the message. He was a youngish man, about my age, with dark hair and blue eyes. "Navy policy is not to negotiate for military hostages," he said. "There's really no point in doing this, is there?" He gave Moira a hopeful little smile, meant to disarm, but only making him look younger and more nervous.

I sighed, leaning back fractionally against Moira's chest. If she had asked me at any point, if she thought before acting at *all*, I could have told her about that policy. As it was, I was going to have to handle this by myself.

I grabbed Moira's sword arm, pulling it down as I hooked my leg around hers. At the comfortable Mars-normal gravity, she was easy to throw. She landed hard on her back. I leaped to straddle her and wrestle the sword away. She struggled against me, not hard enough to get away, but hard enough to look convincing.

I climbed off her, sword in hand. My heart was racing, and it wasn't only from the exertion. Even touching her was a rush, and this sham fight was killing me. "Guess you don't know much about sparring in gravity," I panted out, glaring down at her.

In reality she had beat up any number of people at home, like that one scullery boy who had stolen her diary. He had six inches on her, but she didn't care. She fought dirty. But not today. I fought down a smile. She understood me perfectly.

"Fuck you, Navy scum," she spat at me, clambering to her feet as the marines surged around to take her into custody. "And god fuck the Emprex."

I slid Moira's sword into my belt and sauntered over to the lieutenant, saluting. "Midshipman Prescott-Chin, sir."

He didn't bat an eye. I was in the clear, at least until Brown made more direct contact with the station. "Lieutenant Smirnov-Wilson. Charmed." He gestured for me to follow him anti-spinward. "So there were pirates aboard the *Melpomene*?"

"Evidently! I never would have guessed it while I was on board. They seemed to be everything they said. Perhaps most of them are."

"Impossible to be sure. We have the *Melpomene* targeted and are attempting to raise her on the radio, but there has been no reply as yet. So far, she's shown no sign of aggression."

I glanced back at the marines, who had cuffed Moira and were starting to lead her past us, toward the Navy offices. "You'd better tell them to keep that woman safe through all this," I said. "The Admiralty is going to want to question her when all this is over. If Earth is involved, we'll need a witness to testify to it."

He gave the order, and I relaxed my shoulders a fraction. Not that they normally airlocked prisoners, but one couldn't be sure. Especially not after Deimos.

"You think Earth could be behind this?" he asked me, voice low.

"It wouldn't surprise me," I said. "I mean, look at the complexity of this scheme. You think pirates could work this out on their own? You think they have the resources to?"

He shook his head, a bleak look on his pale face. "Well, Earth would certainly love to be rid of this station. Before the trade war, it was embargoes all the time. Whenever we wouldn't let the corps do whatever they wanted on Mars. If they couldn't buy up estates and strip-mine them, they'd go crying to Earth for another embargo. And what could we do? We had no other source of gasses then."

"But we beat them in the last war," I said. "Like we're beating them in this one."

He shook his head. "I see you haven't been getting the latest news. They're destroying us out there. And if they take this? There goes our independence. We'll have to make terms because we'll have nowhere else to get gasses."

I pictured it. My parents' estate, bought up not by colonist bankers but by Earth corps. Big mining machines tearing up the cliff face, dumping fracking fluid in the Hellas Sea. A lump grew under my heart. Hell, why did the choices have to be like this?

Why was it this or Moira? I couldn't betray Moira, I couldn't let anything happen to her, not if you set a whole planet against her. Not now, when I'd finally claimed her again.

But if anything happened to Mars, it would be like snatching the ground from under my feet. Because I might not be standing there any more, but the thought of Mars remaining as it had been was grounding my soul. A free Mars; a green Mars; a living Mars.

I swallowed hard. A person can only have one north star. I'd chosen Moira. I had to trust that if there were a way to save Mars and us too, she'd have found it.

"Well, we can't let that happen," I said firmly. "So what's next?"

"As soon as the *Nemesis* has contained the fuel spill, both ships will get into position at the hub and attach their grapples. You'll barely feel the pull. They're moving us less than two kilometers north and they won't want to go too fast. As long as they get started within about half an hour, we should be clear of the asteroid in time. Unfortunately…" He stopped at a window and gestured out.

They could now be seen with the naked eye: five blunt black cigars, glowing at the ends as they decelerated toward us. Their sails were furled now, but they were still moving fast enough to see them grow. Hard to say exactly how fast, with the asteroid shadowing the stars behind them. It hung in the sky, bigger than the sun, beginning to blot it out along one edge.

I wanted to stay and gape, but he hurried me along. "The asteroid will be here in an hour and a half. The ships, half an hour or less. We're evacuating the civilians. Can you pilot a launch?"

"To where?"

"Just away. Anywhere. When everything's over you can return to…whatever's left. Hopefully to the station. If not, to the *Nemesis* or anywhere."

I glanced sideways at him, taken aback by the foreboding in

his tone. His face was pale and drawn. Twelve hours ago, everyone on this station would have been cheerful and confident, knowing that the war was as yet far away. Today it was all different. I wanted to reassure him.

At the same time I did not, by any means, want to get on any launch. Not with a crew of loyal Navy men at the thrusters and a load of civilians to keep out of the crossfire. Of all the crew, I was currently the only one still on the station and at liberty. I had to use that, somehow. Being stuck on a launch wasn't what I had in mind.

"I can do it," I said firmly. "But don't worry. It's just a precaution. It won't be needed."

He found me a crew and gave me an airlock number. "They count up spinwise, evens to sunward and odds to lee. Thank you, Prescott, you're a big help."

Damn it, I had taken him for completely fooled, but he was doing the Navy thing again. Trust but verify. Bog me down with three spacers and put me on a launch going as far from trouble as possible. Or was I projecting? Perhaps he was only trying to help. It amounted to the same thing.

The ranking spacer, a lanky, square-shouldered woman, touched her forehead respectfully. "Sir, our launch is this way."

"Will the civilians be there already? Or do we have to round them up?"

"In theory everybody's got an emergency plan with an airlock number to meet at. In practice..."

"All right. You two, go scour the area for anybody who looks lost." The tall woman and I hurried to the designated airlock. I cast her a sideways glance. I was down to one escort, and I could probably take her. I was armed and she wasn't. But the concourse was still crowded, mostly with spacers and marines now, and there was no way I could get away clean.

A knot of civilians crowded the airlock, pushing one another and babbling with panic. On spotting me, they immediately pressed in with questions. Was this only a precaution? Was there a plan for their things here on the station, which they'd been strictly enjoined not to take? Could I perhaps make an exception for one or two items that were very important and couldn't possibly be left?

"The most important thing—" I tried to say. My voice disappeared under the desperate babble of voices.

The tall sailor shouted, "Mouths shut, ears open!" in a stentorian tone, and the babble died out.

"The most important thing," I repeated, "is to get all the people off the station safe. We hope it will be temporary. Your personal belongings should be safe here. Though really," I said, glancing down at the many bundles scattering the concourse, "this is not exactly the safest place. Let's move them upstairs, at least. If they're in the way of the marines as they attempt to do their duty, they may be damaged."

The sailor stared at me, aghast, as I grabbed a suitcase in each hand and started toward the stairs. Her eyes clearly said, *What the hell are you doing? Who cares what happens to these civilians' baggage? We have a mission and you're not doing it!*

But the chain of command stood firm. She'd never question me in front of all these people. So she stood, looking shocked, while several of the civilians grabbed their bags and came with me.

I found a safe-looking corner and helped everyone stow their bags again. "All right, go back and board the launch with the pilot. I'll make a final check for anyone else who is supposed to be aboard. Please tell her not to wait more than five minutes for me."

They thanked me and went downstairs, and I hurried away from the area as fast as I could. I hoped that my escorts would realize taking the civilians to safety outweighed any other considerations. Like quiet instructions from that lieutenant to keep an eye on me.

Free at last, and what was I going to do with my freedom? I

would have liked to free Moira and the others, but I wasn't sure where they would be kept or under how much guard. If I had to guess, I'd say in the Navy offices, where they'd be well guarded. I couldn't break in there by myself. All I'd get is another polite escort and another job to get me out of the way.

So I hurried toward the nearest stairwell, unlocked the door with Bing's key, and started upward. My first thought was to get at the fuel stores somehow, either explode them or set up some kind of leak like I had on the *Nemesis*. But as I rose upward, my weight easing and my head growing dizzy, I realized that was a terrible plan. I didn't have a way off this station, not if the *Mariposa* couldn't send a launch, and more importantly I didn't have a way to get Moira off.

Eyes on the goal. I was beginning to realize that even if I had a singular guiding star to direct my choices, it still meant constantly shifting plans. While Moira had been on the *Mariposa*, my goal had been to help her destroy the station, even though it tore me apart. But now that she was here, I didn't dare hasten its destruction.

Was this what I had meant, when I said her gravity would whip me around? I certainly felt yanked about. Not the gentle, uncomplicated free fall I had hoped for.

Coelho's asteroid plan left time for evacuation, and I had to hope that what I'd told the lieutenant would be enough to get Moira taken along. The chaos of the evacuation would be a perfect time to snatch her out of whatever launch or ship they put her on. But for that to happen, I couldn't interfere. Let them count off the seconds exactly as they expected to. No sudden changes of plan.

I paused and pressed my face to one of the small portholes letting light into the stairwell. Coelho's ships were coasting close, engines off now, the sun picking out their outlines with a glint of silver metal. The space between us was filled with torpedoes and smaller fire. Some came from under my feet, arcing toward the pirate ships, aimed flawlessly despite the spin.

One slammed into the *Sirocco*, Hussein's ship, with terrible force, shuddering it enough to see from here. Those torpedoes were *big*, much more powerful than ship-mounted ones. The *Sirocco* took on a lazy spin, bow over stern, and I held my breath. If anyone was able to move around on board, they'd soon fire thrusters and steady the ship.

But no one did. She kept wheeling, end over end, till she passed the station and out of my vision.

Damn it, this had seemed a flawless plan. But the two defending ships, with help from the station's massive guns, were handling Coelho's force neatly. The *Mariposa* was attempting to engage, but she would take time to build up any speed from her dead stop, and until then she wouldn't be able to manage any broadsides.

And the whole time the ships struggled and rattled each other with arms fire, the *Nemesis* was slowly moving into position to the north. I put my head at the bottom of the porthole and looked up. If her opposite number was ready on the leeward side, they'd be ready to pull the station in minutes. I spared a glance for the asteroid: still at least an hour away. It would come too late.

That thought was enough to pull me away from the window and back up the ladder. I was needed now, or Coelho's plan would come to nothing. Bing had said the station could only be moved by ships pulling it, and that they could only attach their cables in one place, on the spindles projecting on either side of the hub.

So to stop the *Nemesis* from pulling the station out of the asteroid's path, all I needed was to sabotage one of the spindles. With that gone, there would be nowhere else the *Nemesis* could grab on without being swung like a whip by the powerful spin of the station. And her partner ship trying to drag it by the other spindle would only tip the whole station over.

The top level, below the vast storage tanks, was mercifully

abandoned. Thanks to the pipes leading downward, no one needed to come up here to get fuel. I slowly weaved my way among the support struts toward the sunward edge. Here, at least in theory, the spindle should be attached.

The tanks ended barely shy of the wall, leaving a tight crawl space where I could squeeze my way upward. As I wedged myself in, back to the tank and knees against the hull, I realized the tight fit was actually a blessing. Gravity barely existed here, replaced by dizzying forces that changed as I crawled upward. At least this way I was braced.

I made it to the center of the hub and ran my hands over the hull. All there was to mark the presence of the spindle was a wide circle imprinted in the metal, maybe ten feet around. I bit my lip. Of course, how could I have been so stupid? Bing had told me it wasn't the kind of axle that went straight through; it was only attached on the outside. Outside meant no access from here. The only way to reach it would be through an airlock.

I banged the back of my head against the tank. I couldn't possibly get suited up in the time we had, let alone do a solo spacewalk on a strange station. I didn't even know where the nearest airlock might be.

Looking around wildly, I spotted a few portholes, with the radiation glass bowed out like little bubbles for a better view. That would at least let me know how much time I had.

I put my head inside a bubble and looked around. There was the spindle on its disc-shaped base, steadily rotating—or rather, not rotating, holding still while I revolved around it. The sight made me giddy, unless it was my middle ear doing that. And there, to the north, was the *Nemesis*, barely clear of the north edge of the wheel, slowly extending her grapple.

It was time. I had to do something now if I was going to do anything at all. I could sit around agonizing till the battle was over, be the kind of "good person" who never did any actual good.

Or I could keep my forward momentum and just do something, anything, like I'd promised Moira.

Pulling my head out of the porthole, I looked around for some kind of tool. Yes, right outside the circle of the spindle socket was a tool case, the kind ships and stations put everywhere, so repairs could be done right away by whoever found the damage.

I scrambled over and pulled it out, laying it tilted on my lap so the tools wouldn't spill out. Crowbar, spot welder, wrench, tape. Not a lot I could do with that, unless I wanted to vent atmosphere. Here at the hub, the hull plating was thin, not radiation-quality at all. After all, this wasn't a habitation area. I could simply put the welder to the hull and start cutting. Surely all that atmosphere venting into the spindle socket would disrupt it at least a little.

On the other hand, I didn't especially want to die. Especially not for a plan that might or might not work. I stared at the tools. Crowbar, spot welder, tape. Fuel canister for welder. Mask.

Suddenly it clicked. The crowbar was only a big thick piece of metal, with a chiseled edge on each end. But it was four feet long.

Four feet happened to be longer than the depth of the spindle socket. There were maybe two inches of hull plating, two feet of ball bearings, and a foot-thick disk that was the spindle base.

I put the welding mask on and crept back into the circle, clutching the welder in one hand and the crowbar in the other, and braced myself. Picking a spot, I began to melt a hole. The liquid metal bubbled out of the hole, dragged slightly rimward by the spin. Which was a help; without gravity it tended to pool and clog up whatever you were trying to do. I watched carefully to make sure the drips didn't get close to my knees.

It was quiet here at the hub. Quiet enough to hear the faint clank through the hull as the *Nemesis'* grapple hooked on. I breathed in and out through my nose. There was still time. It would take several minutes to build up enough force to even budge the station. I kept welding.

At last air started to hiss in the hole I'd made. I was through. But I had my plug ready. I shoved the crowbar in, hard and fast, on a slant so it would act as a brake on the spindle. It slid between the ball bearings and slammed into the spindle with a jolt that wrenched my shoulders.

The spindle overcame that initial blow, making the crowbar skip and scrape along its underside while I kept the pressure up. But it was only a few hundred pounds. Eventually the resistance lessened, and the crowbar stayed wedged. I released it, arms shuddering from released strain, and went back to the porthole to look.

Sure enough, the spindle now seemed fixed in its socket, rotating placidly with the station. I took a moment to apply heavy-duty tape all around the crowbar, to keep air from sneaking through the tiny gap, and went back again to look. Surely by now the *Nemesis* would have noticed the spindle was turning. Surely she would release the grapple.

But she didn't. Whoever was looking out a gunport window, directing the attachment process, must have wandered off or looked away or failed to notice the slight rotation. Steadily, but with agonizing slowness, the thin cable wrapped around the spindle. First one circuit, then two. A full minute for each one, and nothing I could do but watch in horror.

To the north, the *Nemesis* invisibly crept closer. Perhaps by a foot a minute. But she wasn't very many feet clear of the station's rim. I clenched my teeth as the bar of blackness between them shrank. Maybe the *Nemesis* would stay clear of the station as she came down. Maybe someone would notice their clearance had shrunk and belay, cut grapple, and burn clear.

The belly of the *Nemesis* brushed the rim. Barely a touch, at first. Then the spin—so much faster out there than here at the hub—took her. Accelerated the ship's belly instantly, while the weight of the rest of the ship kept her still. The hull plating sheared off all at once, spilling the fog of atmosphere out into the blackness. And more. Loose bits of equipment. Fuel.

Bodies.

It was far too late to do anything about it. Far too late to warn anyone to suit up in time to rescue them. Far too late to cry out, *that isn't what I meant to happen!*

It was like the jerk that comes, right as you're drifting into sleep and feel yourself falling. No more free fall, painless and fearless; I was suddenly flailing to gain my balance. But there was no ground anywhere, no single truth or loyalty I could rest upon. I had left all of them behind me.

I bit down hard on my knuckle, fighting back tears. Why did everything have to end this way? In the Navy, I had watched helplessly while a man I helped to apprehend was jettisoned into space. So I had left the Navy, out of what? Conscience? And here I was watching helplessly as more sailors decompressed to death and it was still my fault. Always my fault. No choice I could make that didn't lead here: to death. Blood on my hands, only the blood was boiling away under the skin, blooming in bruises as the breath was ripped from their lungs. I couldn't see the details from here, but I knew. I had been trained too well to pretend I didn't know.

Moira wouldn't have been shaken by this. Or Goldstein, or Marron, or anyone but me. I was soft, civilized, born and bred for cocktail parties, not this. I didn't belong out here. Against my will, I was being shaped as a weapon of war. The only thing I was allowed to choose was where I was pointed. And I still didn't know if I was choosing right.

I couldn't. I couldn't sit here and think about that now. What would even be the point, now that it was too late to do anything different? I had rushed forward to avoid thinking about the future. Now I saw nothing left to do but to keep moving to avoid thinking about the past.

Twenty-Two

I climbed slowly down the ladder, weight settling back into my body. I had done what Moira had asked. I had broken something. And now my forward momentum was gone. I had bought the pirates time, at least. Perhaps I had sealed the station's fate for good. Either way, I couldn't think of anything else I could do now.

My adrenaline gone, all I wanted was to rest. I could have stayed at the spindle and done just that, watching the rest like a play through the little window. But that would have allowed me to think, and I didn't want to think. If I thought, I might ask myself what I had done. And wasn't it a little late to suddenly start thinking through actions I'd already taken?

Downstairs, it was much quieter than before. The civilians had all gone. A few people in uniform went running by, one direction or another. I spared one glance out the window. The asteroid was blotting out half the sun now, casting the scene outside in an unnatural twilight. The battle still continued, but one more of the Navy ships was heading sunward, probably disabled and drifting.

The pirate ships, I couldn't be sure. Only one was still firing, but the *Mariposa* was moving on what looked like an intentional course.

I hurried along spinward, not for any particular reason, just because it would look odd to stand still. My eyes fixed on the deck ahead of me. I needed to not think, not yet, not till this was over. Yet I had to think at least of what to do next. Could I find Moira and rescue her? I didn't think so, not when I'd ensured she'd be kept under heavy guard. The next question was whether any of the other pirates were still at liberty.

I stared at the ground with such focus that I narrowly avoided running into someone. I pulled up short and craned my neck. "Bing!"

The poor boy looked terrible, haggard and driven to distraction. His red hair was half out of its queue, straggling on either side of his face, and his freckles stood out against his pale cheeks as if marked with a pen.

"Prescott," he gasped. "I thought you'd be gone by now for sure. They're making everyone who can, fly a launch out of here."

"I'm sure they'll give me one soon," I said. "Why are you still here?"

"I was ordered to check all the stairwells to make sure they're clear," he said. "The officer ran off before I could tell him I'd lost my keys."

I dug in my pocket. "Are these them? I spotted them on the ground near the stairwell you took me up in."

He snatched them gratefully. "Come on, you can help till you get some other orders."

I acceded without protest. Why not help check stairwells? It was as good as any job. Saving lives, at least, could never be wrong. We made it through three stairwells without incident, opening the doors and peering upwards. Bing added a shout up each one.

"Imagine if we forgot someone, if someone didn't get the

order," he said, as we shut and locked the third stairwell. "It's not like we have time to count heads as we're going."

"Why don't you give some kind of general alarm?"

"There may still be pirates at large on the station," he said. "We've caught four, plus the one that was with you. How many were there on the launch that came in?"

"I *think* five?" I said doubtfully. There had been six, including Moira. One was still at large, then. I wondered which. Nguyen? Ntumba? Yao? "You don't want them to get off in time?"

"We're worried they wouldn't," he said. "If they knew the station was getting abandoned, they could just take it. That is, if they have a way to stop the asteroid."

"I doubt anything could stop it now," I said, casting it another glance. The barest scrap of sun flashed over its edge. It looked like a ball ready to come arcing in for a catch, any second now. Of course, it was really the better part of an hour away, despite how large it loomed to the eye. But that still wasn't enough time for anybody to do anything. The station must not have had enough ships left to move the station. Or they didn't know what was wrong with the spindle and didn't have time to find out.

Bing opened the fourth door and gave a surprised shout. I crammed into the stairwell along with him to see what was the matter. There, perched on the ladder, was a small figure in tattered brown. I knew who had been wearing brown on the launch. But would Bing recognize her?

She paused in her work, which was scraping at an oxygen pipe with a file, and looked up. Now that would have been a nasty job if she'd gotten through it. Let the gas reach a good enough concentration, make the tiniest spark, and the whole spoke would fill with fire. Possibly breach.

"Maggie?" cried Bing. "What in the ancestors' name are you doing here?"

I thought fast. Surely there had to be some kind of explanation that would get her off. But Maggie only scowled at him. "Breaking your shitty station," she said, pocketing the file and turning to race up the ladder. "God fuck the Emprex!"

Bing followed close on her heels, and I hurried after. Her quick little footfalls on the ladder gave me hope. She'd outdistance both of us.

But when we reached the top, she wasn't prepared for the spin vectors. She hadn't been up here before. Bing and I stood panting at the top, holding onto the network of struts, while she tried to run, staggered drunkenly, and fell.

Bing was standing over her in a second, sword drawn. "No time to take prisoners," he said. "I guess I'd better just—"

"Bing, are you crazy?" I demanded. "She has the right to a trial!"

"And what could the trial tell us that we don't already know?"

"She's a *child*." That won me a glare from Maggie. Brave idiot, she'd rather be skewered by her old shipmate than belittled. I carefully stepped over to them, standing by Maggie's side as she lay sprawled on the ground, still too dizzy to get up even if Bing would let her.

"Not by the laws of war she's not."

He made a sudden move toward her with his sword, and I whipped mine out of my belt and crossed it with his. He looked up at me in confusion. "Prescott, I outrank you. We can't be squabbling over this. The decision is mine; no one's going to hold you responsible."

He looked so adult in that moment: calm, grave, even though I knew he was as frightened as Maggie. This was the one thing he could control and he wanted to handle it. I wanted to scream at him, but I knew it would do no good. Instead I said, "I'm not going to let you."

He blinked in disbelief. "You want to *fight* me?"

"Yes. This isn't a Navy thing anymore, Bing. This is honor. Fight me if you're any gentleman."

We'd both be court-martialed for dueling; he knew that and he knew I knew it. But the noble code ran deep in all of us. He wasn't going to say no. He stepped back a pace and saluted with his sword.

It was the strangest duel I had ever fought, and I'd fought quite a few. None in such earnest. And none on a spinning station where with every step the ground was in a slightly different place than you expected.

Bing went on the offensive at once. He knew I was a better duelist than him in space, and he might well guess I could do it better in gravity as well. But he also knew I hadn't spent much time up here, and the less time he gave me to adapt to the ground, the better. I parried without moving, one hand on a strut. As long as I kept still, the motion was only distracting.

After a few passes, he figured out what I was doing and hung back to draw me out. Damn. I let go of the strut and lurched forward in an attack. It didn't land, but I didn't fall over, either, which was pretty good considering.

We lunged back and forth at each other, grabbing whatever struts were to hand. Out of the corner of my eye, I saw Maggie rise to her feet. She was closer to the ladder than we were; she could run. But instead she stared, as if mesmerized by our ridiculous duel.

Bing got in a touch on my arm, cutting through my coat and drawing a little blood. "That's enough, don't you think?" he panted. "The launches will be gone soon. We have to move."

"I'm not going on the launches."

"Then what is this *about*?" he cried in frustration.

I took a breath. My cover didn't matter now. And it would be gone soon in any event, as soon as everyone got off the station and started comparing notes, realizing I was never where I had been ordered to be. As soon as Bing got a look at the prisoners and realized the *Melpomene* had to be the *Mariposa*.

"It's about Mars," I said, resuming the offensive. "It's about people like us making the place miserable for everyone else. It's about the flogging and about Maxwell getting thrown out an airlock because he cared about protecting an innocent girl. Did you hear about that one, when the captain was found?"

"I read the report," he answered breathlessly, parrying another one of my strikes. "But that's no reason to turn traitor."

I caught myself on a strut to breathe. "And then I found out what they were keeping on Deimos. Prisoners in terrible conditions. Muscles withered to nothing. Alexei Khan was there, can you believe it? All those years we all thought he was dead."

He stepped closer and tried an attack, which I parried easily. "I remember hearing about him. But still. If you have a problem, you have to take it up with the people in charge. You can't *do* this! Don't you care about Mars? Don't you care about our *home?*"

I hadn't been angry until that moment. Care about our home? I felt sometimes like the only one who cared. The only one who wanted it to be better. I lunged at him wildly, teetered sideways, and fell hard onto my side. I tried to scramble to my feet, but he was on top of me, one foot on my chest, his sword at my throat.

"So it's the same for me then?" I asked him quietly. "Death without trial?"

"You were my *friend,*" he said, his voice heavy with grief. "If you want me to drag you back for a court martial, I will. But for your family's sake, I think it's better if you're marked as lost with the station."

I stared up at him, eyes filling with tears. My family. I had managed to put them out of my mind almost this whole time, but he hadn't forgotten I had one. I hated that this terrible war had pitted us against each other. Because this offer, more than anything else he had said, made me wish we could be on the same side. He grasped immediately the thing Moira had never understood. That I would always choose death rather than shame for my family.

I lifted up my chin, exposing my neck. "Quickly, then," I said, because there was nothing else to say. I closed my eyes and waited for the pain.

Instead I heard quick, light footsteps, a soft wet impact, and a bubbling gasp. My eyes flew open. Bing stood as before, but his sword hung limply in his fingers. He opened his mouth as if to say something, but only blood poured from his lips. He collapsed onto the deck.

Maggie stood beside him, the sword in her hand red with blood. She was pale, staring at her sword stupidly.

I scrambled to my feet. I wasn't sure whether to be grateful she had saved my life, angry at her for killing my friend, or sorry for her own loss. Bing was as much her friend as mine. "Oh, Maggie," I breathed.

She lifted her chin and gave me another glare. "Save it," she said. "If they're evacuating now, we'd better look for a way off this thing." The bravado was good, if it meant she was functional till she was safe. But at the same time it felt wrong. She shouldn't have to be acting this way at her age.

"You go," I said. "I'll catch up in a minute."

She was off without a backward look, and I was alone with Bing. Or rather, Bing's body. Maggie had gotten him right in the back.

I sat down beside him, watching the blood flow along the curved deck. For several minutes, I couldn't even formulate a thought. My mind kept circling over and over the same facts. He was dead. My friend was dead, and my other friend was a murderer, and this was wrong. Everything was wrong.

It shouldn't be this way. These shouldn't have been the choices. There should have been a path to take that hadn't ended in death, but I had never been able to think of any. Kill for Mars, kill for Earth—the only thing I was good for seemed to be killing.

I wanted to say it wasn't my fault. It was Earth's for trying to encroach on Mars's independence. It was Mars's fault for building up a Navy so rigid and cruel. It was Moira's fault for signing on as a pirate when she could have chosen a quieter life.

My conscience wouldn't allow it. I had silenced it for as long as I could, running every moment, shutting down every attempt at a thought. Not just since I had chosen to surrender to falling in love with Moira. Since the first time Brown had insisted I have the men beaten, and I had complied. I had learned, painfully, that a conscience was only a burden and that I should trust the chain of command to make those decisions for me. If the decisions weren't mine, surely the responsibility wasn't? And yet I felt in my bones the weight of every action that had brought me here.

Bing's corpse stared at me glassily. I reached over and shut his eyes. Poor Bing. He had tried to be a good officer, and look where that had gotten him. I didn't blame him for not seeing through it. He'd been no older than Maggie when he'd signed on. The Navy was father and mother to him, more than his parents had ever been. He couldn't see me as anything but a betrayer.

I didn't believe I was. I wouldn't have thrown away my oaths of loyalty just for Moira. I turned my back on the Navy because it was wrong, because I couldn't countenance that much dishonesty.

Yet I could see my disillusionment, too, had been used. Earth scraped up broken men with nowhere else to go and shaped them into weapons to attack Mars. But had we ever wanted to attack Mars? All Moira and Coelho and the others wanted was to live free. Mars offered them chains. Earth offered a bill. And which was worse?

I had chosen Earth, because Moira had. But now Moira was in a cell and I had no way to get to her. I had achieved her mission for her, but if it wasn't going to purchase her freedom, what was the bloody point? I had killed the crew of the *Nemesis*. I had killed Bing. I had possibly doomed Mars to re-conquest. And for nothing, in the end.

There had to be another choice. There had to be. The asteroid was bearing down on us, I had less than an hour to get off this station and no way to do it without turning myself in to be hanged. And yet I could not believe there was no third option.

Maybe I was wrong, that a person couldn't have more than one north star. Didn't we always navigate off three? Let Moira be the sun. Maybe she shouldn't be the sun of my system, but I had long since accepted that she was. That still left Mars and my family as points of reference. Things I should take into account.

But this was ethical figuring far beyond anything I'd done. I felt like Maggie, going straight from sine, cosine, and tangent to celestial navigation. I'd only started making choices for myself a few months ago. I wasn't ready for this level of calculation.

"What would I do if I had no loyalties?" I whispered to Bing. "Not to Mars, not to Moira. What if it were only me?"

He lay silently. There really was only me, here, in the end. I would probably die here when the asteroid hit, so why not, for once in my life, do what I felt like doing?

For the first time since I could remember, I turned inward and listened. What did I want? And it was immediately clear—hadn't I been saying it over and over? I wanted a third choice. I wanted a place where refugees from Mars or Earth could place their feet, breathe the air, drink water.

And I was standing on it.

I leaped to my feet and staggered toward the sunward wall. Out the bubble window, I could see the last launch leaving. I was alone on this station with a corpse, and possibly Maggie. And forty minutes to live, if I didn't work something out.

There was a little radio bolted to the wall, mainly for intrastation communication, and I cranked it up. When it had charged up enough for the light on top to turn on, I tuned it to the channel the pirates used. "Coelho, you there? It's—" I considered my words carefully. There was no reason the Navy ships would be tuned to this channel, but there was nothing stopping them from doing it either. "Moira's girlfriend," I finished.

The radio crackled to life. "You're still on the station?"

"Yes. I think the last Navy launch has gone."

"I think we can manage a pickup. Probably."

I paused. "Don't you want more than that?"

"If you've got something in mind, you'll have to clue me in," he said, annoyance creeping into his voice. "We've got under an hour. That's no time for dithering."

"The station," I said. "It's empty. It could be yours."

"Earth didn't ask us to take it, they asked us to destroy it. Don't know if they'll pay us if we don't deliver."

"Don't you get it?" I blurted impatiently. "If you had the station, you wouldn't need Earth's money. They've got all the gasses you could want, hydroponic gardens—it's like having a planet of your own."

There was another silence. He hadn't seen the inside of the station. He probably hadn't thought of the possibilities at all.

"Give me a second," he said at last. "Or rather, don't wait for an answer. Just tell me, what happened to their ship and is it going to happen to us if we try moving the station?"

"Spindle was broken," I said briefly. "I can fix it."

"Get to work," he said. "Coelho out."

I switched the radio off, letting out a long breath, and went to repair the sabotage job I'd done earlier. It wasn't difficult; all I had to do was slam the crowbar the opposite way, giving the spindle's base repeated shocks until it no longer kept pace with the station. I took a moment to watch and make sure it was steady compared to the stars and the ships around before patching the hole I'd made and looking out the bubble window.

The *Estrela* was moving slowly downstream and to leeward—away from the center of combat, like the other ships were going, but also behind the station. I thought I had an idea what they were doing. I moved across the hub toward the leeward side and watched the bubble there. Sure enough, once the *Estrela* was out of sight of the Martian ships, a launch detached from her side and headed toward the station.

I met them at the airlock. Maggie was waiting there too, having seen what I had. Coelho strode off the ship, bouncing slightly to feel the gravity.

"What g is this?" he asked. "Half?"

"Mars-standard," I said. "You think they saw you coming over?"

"Not yet, but they'll see if we do the maneuver," he said. "They'll shoot us when they see us trying. Both their fighting ships are still active. I don't know why those two aren't moving the station."

"Not enough fuel," I said. "How much have you got?"

"Almost full. We got most of our deceleration from the asteroid. My ship and the *Fuji* could do it, but that would leave the *Mariposa* the only one left to defend from the other ships."

"It's risky," I agreed. "But I'm guessing you've made up your mind."

He gave a tight nod. "I'll be staying here to coordinate the maneuver. Which way to the spindle?"

I pointed out the way, and he disappeared up the stairs with Maggie and the rest of the men he'd brought on the launch. Taking my watch out, I glanced at the time. It was getting close. Li had planned half an hour, minimum, to move the station. That was all we had now, and the ships would take time to get into position and perfectly still relative to the station.

The ships would have to pull the station faster than Li had planned to get it out of the way of the asteroid in time, but if they applied too much force through trying to move too fast, the spindle would snap off. I could only hope there was some padding built into the timing Bing had told me.

Out the window, the *Fuji* was moving north to get into position. The *Estrela* would be doing the same. The Martian ships had to have noticed by now.

I moved to another window and scanned the Martian fleet. So far, they were still moving away. Why weren't they headed over to stop us?

Then it hit me. They were smarter than we had been. They needed this station; Mars' independence relied on it. They had tried everything they could to move it, but had run out of time. Only one ship was loaded with fuel, the spindle was broken, and there was no time to load up a second ship.

We had just handed them a brand new opportunity. Let them hang back and watch. Either we messed up the maneuver, in which case they were no worse off, or we succeeded. If that happened, they could just wait till the asteroid had passed, land all their men on it, and try to take it back.

They had three ships and a number of launches, all full to bursting with civilians, spacers, and marines. We had docked only one launch. They knew they could overpower us. If they acted fast, we'd still be trying to figure out how to work the guns when they came back.

I ran to the stairwell and began climbing as fast as I could. My arms ached: I'd done this far too many times today. When I got to the top, I didn't stop to talk to Coelho, who was wedged at the hub, peering out the bubble window. Instead I grabbed the radio, turned the crank, and switched to the frequency the Martians used. "This is Ares Station, calling Captain Li!"

Coelho twisted around to look at me. "What the fuck—"

The radio crackled. "This is Captain Li. Who is speaking?"

"Midshipman Prescott, sir. I, ah, got left behind."

"Oh, for the love of..." The rest of her words were a mumble, but I got the idea. Me again. Late again. Missing again. I had no idea where she thought I was supposed to be by now, but it certainly wasn't here. I only hoped she wrote it off as still more incompetence. "I am sorry, Mr. Prescott, it won't be possible for us to return. Please wait there."

The idea would have been horrifying, if she didn't know the pirates were moving the station. But she didn't sound upset. My guess was correct.

"There are pirates here, sir," I said. "I've been taken captive."

A staticky sigh. "Well, if they make it through this, we'll negotiate for your—"

"They know what you're planning, sir. They think you might be waiting for them to move the station, and then come in to retake it." I caught Coelho's eye as I let up on the button.

Horror spread over his face. "Holy fuck, of course they are, I can't believe we—"

Li responded, "They couldn't match us, if we did."

"They know that, sir. They are currently applying ignition switches to all the gas pipes. They wanted me to tell you that if you approach the station, they will destroy it." Another lie. For once, I found I didn't care.

There was a silence. Swearing to herself, probably. Then: "How long do they think they can hold the station? We've got reinforcements closer than they do. What's the point of all this when, sooner or later, we're either going to take it or make them destroy it?"

I waited a moment. Let them think I was going back and forth with the pirates. At last I said, "Because you benefit more if you let them keep it, sir. I've been trying to explain our perspective to them. It seems they're in much the same situation we are. The prices they're paying Earth for fuel and necessities have become extortionary. They only want the station so they can have access to their own source. They think ... they think perhaps you would prefer to deal with them than Earth. They could operate the station and sell you gasses for below what Earth is charging. I know it's not the same as having it ourselves, sir, but given the options ..." I trailed off, releasing the button.

She was silent for a few seconds, then said, "Put them on. I can't keep talking through you."

Coelho scrambled over and took the handset. "What about it, Mars boss? You leave us the station, permanently, and we'll make sure you get what you need. Try to get it back and we'll just blow the damn thing. We want it, but we don't *need* it. Feel like the burden's on you to make sure we feel safe staying here."

"We need to discuss terms more specifically," she said.

"Come on over. Just you and somebody to steer your launch. You and I will hash it out while we do the maneuver. We don't make terms, you can sail on back."

❧

By the time Coelho and I reached the rim, the grapples were locked on. Here, we could get a good view of the *Estrela* below our feet for part of every minute before we wheeled around and the ship was too far above our heads to see. Coelho waited by the Navy offices for Li to arrive.

"One second," he said, and reached into his pocket. "You told them you were being held captive, we have to make it real." Ducking behind me, he deftly pulled my arms behind my back and whipped a length of carbon cable around my wrists.

"You going to give me away to them?"

"Temporarily, yeah. Maybe we can trade you for the rest of the *Mariposa*'s boarding party. By the Empire's math, you're worth half a dozen pirates. You can do what you want when this is over."

What I want. Now that was a question I hadn't had a chance to consider in a long time. Not what I wanted for *myself*. But the thought of it could barely find room in my mind beside thoughts of Moira. I would see her again. And then she could finally tell me what she had to talk about.

Li arrived with a lieutenant, and she spared me only a quick glance before starting to negotiate with Coelho. I could see she was eager to reach a deal. Anything to make it look, when she made her report to the Admiralty, that she'd snatched a partial victory from the jaws of defeat.

I couldn't feel the acceleration when we started to move, but I saw the asteroid shift. Slowly a glow built at the edge, until all at once a flash of sun sprang from behind it. I turned my face away from the glare. All around me, the shadows lifted. The station's first sunrise.

I turned my back to the sun and watched the light brighten on the potted plants, the trellised vines, the little fountain.

A new era was dawning here. A new Mars. A new green bubble hacked out of the blackness of space. A place where pirates and exiles could plant their feet and be free. Like Mars and Venus had done. If tyrants took our home from us, we would build another. As many as we had to build to stay free.

Twenty-Three

The final agreement was signed on the concourse outside the Navy offices. Captain Li and Coelho had worked out all the details, from product volumes and prices all the way to equipment that would stay or go. Moira and the rest of the boarding party were formally exchanged for me.

Li shook my hand when I walked across the concourse and let a Marine untie my wrists. "I am very sorry you were left on the station," she said. "We thought we had everyone."

"It's all right, sir," I said. I wasn't sure yet what my excuse was going to be. I wasn't sure yet if I needed one. It would depend on what Moira said. If she wanted me with her ... I didn't think I could say no. Even though I'd lost my original cover story of being presumed dead.

When the last document was signed, there was no applause from the assembled Martian Navy or the pirates. The moment felt somber. Maggie and Yao stood next to each other, tears flowing down both their faces. This was the closest either of them could ever get to returning home. But it was so much closer than they had thought they'd ever get.

After, Moira stalked over to me, stopping several feet short. "They've told me I'll be housed on the upper level," she said. "Can you show me where?"

I nodded and turned to lead her upstairs. Count on her to find a way for us to talk alone. I ought to trust her distant attitude was only to prop up the fantasy that we barely knew each other, but it still stung. I wanted her to lean in, torment me, wink. Anything.

The concierge desk upstairs was vacant, and I ducked behind to grab a key from a hook. Any room would do. I held the door for her and glanced around before following her inside.

I was carefully shutting the door behind us when she grabbed my shoulders and spun me around. I had time for only one breathless gasp of fear before she slammed me against the wall and started kissing me. One hand pressed me up against the wall while the other untucked my shirt and slid down my breeches.

It was a kiss like a torpedo blast is a touch. I could barely respond to it, I was so overwhelmed by her. The taste of her, the strength of her, what she was doing with her fingers.

After a moment she paused and pulled back. "What's wrong?"

I panted for breath. "I thought…well, I said I loved you…and you couldn't answer…so I wondered…"

She threw her head back and laughed. Then she slipped her arm around me and carried me over to the bed. In the Mars-standard gravity, it was nothing to her. Laying me out on the bed, she straddled my hips and started undoing my neckcloth. Under gravity, her hair was just as I remembered, wisps falling across her face.

Pulling off my shirt, she went to work on my stays, dropping kisses as she went. "You…actually…thought…I didn't love you still?" Her last kiss fell below my navel. "I never stopped loving you. Not for a second. Not since I showed you the first time."

I reached up and pulled her head back down to mine. How could she have never doubted? There I had been, lashing out in fury and torn between too many loyalties, and she had never faltered. I twitched my hips under her, making her gasp.

This time there was no hesitation, no thoughts to push from my head. I only wanted her, all of her, all of her against all of me.

Later she lay half on top of me, skin faintly damp, one leg still threaded between mine. "Oh god, Lucy," she breathed. "That was better than last time."

"This time I'm all here," I said, startled by the clear feeling of telling her the honest truth. "I was only falling towards you before. I didn't choose you; I gave up resisting you. It's different."

She nuzzled into my neck. "I'll take your word for it," she said. "It sure felt real then too."

"It *was* real! I just felt…" I hesitated, half embarrassed to say it out loud. "I felt like you were a planet, and I couldn't achieve escape velocity. And so I cut engines and drifted. Let myself orbit you, because you were too much to get away from."

She snorted. "So I'm a planet in this metaphor, and you're, what, a ship? I object."

"I don't mean physically!"

"No, I didn't—" She laughed, a delicious, comfortable laugh that tickled my neck. "I didn't mean like that. I mean, you don't orbit me while I'm standing still. You pull at me too. It's not like Mars and Phobos or Deimos. It's like Pluto and Charon. They orbit each other." Her fingers traced a circle on my sternum.

"You always seem to be on your own course," I said. "Sure of what you want. It's all I can do to even keep up with you. You're miles ahead while I'm still trying to decide whether or not to fire rockets."

"And yet, this was all *your* idea. Not mine. I would be plotting a course away from a debris field by now, if you'd left me to it. With a crew halfway to mutiny because they didn't want to do it."

I turned toward her, touching my forehead to hers so her eyes were almost too close to see. "I never actually said I'm sorry."

She blinked. "For what?"

"For rejecting you all those years ago. For picking a fight instead of kissing you like I wanted to. I feel like you're buttering me up all of a sudden. Like you're afraid I'll go."

"I'm not," she said, drawing back a fraction and half laughing. "I just wanted you to know I appreciated what you did. You made a difference."

I rolled back onto my back. "I know I did. I think anybody could have, maybe. Or anybody in the position I was in." I took a breath. This wasn't really what I wanted to be talking about. "I just want to tell you. I'm not going anywhere. I'm not falling toward you anymore; I'm choosing you. I'm never leaving."

She hiked herself up on one elbow to look down at me. "Except in a physical sense. When you leave the station. The last Navy ship leaves in a few hours."

I looked up at her in puzzlement. "I'm not leaving here. I'm going to tell Captain Li I'm resigning. This ship is your territory now; she can't make me come with her."

She sat all the way up, drawing her long legs against her chest. "Lucy, you can't. They'll mark you a deserter. You'll be exiled from Mars forever."

"I don't care," I said, and was shocked to find I really didn't. If I had her, I had all that had ever made me happy on Mars.

"You will care," she said firmly. "When the afterglow wears off, and you realize you need more than me in your life to be happy. And what about William? You explained it all to me. You've managed to keep your name clean, it seems. They'll take you back and you can support your family."

My heart sank. William. There would be no way I could explain to him why I wasn't coming back. "Maybe I could send them something from here…"

"It'll be years before we turn any kind of real profit," she argued. "The Navy is a safer bet."

I thought about my time in the Navy, Maxwell's airlocking, blood spattering off the end of the lash. "I can't go back to that, Moira," I whispered. "I can't. Are you trying to get rid of me?"

Her dark eyes softened. "Never. It's just, I need somebody to be my eyes and ears back there. To be sure Mars isn't trying to take the station back. To help spread the word that there's a refuge here for people who need to get free. And you still can! You're the only person we have that can go back. I know it's hard. We'd have to be apart for a while. But if you could get yourself an honorable discharge when the war ends…"

I lay gazing up at her, trying to fight against hope. Could I really have it all? Maybe get a place on a merchant vessel, traveling between here and Mars, bringing cargo for the terraforming project.

But who knew how long the war would last, and there was no hope of any discharge before then. That was a long time to endure the service, now that I had fully rejected it. I knew better than to think I could change it. It was a structure that resisted, in every way and on every level, any effort to soften its hard edges.

I thought about refusing Moira's offer. Demanding to stay. I knew she was only trying to make me happy. I had thought she couldn't understand how I felt about my family, but she hadn't forgotten anything I'd told her. She didn't want to keep me here if it would only make me resent her.

And she was right. I would be racked with guilt if I stayed. Not for letting the Navy down; I was beyond any sense of duty to that. But for not coming back for William. For letting a single postcard of concentric circles take the place of ever seeing me again. When I made myself quiet, when I hushed the clamor of the Naval Code and my oath to the Empire and even my desire to please Moira, I could hear my own conscience. It whispered, *go*.

I pulled Moira down beside me and buried my face in her neck. "I don't want to go," I said, hot tears springing to my eyes.

"I know you don't," she said, her own voice husky. "And I don't want you to."

"So long as you understand that. You have to believe me. That it isn't an out, to get away from you."

"I know you better than that, officer," she said, a bit of her old briskness coming back into her voice. "You're getting to be a much better liar now, did you know that? But you're absolute shit at lying to *me*."

TWENTY-FOUR

The sun shone brightly on the sandstone façade of the Admiralty building. I checked my pocketwatch: still ten minutes before my court martial.

According to the orders I'd received on arriving at Phobos Station, it was merely a formality, which was why I was standing outside the building alone instead of being escorted there in irons. But it was the sort of formality that grew teeth if you attempted to evade it. And which would certainly separate my head from my body if they didn't like my answers.

To calm my nerves, I bought a paper from a boy on the corner and flipped it open. The top story was about the first ships returning from the handover of Ares Station, and I skipped it. I knew what had happened better than even the Admiralty did, and I didn't care to read the muddle a journalist would make of it.

But on the inside, in letters to the editor, was a long letter in a style I recognized. It began, "Brothers, equals, Martians," and it was signed at the bottom, "Alexei Khan." On the facing page, the editor insisted that Khan was dead, that the letters were from an imitator, and not to give any credit to accounts of his followers that he had returned, frail and in a wheelchair. Of course they had to print that; the paper operated at the Emprex's pleasure and was hardly going to risk censorship. But even the attempt to refute the story would only give it traction.

I smiled and shut the paper. Progress was slow, but perhaps it would happen in the end. I climbed the steps heavily, still unused to the drag of gravity, and opened the solid front door.

The large paneled room was empty, except for the admirals at the far end and a few clerks beside them. A good sign. No need to put on a show if this was only a formality.

My bewigged questioners got right to the point. "We've already tried Captain Li for losing the station. She has been found to be at no fault, and in fact to have acted admirably to preserve the Empire's interests in such a way as she was able. And she commended you, I might add, for your assistance in that matter. But, as you were a prisoner of war for a matter of months, and then out of contact for several more, you are due for a *thorough* debrief. Perhaps more than a debrief, depending on the facts of your case."

"Thank you, my lord Admiral." I drew in my breath. I had my story; I was well prepared. The question before me now was whether I could lie well enough to convince my judges. "As you know, I was retained by the pirates in the hope that I would assist them with navigation, which, of course, I refused to do."

"And your fellow midshipman, Mr. Borisov?"

I cast down my eyes, as if disappointed. I had Maggie's permission to tell the whole truth in that regard. "She chose to cast in her lot with the pirates, my lord Admiral."

The center admiral nodded. "And when did you get free of them?"

"A few days short of Mars orbit, they loaded me into an escape pod and cast me adrift. I had the impression that they had an important job ahead of them, which they were afraid I might jeopardize. I had been attempting to sabotage the ship at any given opportunity, of course, and I suppose I had become more trouble than I was worth."

"How long did you stay in the pod?"

"Three days, my lord Admiral. On the third day, I was picked up by a ship calling itself the *Melpomene*. It claimed to be a mining ship run by the Tharsis Corporation, which I had no reason at the time to doubt."

"You remained on that ship till you arrived at Ares Station?"

"Yes, my lord Admiral. I went aboard with the captain and a few others. I parted ways with them and reported to Captain Li."

"In her report, she says she ordered you to depart on the *Destiny* that evening. Why did you fail to do so?"

I cringed and scuffled my feet a little. Let them think this was the part I was most uncomfortable to recount. "I was tired, my lord, and decided to take a short rest. Unfortunately I was more tired than I had thought, and since I had neglected to tell anyone where I was, they weren't able to find me before they left."

The admiral made a note. "Captain Li reports that you asked to hail the captain of the *Melpomene* for assistance. You felt that was wise?"

"It was actually Midshipman Abington's idea, my lord. But I thought it seemed harmless. They were, after all, Martians also, and could be assumed to have the Empire's well-being at heart."

"Which turned out to be false."

"Yes, my lord Admiral. When we reached the *Nemesis* to deliver fuel, the captain, Rajasthan by name, opened one of the fuel tanks and caused a spill. They left the marines on the *Nemesis* and rushed back to the station."

"Did you attempt to stop them?"

"I did, my lord, but I had no weapon so my attempts were quickly overpowered."

He made a note. This was the dangerous part. I didn't know what Brown had managed to report before he had died, when I'd accidentally destroyed the *Nemesis*. I was assuming he hadn't had a chance for any more specific report, given everyone's reactions to me thereafter, but if he had given my name, the jig was up and I would be hanged. But it seemed unlikely that they would ship me all the way here and let me find my own way to my court martial if they already had the evidence needed to hang me. They would have wanted to interrogate me as soon as possible.

The admiral looked up blandly. If he was hiding damning evidence, he had as good a poker face as I did. And I had spent the entire trip here practicing mine. "You did manage to break free of the pirates once they were on the station."

"With the assistance of Lieutenant Smirnov and his marines."

"Lieutenant Smirnov says he ordered you to take a launch with civilians away from the station. But Able Spacer Larson says you excused yourself and didn't return. She had to pilot the launch away herself."

"Yes, my lord Admiral. When I came upstairs to move the luggage out of the concourse, I spotted former midshipman Borisov. Recognizing her and knowing she had joined the pirates, I pursued at once."

"Do you know how she got on board the station?"

"No, my lord Admiral. I suppose she had joined one of the pirate crews in the area."

"How long did it take you to catch up to her?"

There was a lot of unaccounted-for time in what they knew. "At least half an hour, my lord Admiral. She eventually made her way to the hub, where I lost her among all the struts. I was not accustomed to dealing with the gravity on that level. I was unable to find her until Mister Abington arrived. The two of us worked together to corner her. However, she escaped from us again and managed to surprise him from behind." I allowed myself to be briefly overcome by emotion. That, at least, was entirely sincere. "I am sorry, my lord Admiral. Mr. Abington was a dear friend."

"Understood, Mr. Prescott. Please continue."

I gave a sharp sniff and dabbed at my eyes. "Borisov escaped down a stairwell. I took Mr. Abington's sword and tried to pursue her, but she eluded me for some time. By this time, all the launches had gone. When the pirates landed their launch, they were able to take me captive due to superior numbers."

None of this made me look very good. In my story, I had failed to save Bing, failed to apprehend Maggie, failed to save the station, and had let myself get taken captive by pirates. I wasn't that incompetent—and I might have single-handedly saved Martian independence by arranging that handover. But then again, it wouldn't have been under threat if I had left well alone. If I got a dressing down, it was no more than I deserved.

The admiral nodded and gathered up his notes, tapping the sheaf of paper sharply on the desk. "You account for your time satisfactorily, I think," he said, exchanging glances with the admirals on his left and right. "Captain Li believes you are due some credit for the negotiations you undertook with the pirates. It could easily have gone much worse. We are willing to overlook the errors due to your inexperience, in light of the help you managed to be at that moment. Mars is still independent, and I think you may feel proud that you served some small part in that."

I bowed my head. He could hardly be more wrong, but it was a better outcome than I had hoped for.

"You are due two months' leave, and I suggest you spend it studying. When you report for duty, I see no reason why you should not sit the lieutenant's exam. Captain Kim-Johnson has recommended you as an excellent navigator, and as you know we are in desperate need of trained officers."

I bowed and took my leave. Outside, I breathed a long, slow sigh of relief. I hadn't hesitated for a second as the lies had poured off my lips. I hadn't had to. Lying had been hard for me before because I had felt confused about what, if anything, lay beneath the lies. Now I knew. I was a citizen of Ares Station—Liberty Station, they were calling it now. The new republic of exiles. Not because I owed it anything, but because I believed in what it could be.

And I was Moira's now. Not shakily falling, but in stable orbit now. The forces that pulled me away from her would pull me back in time, no matter how wide the ellipse.

A flustered figure in wide skirts and a feathered hat came hurrying up the stairs. It took me a second, after so long apart, to recognize my mother. "Lucy," she cried, "they wouldn't let me in, they said it was confidential, but if you're out here I suppose it went all right?"

I stepped down to meet her. "Yes, everything is fine. Did you think it wouldn't be?"

"How was I to know? Last we had heard you were almost certainly dead, and then came a wire saying you were alive but had an inquiry. An inquiry! What sort of business could you ever have had that would have to be inquired into, I'd like to know! Though I don't suppose I shall ever *get* to know, will I?"

I smiled to myself and took her arm to bring her back down the stairs. "The version the public gets to know is already in the papers. I only had to be inquired about because I was on a civilian ship for a while and they didn't have records."

"How much time do I get with you?" Her tone was so plaintive that I shot her a quick sideways look. Her eyes, I could see now, bore new lines around them, and she'd finally let her hair go naturally gray.

"I'll be home for two months, they said. Or at least, I'll be on Mars. Is there—is the house—"

"It's still standing, thank the ancestors, and we still have that, at least. We've been selling off parcels here and there to fund the rest. Not much equity in any of them, but the less we have, the less we owe. The solicitor has finally made me understand that. It's—"

Her gloved hands gave an anxious tremor. "It's all so frightfully embarrassing, but with you in the service, our social standing hasn't seemed to matter so much. Since after all you didn't have to get married—although maybe you still want to?" She cast me a sly sidelong look. "Maybe you met someone out there?"

"No one I can bring home to meet you just yet, Mother." We crossed the street, passing Independence Fountain and a cluster of statues. "And William, how is he?"

"Oh! You've almost made me forget, with all your talk. I brought something from him for you." She reached into her large purse and pulled out a long cylinder. "I tried to get him to understand that you were lost, that you were almost certainly dead, and he simply refused to believe it. Wouldn't let us talk to him about it. I thought it was simply denial, but perhaps somehow he knew. Anyway, the entire time he was working on this for when you came back. When I said I was going to meet you at Landing, he made me take it along."

I took the cylinder and carefully unrolled it. It was a beautiful painting, the kind he makes in winter when the storms get too bad to go down to the shore. From each side of the painting came a separate series of concentric circles—ripples, I realized, exactly as if a stone had been thrown into water at either edge. In the center of the painting, the ripples collided, neither combining nor canceling, but creating a new pattern.

Were the two splashes William and I? Was he trying to say something at all, or was it a technical challenge of his skills, to replicate the exact look of the water when he threw in two stones? What it reminded me of most was Earth and Mars, and the new station that contained exiles from each. But that was only because I had the station so heavily on my mind. And Moira, pirate queen of it all.

"I can't wait to see him," I said, rolling the painting back up. "I'll tell him everything."

The story continues in

THE SEA OF CLOUDS

Mars isn't ready for a revolution, but as violence escalates and a prince goes missing, it might not have a choice.

Lucy sails to the cloud cities of Venus and finds herself ensnared in a diplomatic incident and investigating a murder. Moira visits her family on Mars, where a populist revolution is heating up and violence becomes a regular occurrence in the capital city.

Will the common people finally make their voices heard, or will it all end in blood?

Author's Note

This book was inspired by reading (and loving) *Master and Commander* and other sailing novels, but thinking the whole time that the Navy of the period was dysfunctional at best and cruel at worst. How could I write about the traditions and glamor of the high seas without taking some kind of stance, one way or the other, on impressment, flogging, and the rest?

Then, of course, I had to spend six months intensively studying the physics of solar sailing, calculating the mass and required stores of a ship, and so on. Solar sailing is real and works, though there are a lot of engineering problems to solve before it could carry people.

To learn more about the science behind this book and keep up with my new releases, check out sheilajenne.com.

GLOSSARY

bearing: a ship's position, speed, and direction, as calculated from the stars

beat to quarters: summon the crew to battle stations

bosun (also **bo's'n** or **boatswain**): the spacer in charge of the sails

bow chasers: small guns facing forward

boy: a young spacer of any gender

broadside: cannon fire from all the cannon along one side of the ship

cat: the "cat o' nine tails" used for flogging

chain: a type of ammunition attached with chains so that it will tear a broad swath through the enemy's sails

checked shirt: pattern of welts after a flogging

colonist: someone who came to Mars after the original settlement; also called a commoner

downstream: the direction all the planets orbit

EVA: extravehicular activity, a spacewalk

forecastle (also **fo'c'sle**): a bubble-shaped window at the bow of the ship

Founder: a member of the Martian nobility, descended from the first settlers

hammock: a sack for zero-g sleeping, clipped to the wall

impress: to force a spacer into service for the Navy

leeward: the direction away from the sun

master: the warrant officer responsible for a certain duty on the ship

mate: an assistant or second in command

midshipman: an officer in training, usually a teenager

parole: an officer's word of honor to obey the terms of their captivity

port: left on a ship

prize money: the share of money each crew member receives after taking an enemy vessel

quarterdeck: a raised platform at the stern of the ship, allowed only to officers

Singularity: a disaster in Mars and Earth history in which artificial intelligence caused the deaths of millions

space-bound: unable to return to a planet because of atrophied muscles and bones due to long periods in space

spacer: an enlisted sailor of the Martian Navy, not an officer

starboard: right on a ship

stays: supportive corset

stern chasers: small guns facing aft

sunward: the direction toward the sun

upstream: the direction opposite the planets' orbits

warrant officer: a spacer with a special position on the ship, though not a full officer due to being born a commoner

www.ingramcontent.com/pod-product-compliance
Lightning Source LLC
Chambersburg PA
CBHW061227310726
48971CB00007B/1972